<u>WHISPERS IN THE DARK</u>

All characters in this book have no existence outside the imagination of the author and have no relation whatsoever to anyone bearing the same name or names. They are not even distantly inspired by any individual known or unknown to the author and all incidents are pure invention.

ISBN: 979-8-90329-227-1

Whispers In The Dark

By Makala V.P. Thomas

For

Nevaeh

Brenda

Priscilla

Dean

Damien

Sorcha

To the London Borough of Hackney. No matter how far I go in life, I will never forget where I came from.

x-x-x Mwah x-x-x

Welcome to Whispers In The Dark

Before you turn the first page, take a breath.

You're about to step into six different worlds- each one crafted to pull you in, hold you close, and refuse to let you leave unchanged.

Whispers In The Dark isn't just a collection of novellas.

It's a journey through the spaces we rarely speak about out loud- the places where desire stirs, secrets breathe, magic hums beneath the skin, and danger waits just beyond the edge of the light.

Inside These Pages, You'll Find Five Novellas Under The Genres Romance, Mystery/Thriller, Fantasy, Science Fiction, and Crime.

Whispers In The Dark Is A Collection for the Curious and the Brave.

This book is for readers who crave immersion.

For those who love slipping into new atmospheres, new emotions, new rules.

For those who want stories that linger long after the final line.

So, settle in.

Let the lights dim.

Let the whispers guide you.

Welcome to the dark… and to every world waiting inside it.

WHISPERS IN THE DARK

Novellas 1- 5

1. BETWEEN THE LINES

When a struggling bookstore owner discovers a trail of forgotten love letters tucked inside her vintage novels, she's instantly captivated, but never imagines they'll alter the course of her life. That changes the day a stranger walks into her shop, claiming to be the descendant of the letters' elusive author, a man who disappeared without a trace.

Drawn together by curiosity and a shared desire for answers, the two begin poring over the letters week after week, uncovering a long-buried romance that feels strangely alive between them. As secrets surface and the past slowly reveals itself, the pair find themselves growing closer... connected not just by the mystery they're solving, but by a spark neither expected.

What starts as a search for truth soon becomes something deeper, offering both the possibility of closure... and the promise of a new love story waiting to be written.

2. THE LAST WITNESS

Detective Ruby Walker is running out of time. The only witness to a brutal murder is a woman who swears she remembers nothing about that night-whether from fear, trauma, or something far more dangerous. Ruby knows one thing for certain: someone wants this woman silenced.

As Ruby pushes past dead ends and evasions, she uncovers a pattern that suggests the murder is only the beginning. Each clue pulls her deeper into a web of corruption, hidden crimes, and carefully buried secrets. Allies grow scarce, enemies were once friends, and the truth becomes harder to trust.

Protecting her witness may be the only way to expose what's really happening- but doing so could cost Ruby her career, her safety, and the fragile trust of the woman whose forgotten memories might be the key to everything.

3. THE MOONWEAVER'S APPRENTICE

Seventeen-year-old Elara Romane has always felt drawn to the moon, but the night it speaks her name, she learns why: she is the first Moonweaver's Apprentice in three hundred years. Gifted with the rare ability to see and wield living strands of moonlight, Elara is thrust into a destiny she never asked for. As she begins her secret training under the enigmatic Moonweaver Lysander, a darker truth emerges- an ancient force that feeds on fear has taken root inside her own sister. Torn between loyalty and survival, Elara must master her lunar magic before the darkness consumes her family and her village. With danger rising and secrets unravelling, she discovers that the moon didn't choose her by accident… it chose her because only she can face what's coming.

4. THE ECHO PROTOCOL

When Dr. Maya Tessler intercepts a distress signal coming from her own research station, she faces an impossible choice: heed the warning or risk triggering the very catastrophe she's sworn to stop.

Then a message arrives- from her partner, Adrian Vaelle- delivered through digital channels that shouldn't be able to reach her... and may not be coming from the living. With time running out, Maya must unravel the truth before she shares his fate, or something far worse.

Gifted with the rare ability to communicate with any form of technology; from phones and computers to televisions and microwaves, Maya is the sole conduit for a mysterious entity that calls itself the Echo.

The Echo listens only to her. It obeys only her.

Now Maya must decide whether to wield the Echo as a force for good... or bend it toward her own desires, no matter the cost.

5. THE WHISPER THAT BROKE THE NIGHT

When Carmen Cruise hears her husband whisper, "She won't wake up," everything she thought she knew about her marriage shatters. What begins as a chilling late-night confession spirals into a maze of half-truths, buried secrets, and a past her husband swore never existed.

As Carmen pieces together the fragments of that night, she uncovers a trail of lies that point to one impossible question: is she the one in danger- or is she the danger herself?

A story where memory twists, trust fractures, and every revelation cuts deeper than the last, nothing stays buried forever.

And the truth, once awakened, refuses to sleep again.

BETWEEN THE LINES

When a struggling bookstore owner discovers a trail of forgotten love letters tucked inside her vintage novels, she's instantly captivated, but never imagines they'll alter the course of her life. That changes the day a stranger walks into her shop, claiming to be the descendant of the letters' elusive author, a man who disappeared without a trace.

Drawn together by curiosity and a shared desire for answers, the two begin poring over the letters week after week, uncovering a long-buried romance that feels strangely alive between them. As secrets surface and the past slowly reveals itself, the pair find themselves growing closer... connected not just by the mystery they're solving, but by a spark neither expected.

What starts as a search for truth soon becomes something deeper, offering both the possibility of closure... and the promise of a new love story waiting to be written.

Before the Letters

The morning Ember Richards found the first letter had begun like every other: quietly, with the soft hum of the old radiator and the faint smell of rain drifting through the cracked window above the classics section. But what she didn't know, what she couldn't have known, was that her life had already begun to shift long before she flipped the bookstore's sign to OPEN.

For weeks, she'd been waking up with a strange restlessness, a sense that something was missing. Not something physical… something internal.

A spark.

A direction.

A reason to believe her life wasn't just a slow fade into obscurity alongside the dusty shelves she tended to like a caretaker of ghosts.

She'd inherited the shop from her grandfather who'd raised her and sadly passed when she was twenty-five, too young to understand what it meant to anchor herself to a sinking ship.

Now, at thirty-two, she felt the weight of every decision she hadn't made. Every risk she hadn't taken. Every dream she'd quietly folded and tucked away like a forgotten bookmark, buried under the weight of her inheritance that was meant to be her legacy, The Last Chapter bookstore.

Her friends had moved on; marriages, babies, careers that involved promotions and conferences and health insurance.

Ember had books.

And silence.

And a creeping fear that she was becoming a footnote in her own life.

That morning, she'd stood in front of the mirror brushing her thick black hair, wondering if she should cut it.

Change something.

Anything. But she'd sighed, tied it back, and told herself she'd think about it later.

She always told herself that.

The Bookstore's History

The Last Chapter bookstore had been in her family for three generations. Her grandfather, Ivan Richards, had opened it in 1951 with nothing but a loan, a dream, and a stubborn belief that stories could save people.

Her grandmother, Melody, had joined him a year later, shelving books with one hand and holding their newborn daughter Eloise with the other.

Ember had grown up hearing stories of the shop's golden years: lines out the door on Saturdays, book clubs that filled every corner, authors who stopped by just to chat. She'd spent her childhood curled up in the reading nook behind the counter, devouring everything from children's books to adult novels she shouldn't have been reading at twelve years old, but she lapped them up anyway.

But the world had changed. People didn't linger in bookstores anymore. They clicked. They scrolled. They downloaded.

Disaster struck the small family when Ember was ten. Both her mother and grandmother were killed when their bus was hit by a lorry which had spun out of control on the busy road of their town.

They weren't the only ones to have been killed, it was a local tragedy. But it was never the same after that, with just Ember and her grandfather Ivan.

There was no more singing from her mother, no more apple pie on the weekends along with cookies baked by her grandmother.

Ember was forbidden to enter her mother's bedroom after her funeral. The door remained locked, with Ivan keeping the key hidden.

The bookstore closed for almost three years.

Things became a little colder around the once happy home.

Ivan never fully recovered from the shock and trauma of losing his wife and only child. He'd mutter to himself as he did his best to cook for himself and Ember, soon hiring a housemaid to do the work when the meals weren't up to par.

Trudy was a very nice maid.

She brushed Ember's hair and helped her with her homework, ironed her school uniform and made sure Ember was always looking presentable.

It was nice, but Trudy wasn't Melody, nor was she Eloise.

Both Ivan and Ember felt that, for years.

And Ember… she clung to the memory of her mother like it was a life raft.

Ember's Emotional Landscape

Ember wasn't unhappy, not exactly. But she wasn't living, either. She was maintaining. Preserving. Surviving.

Sometimes, late at night, she'd sit on the floor of the shop with a cup of tea and whisper to the shelves, "Tell me what to do." As if the books might answer. As if the stories might offer her a way out.

But they never did.

Not until the letters.

Finding the First Letter

When the first letter slipped from East of Eden, a thick book which was an olden-day fantasy novel, Ember didn't notice it at first.

She was too busy muttering to herself about reorganizing the Sullivan section, *again-* because customers kept putting Magpie's Crow in the wrong place.

The letter fluttered to the floor like a leaf, landing face-down.

Ember frowned down and it, then bent to pick it up, expecting a receipt or a forgotten bookmark.

But the paper was too thick.

Too old.

Too deliberate.

Her breath caught as she turned it over.

The handwriting was elegant, looping, the kind of script people didn't use anymore. The ink had faded to a soft brown, and the edges of the paper were worn, as if it had been handled many times before being tucked away.

She hesitated before opening it, a strange sense of trespassing prickling her skin.

But curiosity won.

It always did.

As she read the first line…:

My dearest, I saw you today in the market…

Something inside her shifted as she continued to read.

A door in her mind she hadn't realised was closed, creaked open.

She read the letter twice.

Then a third time.

Each reading pulled her deeper into the world of the writer- this mysterious J. who had loved someone from afar with a tenderness that felt almost sacred.

For the first time in months, Ember felt something spark in her chest.

Hope.

Possibility.

A whisper of something she couldn't yet name.

Ember's Reaction That Night

That night, after closing the shop, Ember sat cross-legged on her living room floor with the letter in her lap.

She'd made tea, but it had gone cold. She'd turned on the lamp, but the room still felt dim.

She kept rereading the letter, tracing the loops of J.'s handwriting with her fingertip.

Who had he been?

Who had *she* been?

Why had the letters been hidden?

Why had no one found them until now?

She imagined J.'s woman with copper hair- imagined her laughing, imagined her unaware of the man who watched her with such aching devotion.

Ember pressed the letter to her chest.

"No one has ever written anything like this for me," she whispered into the quiet.

And for the first time, she admitted the truth she'd been avoiding:

She was lonely.

Deeply, profoundly lonely.

And she didn't want to be anymore.

The Second Letter's Impact

Finding the second letter felt like fate.

Finding the third felt like destiny.

By the time she'd uncovered the seventeenth letter three weeks later, Ember was no longer simply curious.

She was invested. She felt connected to J. in a way that startled her. His vulnerability, his longing, his poetic desperation… it resonated with something inside her she'd buried long ago.

She began to imagine him; not as an old man, but as he'd been when he wrote the letters.

Young.

Hopeful.

Terrified.

Brave in the only way he knew how to be.

She wondered if anyone had ever loved *her* like that.

She wondered if anyone ever *would.*

Braxton's Entrance

When Braxton walked into the shop the following evening, Ember didn't notice him at first. She was behind the counter, sorting the letters into chronological order, some of her loose curly hair falling into her face as she worked.

He cleared his throat softly.

"Excuse me? Miss?"

Ember looked up, and she froze.

He was handsome, yes, but that wasn't what struck her.

It was the expression on his face.

A strange mix of hope and fear.

The same expression she imagined J. wearing as he wrote those letters.

"Can I help you?" she asked, her voice steadier than she felt.

He hesitated, glancing around the shop as if searching for treasure.

"I'm looking for something my grandfather left here," he said. "A long time ago."

And just like that, Ember's world shifted again.

Braxton's Backstory: Before the Bookstore

Braxton Stevens had not planned to come to this small town.

Three months earlier, he'd been sitting in his grandfather's study in London, surrounded by the smell of cedar and old books, listening to the soft, laboured breaths of a man who had once been larger than life.

Justin Stevens had been a storyteller- one of those rare people who could make even the most ordinary memory sound like a legend.

But in the final weeks of his life, he spoke only of one thing: *a woman with dark brown skin like theirs, and naturally auburn hair.*

Braxton had grown up hearing fragments of the story.

A bookstore.

A girl, who grew into beautiful woman.

A love so fierce and silent it had shaped the rest of Justin's life. But it wasn't until the night before he died that Justin finally told the whole truth.

"She never knew," he whispered, his voice thin as paper. "I wrote her a hundred letters. Hid them in the books she loved. I thought… I thought she'd find them. I thought fate would do the rest."

Braxton had held his grandfather's hand, feeling the bones beneath the skin.

"Why didn't you tell her?"

Justin had smiled, a sad, distant smile. "Because I was a coward. And because I thought she deserved someone braver."

He'd pressed a small brass key into Braxton's palm.

"A box," he said. "In my closet. Read what's inside. And if you ever feel what I felt… don't wait. Don't hide. Don't let fear write your story."

Justin died the next morning.

Inside the box were copies of the letters; drafts, notes, unsent versions. And a single envelope addressed to Braxton.

Inside, Braxton read:

Find them.

Find the letters I left behind.

And find the courage I never had.

Grandfather.

Braxton had cried- really cried- for the first time in years.

And then he'd packed a bag and driven to the town he'd only ever heard about in stories.

Braxton's First Impressions of Ember

When Braxton first saw Ember, he felt something he couldn't explain.

It wasn't love at first sight.

It wasn't even attraction, not in the usual sense.

It was recognition.

As if he'd walked into a memory that wasn't his.

Her dark glossy hair shone in the light in a way that made his breath hitch- just like his grandfather had described.

Her posture, slightly tense but determined, reminded him of someone carrying more weight than she let on.

And her eyes… they were light brown… tired, but not defeated.

Instantly, he knew she was innocent.

He knew she hadn't experienced life they way she should have.

Staring at her, he thought absurdly: *she looks like someone who needs a letter.*

He didn't know yet that she'd already found them.

"We're soon closing," Ember said a little nervously. "In the next half hour."

"Half an hour is all I need," Braxton said quickly. "I'm looking for a woman named Eloise Richards."

He saw her cringe big time, and he knew something was wrong.

"Do you know her?"

Silence.

"You must know her," pressed Braxton. "You fit her description had you been born many years ago. But your hair is a different colour."

Ember took a deep breath, then she replied "Yes. She was my mother."

“Was?” Braxton’s heart sank. “You mean-”

“She died a long time ago,” Ember said a little coldly. “Twenty-two years ago, to be exact.”

“Damn,” Braxton said softly. “After all this time… he never knew.”

“Who?”

Braxton sighed heavily. “My grandfather. Justin.”

Ember froze. “J?”

Braxton frowned at her. “What do you mean?”

“What are you looking for exactly?” asked Ember. “Who was your grandfather to my mother?”

“Nobody,” confessed Braxton. “He was an admirer. Just a teenager who loved her from afar. Then, when both he and your mother grew into adults, he felt he loved her more than anything. She was beautiful in his eye.”

“She was beautiful in *everyone’s* eye,” Ember corrected. “Many men came in here trying to date her.”

“Oh.”

It was quiet for a moment, then Ember asked “So what exactly did your grandfather leave here?”

“Letters,” Braxton replied quietly. “In your mother’s favourite books.”

Ember frowned at him. “If he was a stranger, how did he know what her favourite books were?”

“They were books of the week, changed every Friday,” Braxton answered. “I think he assumed they were her favourite books. She’d convince customers to purchase them, succeeding each time.”

“And he snuck a letter in the leftover copies?”

Braxton nodded. “I’m guessing so.”

A clock chimed through the store, making them jump.

"It's closing time," Ember said apologetically. "Can we finish this conversation tomorrow?"

"Tomorrow?" Braxton repeated slowly.

Ember nodded, a little nervous.

"Alright. What time do you open?"

"At eleven. We're not open on Sundays," she replied, "So tomorrow is best. Unless you want to wait until Monday to continue our conversation."

Braxton was startled as he realised it was Friday evening.

"Alright. I will see you tomorrow afternoon."

"What time?"

"Around two," Braxton answered as he straightened up, Ember as well as she said ok. "I didn't get your name, Miss."

Silence.

Braxton waited, his heart hammering.

"It's Ember," she said quietly. "Ember Richards."

Braxton nodded. "Nice to meet you, Ember. I'm Braxton Stevens."

He held out a hand.

Ember hesitated, then she reached across the counter and shook it slowly.

His skin was soft, his grip firm.

Ember's heart pounded as he smiled a little, then he ended the handshake.

"See you tomorrow," he said warmly. "Ember?"

"Yes?"

"Can you do me a favour and try and find those letters?" he asked, and he reached into his pocket and pulled out a sheet of paper. "This is the list of the books my grandfather hid them in."

"Of course," Ember said quickly, accepting the sheet of paper. "I'll do my best."

"Thank you."

Braxton straightened up, and he turned and walked away.

Ember hesitated, then she called after him. "Where in town are you staying, Braxton?"

"At the Macy's Hotel, across town."

"That's over an hour away."

"I know. I'll be alright." Braxton glanced back, and he smiled at her. "See you tomorrow, Ember."

"See you," she answered softly, and Braxton Stevens left the store.

Ember quickly closed the bookstore, then she ran back and looked at the list of books that contained the hidden letters that were intended for her late mother.

She'd discovered seventeen already.

There were thirteen books left.

Ember went back into the main part of the massive house that was connected to the bookstore, and she headed up to the master bedroom and placed the list down on her bedside table.

She couldn't help wishing that this Justin Stevens had been a little braver and told her mother directly how he felt about her.

Maybe things would have been different.

Maybe she would still be here.

But then, maybe *Ember* wouldn't be here.

Ember sighed, and went into her bathroom for a quick shower.

She got into bed afterwards, and fell asleep before nine p.m.

Braxton Broods At Macy's Hotel

It was two in the morning.

Braxton browsed on his phone, looking at Ember Richard's photos on her social media.

She was a very pretty woman.

But she hardly interacted with men who commented on her photos, trying to get to know her, asking her out on dates.

Braxton was glad about that.

He kept scrolling desperately, hoping to find a photo of her mother.

It just reached four in the morning, and Braxton, with very heavy eyes, had almost given up when he finally found a family photo on Ember's Facebook, of Ember, her mother Eloise, and her grandparents.

"Grandfather wasn't lying," he muttered. "She was beautiful."

Eloise had sepia coloured skin, naturally auburn hair which she had inherited from her father, Ember's grandfather. Her grandmother Melody had jet black hair, just like Ember's, and they all had light brown eyes.

There was no father of Ember posted anywhere. Braxton assumed he was either dead or a deadbeat father.

"Gorgeous family," yawned Braxton, and he placed his phone down. "I'd better rest."

Sleep didn't come for another two hours.

Braxton was tossing and turning, wondering why his grandfather was so afraid to approach Eloise Richards.

"It's sad," he muttered. "So sad."

Saturday Afternoon

Ember's heart raced as she stood behind the counter, looking up at the clock above the bookcase opposite.

It was almost two p.m.

Braxton Stevens would be there very soon.

Ember swallowed hard.

She'd be a fool to deny that Braxton was extremely handsome.

It was an odd situation.

Like fate, she mused.

She'd discovered the beautiful letters, and in less than a month later, the mystery man's grandson turned up.

It was very odd, but Ember was a slight romantic, very skeptical, but not afraid to let her heart lead the way for once instead of her brain.

The bell above the shop's chimed as someone entered, dragging her out of her thoughts as she whipped round.

Her heart sank; it was an elderly woman with a young boy, around eleven years old.

"Welcome to The Last Chapter," she said warmly. "How can I help you?"

"My grandson Eric refuses to read proper books," the elderly woman said with a sigh. "You know, novels. I've come for a few age-appropriate books for him to read for two weeks. There will be no screen-time during then, at all."

"Come on Nana!" the boy called Eric protested. "I can read and have screen time!"

"His school suggested this," the elderly woman said to Ember. "All he does when he gets home is go straight on his phone or computer, or games console. It's getting out of control. What do you suggest, Miss?"

"I have just the series he may be into," smiled Ember, and Eric scowled. "Follow me."

Just as she walked around the counter with a smile, the bell chimed again, and in walked Braxton Stevens, looking ever so handsome in black jeans and a black shirt.

"Braxton," breathed Ember, and he smiled at her.

"Ember. Good afternoon."

Ember smiled back, then she pouted at him. "You're late."

"My apologies. There was a lot of traffic. As to be expected on a weekend, am I right?" his smile grew, Ember's heart pounded.

Then she remembered her customers.

"Um- Braxton, head into the back. The living area in just down the hall. I'll be right in."

"Thank you."

Braxton left the main part of the store, and Ember turned and smiled at Eric.

"Have you heard of A Series of Unfortunate Events, Eric?"

Eric shook his head.

"Well, it's an awesome series," smiled Ember. "I loved it. Some parts are a little freaky, but I think you'll be into it. I can tell from the skull on your t-shirt that you like a bit of horror."

"Horror?" his grandmother repeated disdainfully. "I don't want my Eric getting any funny ideas."

"Not to worry Ma'am. This series isn't too gory," smiled Ember as she led them deeper into the bookstore, and she reached up and pulled down Book One of the series. "Here Eric, read the blurb of the first one."

Eric obeyed, muttering as he read.

His eyes seemed to light up with interest, his grandmother looking surprised at him.

"Does that seem like something you could finish in two weeks?" smiled Ember; Eric nodded. "Very good. And if you want to know what happens next, come back for Book Two. I'll make sure I have a brand-new copy waiting just for you."

"Thank you," mumbled Eric, and his grandmother smiled broadly.

"Excellent. Let's pay and be on our way. Eric, if you like this book, we'll be back."

"Yes Nana."

Ember served the woman and her grandson with a smile, then she closed the store temporarily, the sign saying "Closed For Lunch", but she was really excited to talk to Braxton.

She joined him in her living area, finding him sat on her three-seater sofa.

She sat opposite him in a matching two-seater, and she said "Hey."

"Hey," he responded, and he smiled a little. "Sorry for being late."

"It's alright."

"I heard you out there with your customers." Braxton's smile grew. "You're great at what you do."

"Thank you. It wasn't my plan to own this big house along with the store though. I inherited it all when my grandfather died."

"Oh," said Braxton. "I'm sorry. What were your plans then?"

Ember hesitated. "We should stay on topic."

"The topic being?" smiled Braxton, and she felt butterflies in her stomach as she replied "The letters from your grandfather to my mother."

"That can wait a moment," smiled Braxton. "What were your plans? Your dreams? If you didn't want this, why didn't you sell the store and this house?"

"Because I just couldn't. It meant a lot to my family, my grandfather especially. He built the store on top of his house and it became a legacy. People would travel from far and wide just to come here and purchase the unique books. The press was always here."

"So what happened?" asked Braxton, and Ember sighed "The deaths of my mother and grandmother happened."

"Oh. I'm sorry. Did things change?"

"Yes. The store was closed for three years. Its popularity faded. Things were never the same when it reopened." Ember sighed again. "It pretty much faded into the background, especially when more and more technology surfaced in the following years. People preferred reading on their tablets, phones and computers instead of reading from physical books. I did too, to be honest/"

"I understand that." Braxton nodded. "I guess time changed everything, huh."

"Yep."

It was quiet for a moment, then Ember straightened up.

"Would you like some tea?"

"Tea would be lovely." Braxton smiled at her, and Ember called for her housemaids.

"Trudy! Selena!"

"Yes Miss Richards," two voices called, surprising Braxton as two women entered the living area and bowed respectfully.

"Please, serve my guest and I some tea and cake."

"Yes Miss Richards."

The two women bowed again and left the room, heading for the large kitchen.

"You must be loaded to have housemaids," smiled Braxton, and Ember smiled back as she replied "I have cleaners too, and a butler."

"Really??"

"Of course." Ember shrugged a shoulder. "My grandfather made sure I was set for life. The staff who reside here too."

"That's awesome," smiled Braxton. "All I have is a two-bedroomed flat in the city that I tend to myself."

Ember smiled back. "Definitely better than nothing."

"Of course." Braxton nodded. "Um- I hope you don't mind, but I did some digging last night."

"Oh? How so?"

"I went through your social media." Silence. "Please don't think I'm a creep. I just wanted to see what your mother looked like, if she was the same as my grandfather described."

Ember relaxed a little as she smiled. "And was she?"

"Of course. Your mother was stunning."

Ember felt her eyes well up. "Yes, she was."

"And so are you, Ember. You look just like her."

Ember felt like she'd taken a blow to the head. "You think I'm stunning?"

"Of course. I'd have to be blind to think otherwise," smiled Braxton; Ember's heart raced.

She swallowed hard, then she mumbled "Thank you."

The maids entered, pushing a trolley with a tea set and four slices of chocolate cake.

"Sebastian will start on a late lunch at four, Miss Richards," Trudy announced as Selena served them both. "He wanted to know if you'd like soup and toast, or

spiced meat and rice with a light salad."
"Both sound yummy," smiled Ember, and she looked at Braxton. "Braxton? What do you fancy?"
Braxton was surprised. "You want me to stay for the next two hours or more?"
"Well, I'm assuming we'll be reading your grandfather's letters together and that may take a while," smiled Ember; Braxton relaxed big time.
"Well, then I think spiced meat and rice would be great."
"Let Sebastian know," Ember ordered her maids, and they bowed and left the living room.
Ember and Braxton conversed contentedly over tea and cake for the next forty-five minutes, and then Ember took a deep break as the maids took everything away.
"Are you ready to go back in time and read your grandfather's letters?"
Braxton nodded. "I am."
"Alright." Ember stood. "I'll be right back."

Ember Brings Down the Letters

When Ember returned with the stack of letters, Braxton felt his throat tighten. He hadn't expected her to actually find them.

He hadn't expected anything, really.

He'd come here on a whim, a grief-fuelled pilgrimage.

But seeing the letters- real, tangible, worn by time- made everything inside him shift.

He picked one up carefully, as if it might crumble.

"This is Grandfather's handwriting," he murmured. "He used to write like this even when he was old. Said cursive was the closest thing to music he'd ever make."

Ember watched him, her expression softening. "He must have loved my mother very much."

Braxton nodded. "He did. But he loved her quietly. Too quietly. My grandmother had no clue about it and neither did my parents. He told me so."

He looked up at her then through tear-filled eyes, and her eyes filled too.

Something passed between them, something fragile and electric.

A question neither of them dared to ask yet.

Ember and Braxton Tidy Up

They began poring over the books Braxton's grandfather had chosen, just for both of them to get a feel of the ones they'd loved and lost.

But this time the air between them felt charged. Every time their hands brushed, Ember felt a spark shoot up her arm. Braxton felt it too- she could see it in the way he paused, the way his breath caught.

At one point, Ember climbed a small ladder to reach the top shelf. Braxton steadied it instinctively, his hands warm against the wood.

"You don't have to do that," she said, glancing down.

"I know," he replied. "But I want to."

She swallowed hard.

She wasn't used to people wanting to help her.

Wanting to stay.

"Wait," she said, pausing. "Jane Eyre. That was on the list, right?"

Braxton nodded. "Right."

"There should be a letter in here," Ember said, reaching for the old book, and she rifled through it, Braxton's hands holding the ladder steady. "Got it!"

She climbed down, holding the worn paper with swirly writing.

"Read it," Braxton said softly. "Read it to me, Ember."

Ember hesitated, and he quietly said "Please."

She swallowed hard, then she nodded and unfolded the paper carefully.

"*My dearest, Today, you handed a book to a customer and smiled in that way that makes the whole room feel warmer. I realised then that I don't love you because you are beautiful- though you are. I love you because you make the world feel less lonely. If I could borrow even a fraction of your courage, I would tell you everything. But for now, I hide my heart in the stories you love. Yours in silence, J."*

Ember read it aloud, her voice trembling slightly.

Braxton listened, his eyes soft. "Grandfather wasn't just in love. He was transformed."

She nodded. "It's… overwhelming."

"Love usually is."

"Let's read the last letter. You can read it this time, Braxton."

Braxton nodded his okay as he reached for the stack of papers and pulled out the one at the bottom.

"My dearest, I saw you crying today. You tried to hide it, but I noticed. I wanted to ask what hurt you, to offer comfort, but I froze. I always freeze. I am a man made of words, yet none of them seem worthy when I'm near you. Forgive my cowardice. J."

Ember's breath hitched.

Braxton touched her arm gently. "Are you okay?"

She nodded, but her eyes were shining. "I just… I know what it feels like to cry in a bookstore."

Braxton didn't ask why. He simply stayed close.

"Did you cry a lot in this bookstore?"

"After my grandfather died, yes. I was alone here, in this big house and store. I had and still have no family. I just…" Ember swallowed hard. "Even though I have the staff here, I still felt… well, so… *alone."*

Braxton's breath hitched this time.

He swallowed, then he reached out and took her hand. “I’m sorry you felt that way. Aside from your staff, do you have many friends?”

“Yes, but they’re long distance now, or doing their own thing, or they just feel awkward around me because of how much I’ve lost.”

“I suppose they didn’t know what to say, or understand.”

“Yeah. I figured.”

It was quiet for a moment, then Braxton decided to grow caution to the wind.

“Would you like to get out of the bookstore and your big house, and go to a café with me tomorrow?”

“What?” Ember looked startled. “The town is practically a ghost town on a Sunday. Not many cafés are open.”

“Well which ones are open?” smiled Braxton, and Ember replied “Carter’s Café is always open. It’s a twenty-minute walk from here.”

“So… can I pick you up from here and we go there together?” asked Braxton, his heart pounding. “I promise, it will be great. We can get to know each other a little more, and understand my grandfather, and your mother. You’d like to know about him, and I’d like to know about her.”

Ember thought about that.

Braxton held his breath.

Moments passed before Ember nodded.

“Ok. Tomorrow it is then.”

“Great,” gushed Braxton, then he cleared his throat. “Um… great.”

Lunch at the Café the Next Afternoon

The café Ember mentioned was small and cluttered, with mismatched chairs and a chalkboard menu that hadn't been updated in months.

The coffee was terrible, just as she'd warned Braxton, but the sandwiches were warm and comforting.

They sat by the window, watching rain streak down the glass.

"So," Braxton said, stirring his coffee with a grimace, "Tell me something about you that isn't about the bookstore."

Ember blinked. "That's… most of my life."

"Then tell me the part that isn't."

She hesitated, then said quietly, "I used to write."

Braxton's eyebrows lifted. "Really?"

Ember nodded, confessing "Poetry. Short stories. Novels. I wanted to wrote a ton of books. But life happened."

"Life always happens," Braxton said. "But that doesn't mean you stop being who you are."

She looked at him, surprised by the conviction in his voice.

"What about you?" she asked. "What do *you* write, Braxton?"

Braxton was surprised at that. "What makes you think I write, Ember?"

Ember shrugged a shoulder. "I just have a feeling."

He laughed softly. "Well… you're right. I write about… everything. Nothing. Mostly drafts of novels I never finish."

"Why not?"

He hesitated, then he confessed "Because I'm afraid they won't be good enough."

Ember stared at him. "You're afraid of not being enough?"

He nodded.

Ember looked down at her coffee, then she whispered “Me too.”

And just like that, something deep and unspoken connected them.

They hesitantly changed the conversation, very aware of what had just transpired, not knowing what to do about or how to react to it.

“So, um. I was thinking,” Ember said, “The weather’s meant to get nasty and the buses come every hour, You’ll probably get soaked.”

Braxton nodded. “Probably.”

“So, um, would you like to stay until tomorrow?” Ember asked a little shyly. “I have more than enough room. And each bedroom has its own bathroom.”

“That sounds nice, but I don’t have a change of clothes, or pyjamas.”

“Don’t worry. My butler will sort that out.”

Braxton hesitated. “Are you sure?”

Ember hesitated too, not knowing the answer to that herself. Then, she nodded bravely.

“I’m sure.”

Braxton smiled at her.

Ember smiled back.

The Afternoon Search... Growing Closeness

After lunch, they returned to the bookstore with a quiet, unspoken shift between them.

The air felt different- charged, expectant.

Ember noticed the way Braxton walked beside her now, closer than before, as if drawn by an invisible thread.

They resumed searching the shelves, but the task had become secondary. What mattered was the conversation that flowed between them-effortless, warm, surprising.

Braxton told her about his childhood summers spent in his grandfather's garden, listening to stories about "the girl in the bookstore." Ember told him about the first time she'd ever felt truly seen- by a teacher who told her she had a writer's heart.

"You still do," Braxton said softly.

She looked up, startled. "How would you know?"

"Because I've read your eyes," he said. "Writers look at the world differently. You see the story in everything."

Ember felt heat rise in her cheeks. No one had ever said something like that to her. Not with such certainty.

Braxton cleared his throat as he looked around, then he said "There! A letter is in that book."

Ember was surprised. "Are you certain?"

"Yes. Grandfather had a second list of books he put letters in for your mother," Braxton told her, "But I took a picture of it with my phone. I misplaced the original sheet of paper. I memorised the book titles on my way here."

Ember pulled down a battered copy of *The Catcher in the Rye*, and a folded page slipped out. She caught it before it hit the floor.

"You were right," she whispered.

Braxton joined her, leaning close enough that she could feel the warmth of him.

“Read it Ember,” he said softly, and she felt like she’d melt through the floor.

She unfolded the letter.

“My dearest, I walked past the shop today but couldn’t bring myself to go inside. I’m afraid that if I see you again, I’ll say something foolish. Or worse- I’ll say nothing at all. I am trapped between longing and fear, and both feel like home. J.”

Ember exhaled shakily. “He was so… vulnerable.”

Braxton nodded. “He always was. Even when he pretended not to be.”

She looked at him. “Are you like him?”

Braxton hesitated. “I think… I think I’ve spent most of my life being afraid of wanting things too much.”

“Why?”

“Because wanting means risking. And risking means losing.”

Ember swallowed. “Maybe. But sometimes wanting means finding.”

Their eyes held for a long moment.

“You’re right,” he said quietly, after a while. “I guess staying positive is key.”

Ember smiled and nodded.

Braxton smiled back.

A Storm Rolls In

By early evening, the rain had turned into a full storm. Wind rattled the windows, and thunder rolled in the distance.

The house felt smaller, cozier, wrapped in the sound of rain hitting the windows.

Ember turned the lamps on, casting warm pools of light across the shelves.

Braxton watched her move through the bookstore, her hair glowing like fire in the lamplight.

“You belong here,” Braxton said quietly.

Ember paused, turning to smile at him. “Do I?”

“Yes. But not because you’re stuck. Because you care. Because this place is part of you.”

Ember looked down at the letter she’d found her hands. “Sometimes I wonder if I’m holding onto something that doesn’t want to be held.”

Braxton stepped closer. “Or maybe you’re holding onto something that’s waiting for you to let it grow.”

She looked up at him, startled by the tenderness in his voice.

“Braxton…”

He stopped, giving her space. “Sorry. I didn’t mean to-”

“No,” she said quickly. “It’s just… no one talks to me like that.”

“Then they’ve been talking to you wrong.”

Her breath caught. “I… um-”

“Shh,” he said softly, and he raised a hand and caressed her soft cheek.

Ember’s eyes closed at his touch, then they both whipped round, startled as the butler Sebastian cleared his throat and announced “Dinner is served, Ma’am.”

“Great,” gushed Ember, quickly stepping away from Braxton. “We’ll be there in a moment."

Sebastian bowed and left them alone, a smile on his face.

He hoped that Ember had finally found love, even in a hopeless place.

The Power Goes Out

A sudden crack of thunder shook the building, and the lights flickered… then went out completely.

Ember gasped. "Oh, great. The wiring in this place is older than I am."

Braxton pulled out his phone, turning on the flashlight. "Don't worry. I've got you. I'll check out the fuse box."

The beam of light illuminated his face- soft, warm, steady. Ember felt something inside her shift.

"You don't have to fix anything. We can just go to bed," she said, though she didn't want him to leave. "Plus Sebastian normally sorts the power."

"I know," Braxton replied. "But I want to help. I can assist him, at least."

He said it so simply, so sincerely, that Ember felt her chest tighten.

They moved through the house together, holding up torches as Sebastian called "Not to worry, Miss Richards and guest. I'll have the power on in ten minutes."

"Thank you, Sebastian," Ember called back, and she smiled up at Braxton. "See?"

Braxton smiled back, thinking that she was so cute. "I see. Let's wait in the living area for everything to get sorted then."

Ember nodded.

The storm raged outside, but inside, everything felt strangely intimate.

As they sat on the sofas in slightly awkward silence, Braxton remembered something.

"The Misery of Sarah Gumphrey."

"What?" Ember looked at him curiously, shining her torch on his face.

Braxton looked excited. "That book holds another letter."

Ember felt a rush of excitement too. "Really?"

"Yep."

Just then, the power came back on and everyone cheered.

"Thank you, Sebastian!" Ember called happily, and she smiled at Braxton. "Well, come on. Let's find that letter!"

Braxton smiled back and nodded, and they headed into the bookstore.

Ember climbed a ladder again to reach a high shelf. Braxton steadied it, his hands brushing her ankle.

"You okay up there?" he asked.

"Yes," she said, though her heart was pounding. "I'm fine."

But when she reached for the right book after scanning the shelf excitedly, her fingers slipped. She wobbled and slipped down a little, unsteady as she gasped "Whoa!"

Braxton caught her waist instinctively.

For a moment, they froze- his hands steadying her, their faces inches apart.

"Got you," he whispered.

Ember's breath trembled. "I know."

She climbed down slowly, aware of every point where their bodies almost touched.

When her feet hit the floor, they didn't step apart. They stared at each other, the rain hammering hard on the windows.

Ember swallowed hard, then she whispered "Next letter."

"Read it," Braxton whispered back, and she nodded and opened the book with shaking hands, pulling out the letter.

"My dearest, I dreamed of you last night. Not your face- I can never quite capture it- but your presence. The feeling of you. Warmth. Light. A quiet kind of joy. If love is a story, then you are the chapter I keep rereading. J."

Ember's voice broke on the last line.

Braxton reached out, gently brushing a tear from her cheek with his thumb.

"Hey," he murmured. "Talk to me."

"It's just…" She swallowed. "No one has ever loved me like this. Not even close."

Braxton's expression softened. "Maybe you've been waiting for the right person."

She looked up at him. "And what if they never come?"

Braxton held her gaze, his voice low and steady.

"Then they're a fool. Because anyone who sees you- *really* sees you- would never walk away."

Ember's breath caught.

"Braxton…"

He stepped closer, slowly, giving her time to back away.

She didn't.

The storm outside roared, but inside the store, everything went quiet.

Braxton lifted a hand, brushing a strand of unruly hair behind her ear. His fingers lingered, tracing the line of her jaw.

"Tell me to stop," he whispered.

Ember's heart pounded. "I don't want you to stop."

He leaned in… slowly, carefully, as if giving her every chance to change her mind.

Their lips were a breath apart.

Then-

“A last tea and snack before bed, Miss Richards?” Trudy offered as she walked in, and they both jumped and whipped round, startled.

Ember stepped back, flustered. “I- um- yes please, Trudy. Braxton, let’s change for bed, and meet in the dining room.”

Braxton exhaled shakily. “Right. Yes. Good idea.”

Ember walked away, taking a deep breath, and he whispered to himself “This is going to change everything.”

And he was right.

After the Almost-Kiss

Ember fled to her bedroom and sat down after changing into her black pyjamas, telling herself she'd go down for tea immediately, but really, she just needed a moment to breathe.

Her heart was pounding so hard she could feel it in her fingertips.

She pressed her palms to her cool face and whispered "What are you *doing?"*

She was talking to herself.

To the part of her that had woken up the moment Braxton walked into her store that very first time.

To the part of her that wanted something- *someone*- so badly it terrified her.

She closed her eyes.

This is too fast.

This is reckless.

This is everything you've been afraid of.

But another voice whispered back.

This is what you've been waiting for.

Downstairs in the dining area, Braxton paced up and down, running a hand over his curly hair as he held his grandfather's letters.

He carefully placed the letters down on the table, his heart racing.

He felt like he'd been struck by lightning.

He hadn't meant to lean in.

He hadn't meant to get that close to Ember.

He hadn't meant to want her this much.

But he did.

God, he *did.*

He looked at the letters spread across the table and whispered, "Grandfather, what are you doing to me?"

He wasn't sure if he meant it as a complaint… or a thank you.

The Conversation They Can't Avoid

When Ember finally returned downstairs into the dining area, she looked steadier, but her eyes gave her away.

Braxton could tell she was nervous.

"Sorry," Ember said quietly. "I just needed a moment to clear my head."

Braxton nodded. "Me too."

They stood there, the silence thick with everything they weren't saying.

The maid Selena entered, saying warmly "Tea and cake is served, Miss Richards."

"Thank you, Selena," Ember said just as warmly, and she looked at Braxton. "Let's sit down."

Braxton nodded, and they sat opposite each other in silence as the tea, cake and some biscuits were served.

Ember picked up her favourite mug and sipped, avoiding his eyes. Braxton watched her look anywhere but at his face, and he picked up his mug and sipped too.

Moments passed.

Ember fidgeted.

Finally, Braxton spoke.

"Ember… about what almost happened-"

"It was the storm," she said quickly. "And the darkness. And the letters. And-"

"It wasn't the storm," Braxton cut across softly, looking at her through smouldering eyes, and Ember froze.

Braxton stood, and she quickly got to her feet also, her heart racing as he walked around the dining table towards her slowly.

Ember backed away at first, then she bravely stood her ground as he came closer.

"It wasn't the darkness either," Braxton continued calmly. "And it wasn't the letters. It was *you.*"

Her breath caught.

"And me also," he added. "It was both of us."

Ember looked down at her hands. "I don't know how to feel about that."

"Neither do I," Braxton admitted. "But do I know I don't want to pretend it didn't happen."

She looked up at him then, and the vulnerability in her eyes nearly made him want to hold her close and kiss her right there, right then.

"Braxton… I'm scared."

Braxton stepped closer… not touching her, but close enough that she could feel his body heat.

"So am I," he said softly. "But maybe we don't have to be scared alone."

The First Kiss

It happened quietly.

There was no dramatic music.

No thunder.

No flickering lights.

Just two people standing in a at the foot of the large staircase, surrounded by forgotten stories, finally choosing to write their own.

“Well… goodnight, Braxton,” Ember said quietly. He didn’t respond, staring at her with those breathtaking dark eyes. “Braxton? Are you ok?”

Braxton lifted a hand without speaking, slowly, giving Ember time to move away.

She didn’t.

His fingers brushed her cheek.

She leaned into the touch.

And then, he leant down, their lips brushing for a moment, and then he kissed her.

Softly at first, like he was asking a question.

Did she really want this?

Ember answered by reaching up, sliding her hands into his hair and pulling him closer.

The kiss deepened; slow, warm, full of everything they’d been holding back.

They stood lip-locked for a full two minutes, holding each other tightly.

When they finally broke apart, both were breathless.

“Wow,” Ember whispered as she took deep breaths, and Braxton laughed softly.

“Yeah. Wow.”

She rested her forehead against his chest, and Braxton wrapped his arms around her as she mumbled “This is insane.”

Braxton nodded, resting his chin atop her head. “Completely insane.”

“We barely know each other.”

“I know.”

“But it feels… I don’t know. Just… it feels so-”

“Right,” Braxton finished softly. “It feels so right.”

Ember nodded, shyly answering “Yeah. It does.”

They smiled at each other, and Braxton said “We’d better go to bed, Ember. It’s getting late.”

“Alright. Are you content with the guest room you have?”

“Of course,” smiled Braxton. “It’s huge. I love it. And these pyjama bottoms and vest are great too. They’re exactly my size.”

Ember nodded, and she murmured “Goodnight Braxton.”

“Goodnight Ember.”

Neither of them moved, both staring at each other hungrily.

And then Ember reached up and kissed him again, tenderly, before she broke the kiss and turned away, heading up the staircase.

She didn’t dare look back, entering her bedroom and closing the door behind her.

Braxton heard her bedroom door close, and he exhaled.

“I’m in trouble.”

Then Braxton heard someone clear their throat from behind him.

He whipped round, startled. “Sebastian!”

Sebastian the butler was right behind him, a grave look on his face. Braxton knew he had witnessed everything that just transpired between him and Ember.

“I- um- what can I do for you, Sebastian?” Braxton asked warily, and Sebastian replied "I shouldn't speak out of turn."

"Then don't," Braxton said haughtily, but Sebastian was determined to have his say.

"Miss Ember is the last living member of the Richards family. She has been alone, for so many years."

"Yeah, I know that."

"I don't want you to sweep her off her feet in a romantic haze before disappearing for good, Mr. Stevens." Sebastian stepped closer. "We all know you are only here because you are honouring the memory of your grandfather."

Braxton opened his mouth, then he closed it.

"After you read and collect the last letter, what next?" Sebastian asked quietly. "You will leave, yes? And you won't look back."

"That's not true." Braxton's tone was cold. "I care about Ember."

"You don't know her to care about her."

"I know enough."

"Is that so."

"Yes, it is."

"So what will happen after you wrap things up and end this chapter, no pun intended? You live three hours away, in London city."

"Three hours is nothing," Braxton replied flatly. "I will make it work."

Sebastian eyed him curiously. "That is what the last gentleman she opened her heart to said. He vanished after he got what he wanted. Just like you will."

Braxton stiffened at that. "She had a boyfriend?"

"He was her high school sweetheart. After she lost her grandfather, he promised that he was fine, and they would stick together, that they would make it work." Sebastian's voice grew cold. "Her tears, her sadness, was too much for him. He vanished, making Miss Ember spiral into a deep depression. But she is strong," the butler added. "She pushed on regardless."

Braxton was curious. “What kept her going?”

“The bookstore.” Sebastian’s voice grew icy. “The memories of her family, her childhood, her entire *life*- are in these walls. She feels deep down, her legacy is her strength. And we have watched Miss Ember grow from a scared child who lost her maternal figures into a wonderful woman. We won’t have her hurting, Mr. Stevens. We are very protective of her.”

Braxton nodded. “I understand, Sebastian.”

“Do you really?”

“Yes. I do.” Braxton’s face was hard. “I know how it feels to lose my parents at a young age. My grandfather raised me from the age of thirteen.”

Sebastian eyed Braxton a little sceptically. “It seems you have some things in common with Miss Ember.”

“Yes. And we have a deep connection also.” Braxton rubbed his cheek. “You can’t deny that. None of the staff can. I know you’ve been watching us, out of curiosity if not nosily.”

Sebastian smiled a little. “Miss Ember is like a daughter to us. We care, deeply.”

“I’m not surprised.” Braxton smiled back. “I think that concludes our conversation, Sebastian. Thank you for letting me know how you and the rest of the staff feel about my presence.”

Sebastian nodded. “Goodnight, Mr. Stevens.”

“Goodnight.”

Braxton turned and headed up the staircase, not looking back.

He entered his room, and he breathed out after closing the door.

He slipped into bed, and then he looked at his phone curiously.

There were a lot of messages from friends in the city, and work emails.

Braxton had already taken a lot of time off work due to the passing and burial of his grandfather. He still wasn’t ready to go back.

He sent his friends a group message, letting them know he was alright, that he just needed some alone time.

He sent his boss Carlton the same message via email, requesting a few more weeks off, possibly months, as he wasn't ready to go back to the office.

Even though it was late, Carlton responded.

"Take as much time off as you need Braxton. If you'd like to change your role to working from home instead of the office, we can arrange that. Just let me know when you're ready."

Working from home was a perfect idea.

Braxton thanked Carlton, and then he settled down to sleep.

The Aftermath

Ember and Braxton didn't rush anything after they'd kissed. They didn't make grand declarations or promises they weren't ready for.

Over the next few days, they sat on the floor between the shelves in Ember's bookstore, sharing a blanket Ember kept behind the counter for cold mornings.

The storm softened outside, rain tapping gently against the windows.

Braxton held Ember's hand, tracing circles on her palm.

Ember leaned her head on his shoulder, feeling more at peace than she had in years.

"Tell me something real," she said quietly.

Braxton thought for a moment.

"I haven't written anything in nine months," he admitted. "Not since my grandfather got sick, passed away, and was buried. It felt like… like the words dried up."

Ember squeezed his hand. "They'll come back."

He looked at her with a smile. "They already have."

Her breath caught.

"Your turn," Braxton said gently. "Tell me something real."

Ember hesitated, then whispered "I'm afraid that if I let myself want this… want you… it'll disappear."

Braxton turned to face her fully.

"Ember. I'm not going anywhere."

She closed her eyes, letting the words settle into the places inside her that had been empty for too long.

"Promise?" she whispered, and he leant close and kissed her temple, whispering in her ear "I promise."

“This feels like a dream,” she murmured. “I… I can’t believe we’ve come so far in so little time. And we’re connected by love. Love that isn’t ours, but that connects us regardless.”

Braxton nodded. “It broke my heart when I realised that my grandfather wasn’t aware that your mother died. He died believing she’d find those letters eventually.”

“I know. It’s very sad. But I’d like to think that they’ve met now, in the afterlife,” Ember answered. “And I’d like to think that my grandparents are finally back together.”

Braxton turned to look at her properly, a smile on his face. “I’d like to think so too.”

Three Weeks Later

Ember woke before dawn, curled against Braxton on the couch in her living area inside her massive home.

They hadn't planned to fall asleep together. They'd just been talking-about books, about their families, about the strange ways life brings people together.

She watched him sleep for a moment, his curly hair falling across his forehead, his breathing soft and steady.

He looked peaceful.

Safe.

Like someone she could build a life with.

The thought terrified her.

And thrilled her.

She brushed a kiss against his temple and whispered, "Please don't disappear, Braxton Stevens."

Braxton stirred, his eyes fluttering open.

"I'm not going anywhere," he murmured, half-asleep.

Ember smiled and kissed him gently.

Maybe, she thought, this was their new beginning.

The Morning After: Reality Creeps In

The next morning, Ember and Braxton walked downstairs to the bookstore together. The

It was finally springtime, leaving the world bright and glistening. Sunlight streamed through the windows, catching dust motes in golden suspension.

Ember unlocked the door, but her hand trembled slightly.

Braxton noticed. “You okay?”

She nodded, but her voice was soft. “I just… the store has been closed for quite some time. I don’t want this to disappear when the sun comes up. Me and you, I mean. How we are now, how close we’ve become these past few weeks.”

Braxton stepped behind her, wrapping his arms around her waist. “It won’t.”

She leaned back into him, letting herself believe it.

For a moment.

But as the day went on, reality began to seep in around the edges.

Customers came and went.

Deliveries arrived.

The phone rang.

Life resumed its usual rhythm.

And with it came the quiet, creeping fear in Ember as she assumed Braxton would eventually have to return to his regular life in the city.

He can’t stay with me forever.

Braxton's Phone Call

Around noon three days later, Braxton stepped away from Ember and walked between the bookshelves to take a call.

Ember tried not to listen, but the shop was quiet, and his voice carried.

"Yes, I'll be there Monday to finalise everything. No, I haven't changed my mind. Yes, I understand it's a big opportunity."

Ember's stomach dropped.

When he came back inside, she was shelving books with unnecessary force.

She was angry.

He was going to leave her.

Just like everyone else did.

"Everything okay Ember?" Braxton asked gently.

"Fine," she said, too quickly, too coldly.

Braxton frowned at her.

Ember held her gaze for a moment, then she turned away.

Braxton didn't push.

Not yet.

The Tension Breaks

It wasn't until closing time that the truth finally spilled out.

Ember was wiping down the counters when Braxton approached her.

"Ember… talk to me."

She kept her eyes on the cloth in her hand. "About what?"

"You know what. You've been reserved and icy all day."

Silence.

Braxton watched her, but she continued wiping invisible dust.

"Ember. Please. Stop."

Ember threw the cloth down and turned to face him, angry tears in her eyes.

"I overheard your phone call. To your boss, I'm assuming. About a big opportunity."

Braxton exhaled. "I was going to tell you tonight."

"You didn't have to," she said, her voice tight. "I heard enough."

Braxton stepped closer. "It's just some changes, Ember. It doesn't mean I'm leaving."

"But you *are*," she whispered. "And I barely had you."

Braxton reached for her hand, but she pulled away.

"Ember, please listen to me. You don't understand what-"

"I don't want to be another chapter you leave behind," she said, her voice cracking. "I don't want to fall for someone who's already halfway out the door."

Braxton's expression softened with something like heartbreak.

"You're not a chapter," he said quietly. "You're the whole damn book."

She looked up, startled.

“But I can’t pretend I don’t have a life in Londin,” he continued. “A successful career I’ve had for years.”

“And I can’t leave this place,” she whispered. “It’s all I have left of my family.”

They stood there, the space between them suddenly vast.

Then Braxton grabbed her hands.

“I wanted it to be a surprise. But I think I need to explain.”

“Explain that you have to leave?”

“No! Well, yes, but-”

“Then go.” Ember’s voice cracked. “You don’t need to explain, Braxton. Just… just get your things together and go back to London city. It’s where you belong.”

Braxton stared at her, stunned and a little hurt.

“You mean that?”

“You have a great career waiting, like you said. I don’t want to hold you back.”

“You could never hold me back, Ember Richards.”

Braxton stepped closer, but she stepped away again and cleared her throat.

“I need to make sure these books are arranged. A new delivery is coming in today.”

“Ember-”

“You should sort your things out and be on your way.”

“Ember.” Braxton’s tone was firm. “Stop pushing me away. We need to talk.”

“We’ve done plenty of talking, Braxton.”

The Letter That Changes Everything

Ember turned away, blinking back tears. She reached for a stack of books to distract herself from the man watching her- and a letter slipped out.

Another one.

Ember froze.

Braxton stepped beside her, his breath catching.

“Read it,” he whispered.

Her hands shook as she unfolded the page.

“My dearest, I am leaving soon. Not by choice, but by necessity. Life is pulling me in a direction I never intended to go. But I cannot leave without saying this, even if you never read it: You were the moment I realised I wanted more from my life than safety. You were the moment I understood that love is worth the risk. If I go, it is not because I do not care. It is because I care too much to stay the man I am. But if fate is kind, perhaps our paths will cross again. Yours, always, J.”

Ember’s breath trembled.

Braxton closed his eyes.

“That’s it,” he whispered. “That’s the letter Grandfather told me about. The one he regretted most. The one he said he should have delivered.”

Ember looked at him, tears slipping down her cheeks.

“He left,” she said softly. “He left because he was afraid.”

Braxton nodded. “And he spent the rest of his life wondering what might have happened if he’d stayed. Even after building a new life, your mother never left his mind.”

They stared at each other, the weight of the moment settling around them.

"I don't want to be like him," Braxton said quietly. "I don't want to spend my life wondering what would've happened if I'd stayed with you."

Ember's heart stuttered.

Then she whispered "Your life is in London city."

He cupped her face in his hands. "No, Ember. My life is wherever you are."

"But- but I want you to chase your dreams, not bury them."

Braxton smiled, and he murmured "Maybe you're part of my dreams, Ember Richards."

It was silent for a moment, then she whispered "And maybe you're part of mine."

Braxton's Choice

That night, Braxton and Ember sat together on the floor of the large living room, surrounded by letters and books and the ghosts of choices made decades ago.

Ember handed Braxton a leather file, softly saying "For your grandfather's letters. They'll be safe in this file."

"Thank you," Braxton said just as softly, and he began gathering up the many pages, and he carefully began putting them into the file one by one.

It was quiet as she watched him work.

Ember's heart was heavy. She knew everything was coming to an end.

Braxton would leave, and she would never see him again.

He got what he came for.

He had closure.

Why would he come back??

As if knowing what she was thinking, Braxton placed the file down and took her hand.

"I'm going to London in two days," he said quietly. "But it's to do with my job."

Ember nodded, tears already slipping silently down her cheeks.

"But I'm coming back," he said firmly. "I'm coming back to you. And then we'll figure out the rest together."

She looked at him in surprise, searching his face for any hint of doubt.

There was none.

"Promise?" she whispered.

He kissed her, slow, deep, certain.

When they broke apart, he gently wiped her tears away and whispered "I promise."

“Do you know how long everything will take before you come back?”

“No,” he admitted. “But I will call and text you every day. You’ll never be in the dark when it comes to me. I swear it.”

Ember believed him.

She felt a calmness settle in her chest, a feeling of acceptance about the way things were headed, and she nodded.

The Goodbye

Two days later, Braxton packed his bag. Ember walked him to the taxi waiting outside the bookstore, her hand in his, her heart in her throat.

"I'll call you every day," Braxton said, turning to her as the driver opened the taxi door for her. "Like I promised."

"You'd better," Ember whispered.

He brushed a kiss against her lips. "This isn't an ending."

"No," she said. "It's a comma."

Braxton laughed softly. "Leave it to a writer to say that."

Ember smiled, but it trembled. Braxton saw.

"I'll be back in five days," he said, surprising her.

"Five days," she echoed. "Are you sure?"

"I've never been surer," he smiled, and he got into the car.

The driver started the engine.

Braxton rolled down the window.

"I love you," he said softly; Ember's breath caught.

But she wasn't scared to confess the same. "I love you too."

The taxi pulled away, Ember watching it go.

She stood there long after the car disappeared, cool wind blowing over her,

She whispered into the quiet afternoon "Five days. Please come back like you promised."

A Life That Doesn't Fit Anymore

London greeted Braxton with its usual bustle of many vehicles, crowded sidewalks, the smell of all kinds of food and coffee from almost every street.

Normally, he loved this city. It was familiar, structured, full of ambition and noise.

But now, it felt… wrong.

Braxton entered his home, dropped his suitcase on the floor, and he sank into his armchair in the living room and stared up at the ceiling.

He should have been excited to be home.

He'd already made arrangements with his boss about transferring his job to a sister firm exactly away one hour from Ember's bookstore.

A position at a respected publishing house had opened up, and Carlton, being a very kind and understanding man, offered Braxton that position. It was a chance to edit real manuscripts, with triple his current pay.

Definitely a career-defining opportunity, and Braxton was definitely excited about it.

He'd start in five weeks.

That would give him enough time to tell his landlord he was leaving, say goodbye to his friends, and start a new life with the woman he loved.

That night, Braxton ordered himself a small pizza and sat watching his television, but he couldn't concentrate on the crime series he'd been so engrossed in before leaving London.

All he could think about was Ember.

Her laugh.

Her bookstore. The way she'd whispered "I love you" when they were parting like it was both a confession and a prayer.

Braxton smiled a little, knowing they'd both meant it.

He closed his eyes, murmuring “We love each other.”

The Realisation

The next morning...

Braxton felt lighter than he had in years.

The sky seemed brighter.

The air felt warmer.

He called his best friend Douglas first.

He answered on the second ring. “Braxton? Everything okay?”

“Yeah,” he said, smiling. “Everything’s... *really* okay.”

“You sound different.”

“I *feel* different.”

Douglas hesitated. “Is this about your grandfather?”

“In a way,” Braxton said. “But it’s also about *me.* And someone I met while hunting on behalf of my grandfather.”

Douglas chuckled. “Your grandfather always said love was the only thing worth being brave for.”

“I know,” Braxton answered. “And I think I finally understand what he meant.”

“So... I guess you’re leaving then.”

It wasn’t a question.

Douglas knew Braxton too well.

Braxton took a deep breath, then he said “Yes, I’m leaving. But I want to leave you my keys. I want you to go to my flat, and if you see anything you want, take it. The television, the furniture, whatever. I’m leaving everything but my clothes and my gadgets. So take a few friends and get a few things in the next two weeks, ok Doug? After that, everything will belong to the landlord.”

“Wow. Alright. You know you have to come say bye to me and the rest of the gang before you jet off to your new life.”

“Consider that arranged, Doug.” Braxton smiled. “Just make it quick.”

“Seriously?” Douglas said amusedly; Braxton replied “Seriously.”

“Ok, ok.”

The Drive Back

Four more days passed quickly.

Braxton didn’t wait for anymore goodbyes or for the planned send-off from his friends that evening.

Evening was too far away.

He couldn’t wait to see her again.

He didn’t check out of the hotel he was staying in after he’d told his landlord he had given up the flat.

He just called the taxi, got in, and zoomed away.

The journey would take three harrowing hours.

He didn’t care.

He just needed to get back to her.

Ember's Worst Day

While Braxton was driving back, Ember was having the worst day she'd had in months.

The shop was quiet.

Too quiet.

Every creak of the floorboards reminded her of Braxton's footsteps.

Every book she shelved reminded her of the letters.

Every customer who walked in made her heart leap, hoping it was him.

By late afternoon, she was pacing behind the counter, chewing her lip.

What if he changes his mind? What if he realises he wants London more? What if I'm just a chapter after all?

She sank onto the stool, burying her face in her hands.

"I'm such an idiot," she whispered. "I fell in love with a man who doesn't even live here."

The bell above the door chimed.

She didn't look up, her head still in her hands.

"We're closing soon," she said, her voice thick with tears that were threatening to leave her eyes. "Please browse or purchase quickly. You only have twenty minutes before I close the store.

Braxton chuckled at that, and he responded "Good thing I made it in time."

Ember's head snapped up.

Braxton stood in the doorway, holding two suitcases, smiling at her.

Ember's heart nearly stopped. "Braxton?"

He crossed the room in three long strides; Ember scrambled to her feet. They stared at each other for a moment, then she mumbled "You… you came back."

Braxton chuckled and pulled her into his arms.

"Of course I came back," he whispered into her ear. "I told you I would."

She clung to him, tears spilling down her cheeks. "You're a day early."

"Another day away from you would have killed me."

She pulled back just enough to see his face. "How did everything go?"

He smiled at her. "My boss transferred me to a sister company just across town."

Her breath caught. "This town?"

"This town. And the pay is triple, Ember."

"That's amazing," she whispered. "I can't believe you did this."

"I did this because I realised something," Braxton said, cupping her face in his hands. "I don't want a life that doesn't have you in it."

Her tears started falling again.

"Braxton…"

"I want you," Braxton said softly. "I want this. I want *us.* And I'm done being afraid of wanting things. Like I implied, I don't want to be like my grandfather."

She kissed him then; hard, desperate, relieved.

He kissed her back with everything he had.

When they broke apart, Ember whispered "Let's go to my room."

Braxton looked at her, surprised, knowing what she meant.

"Are you sure?"

"Yes, I'm sure. If I wait any longer, I will go mad."

Braxton kissed her tenderly, and he whispered "Me too."

The Decision They Make Together

The next morning, they laid tangled in bedsheets, their arms around each other.

"So what now?" Ember asked softly, her head on Braxton's bare chest.

"Now," Braxton said, "We build something. Together."

She smiled. "Here?"

"Here. And anywhere else we want. We don't have to choose one life. We can make our own."

Ember rested her head on his shoulder. "I like the sound of that."

Braxton picked up one of his grandfather's file of letters that he'd kept on the bedside table, running his thumb over the leather.

After Ember had fallen asleep after three rounds of passionate love-making, he'd retrieved the file and read through every single letter, feeling sorry for his grandfather, who'd just never been brave enough to shoot his shot.

"Grandfather never got his chance," he said softly. "But we do."

Ember took his hand.

"Then let's not waste it."

Building a Life Together

The months after Braxton returned were some of the happiest of Ember's life.

They fell into a rhythm, gentle, steady, full of small moments that felt like magic.

Braxton wrote every morning on weekends in his new study, sunlight catching in his curly shiny hair. On weekdays, he went to work.

Ember worked downstairs in the bookstore, greeting customers with a brightness she hadn't felt in years.

At lunch, they'd meet in the café across the street, sharing sandwiches and stories about work and how they couldn't wait to see each other afterwards to tell them more.

They'd searched for more letters, but only found one more.

This one felt like a blessing.

This one felt like a reminder.

"Don't waste time. Don't hide your heart. Don't wait years to say what matters. J."

Ember's New Dream

One evening, as they sat together on the couch, Ember said quietly "I think I want to start writing again."

Braxton looked up from his laptop. "You should."

"But I'm scared," she admitted, and he smiled.

"Good. That means it matters."

Ember laughed softly. "You always know what to say."

"That's because I'm in love with you," Braxton said simply. "And I want you to have the life you deserve."

Ember leaned her head on his shoulder. "I want to spend forever with you, Braxton. The rest of my life, me and you. That's my dream."

"And we will make that dream come true," he whispered. "I promise you."

The Book Takes Shape

Ember spent months writing a fiction novel that involved Braxton's grandfather's letters and characters that were greatly based on the mysterious man in the bookstore and her mother. She referred to the letters, transcribing them, arranging them in order, placing them in sections of the novel.

This time however, the ending was different to real life.

The mysterious man's letters were found by the beautiful woman, after after being afraid at first, finding the man a little strange and creepy, the woman settled down, read each letter, and began to fall as deeply for him as he had for her.

The novel was raw, honest, beautiful.

Braxton edited the manuscript, adding footnotes about his grandfather's life, his regrets, his legacy.

When they submitted it to a small press in London that Braxton had connections to due to his job, Ember didn't expect much.

But the editor called them within a week.

"This book," she said, her voice thick with emotion. "It's extraordinary. We want to publish it and give it the publicity it rightly deserves."

Ember cried.

Braxton held her.

And Justin Stevens's words -silent for sixty years- finally found its voice.

The Book Launch

The launch of Ember's book was held in her newly renovated bookstore- now a cozy blend of old charm and modern warmth. She had kept the oak shelves, the reading nook, the vintage lamps. She'd added another large room that was connected to the store which had sofas and armchairs, a small space for readers.

"It's like a little library," she mused happily, watching her customers settle with their books that they were reading a before buying. "This is good."

"Very good," Braxton murmured from behind her. "Are you ready for this? The press are outside and many are waiting for signed copies of your novel."

Ember's grip tightened on of *Between the Lines: The Love Letters of Justin Stevens*.

Her hands trembled, the book shaking.

Braxton squeezed her shoulder. "You've got this."

Ember took a deep breath, then she said "I'm ready."

"Let's go then."

Ember walked out into the main part of the bookstore; immediately cameras flashed, and cheers went up.

"Miss Richards! Please, look this way!"

Ember held her book and smiled, the press taking their photos for their papers and magazines.

"Alright Ember," her agent Samantha said with a warm smile, joining her. "We're going to film a small clip of you reading the introduction of Between The Lines, and then film you signing copies for your customers."

Ember looked nervous.

Samantha squeezed her arm. "You can do this."

And Ember could.

Shaking off her nerves, she read the introduction aloud, her voice steady and full of emotion.

When she finished, the room erupted in applause.

Ember spent the next three hours posing for photos with her fans, excited readers young and old, and signing copies of her book, over and over again, until her fingers were sore.

When the book store closed at five and she was congratulated one more time by her readers, agent, and the press before the store gradually emptied, Ember breathed out.

“I didn’t mean to become a popular author in the blink of an eye.”

“Dreams really do come true,” smiled Braxton, and she smiled back.

“My dreams would have stayed dreams if it wasn’t for you.”

Braxton kissed her temple. “Your grandfather would be proud of you.”

She smiled up at him. “So would yours.”

The Proposal

Six months later, Braxton asked her to meet him at the bookstore after closing.

When she arrived, the lights were dim, and a single book sat on the counter.

A first edition of *East of Eden*.

The book which had the very first letter from Braxton's grandfather.

Ember's breath caught as reached for the book.

She opened it.

Inside was a letter.

Not one of Justin's.

One written in Braxton's handwriting.

"My dearest Ember, I walked into this shop looking for the past. I found my future instead. You are the bravest person I know. You took a chance on a stranger with a box of old letters, and you changed both of our lives. I don't want to spend another day without you. I don't want to write another chapter that doesn't have you in it. So I'm asking you, here in the place where it all began: Will you marry me? Yours, always, Braxton."

Ember looked up, tears streaming down her cheeks.

Braxton was on one knee before her, holding a ring.

"Yes," she whispered. "Yes, yes, yes."

He slipped the ring onto her finger and kissed her, the bookstore glowing around them like a blessing.

The Wedding

They married in a library of course. Surrounded by books, friends, and the quiet hum of stories waiting to be read.

Ember wore a vintage dress the colour of old paper. Braxton wore a navy suit and a smile so wide it made everyone else smile too.

Their vows were simple.

Ember: "You walked into my life and made me brave."

Braxton: "You walked into my heart and made me whole."

Everyone cried, even the officiant.

The Journal

On their wedding night, Braxton handed Ember a leather-bound journal.

"For our story," he said.

She opened it.

On the first page, he'd written:

"My dearest Ember, This is me being brave. This is me promising to write our story every day, for the rest of our lives. Yours, always, Braxton."

Ember's eyes welled up, and she took the pen he offered and wrote beneath it:

"My dearest Braxton, Thank you for finding me between the lines. Yours, forever, Ember."

The Final Letter

Five years later, on their anniversary, they went down into the bookstore.

They slipped a letter into a worn copy of *Between The Lines*.

A letter addressed to a stranger.

"To whoever finds this, We met in this shop five years ago, brought together by love letters written sixty years before. If you're reading this, maybe you're searching for something too. Maybe you're afraid to speak your heart. Maybe you're waiting for a sign. Let this be it. Be brave. Say the words. Take the leap. Don't let your love story become a collection of letters no one ever reads. With hope, Ember and Braxton Stevens."

They placed the book back on the shelf.

Hand in hand, they walked out into the sunlight.

"Shall we have lunch in the local park?" smiled Braxton, and Ember smiled back.

"I'd love to."

They walked down the road, talking softly, hand in hand.

And somewhere, Justin Stevens's spirit smiled.

Because his story had finally found its ending.

And through it, Ember and Braxton had found their beautiful beginning.

THE LAST WITNESS

Detective Ruby Walker is running out of time. The only witness to a brutal murder is a woman who swears she remembers nothing about that night-whether from fear, trauma, or something far more dangerous. Ruby knows one thing for certain: someone wants this woman silenced.

As Ruby pushes past dead ends and evasions, she uncovers a pattern that suggests the murder is only the beginning. Each clue pulls her deeper into a web of corruption, hidden crimes, and carefully buried secrets. Allies grow scarce, enemies were once friends, and the truth becomes harder to trust.

Protecting her witness may be the only way to expose what's really happening-but doing so could cost Ruby her career, her safety, and the fragile trust of the woman whose forgotten memories might be the key to everything.

The Night of the Murder

The alley behind the Blue Lantern Bar was the kind of place where secrets went to die.

Rain slicked the pavement, turning puddles into mirrors that reflected the neon sign flickering above. A cat darted between trash cans. Somewhere in the distance, a siren wailed.

And then-

A scream.

Short.

Sharp.

Cut off too quickly.

A woman stumbled into the alley, her breath ragged, her hands shaking. Her clothes were soaked, her hair plastered to her face. She pressed her back against the brick wall, eyes wide with terror.

Footsteps pounded behind her.

She turned.

A shadow loomed.

A flash of metal.

A voice, low and cold: "You shouldn't have seen that."

Then everything went black.

Detective Ruby Walker's Arrival

Detective Ruby Walker pulled up to the scene at 2:14 a.m., coffee in one hand, badge in the other. She was exhausted, but she'd learned long ago that homicide didn't care about sleep schedules.

The alley was cordoned off with yellow tape. Uniformed officers milled around, their breath fogging in the cold air. The crime scene techs were already at work.

Ruby ducked under the tape.

"What do we have?" she asked.

Officer Ramirez approached her, his expression grim. "Male victim. Late thirties. Multiple stab wounds. No ID yet."

Ruby crouched beside the body. The man laid face-down, blood pooling beneath him. His jacket was torn, his knuckles scraped.

"Looks like he fought back," she murmured.

"Yeah," Ramirez said. "But that's not the weird part."

Ruby raised an eyebrow. "There's always a weird part."

Ramirez nodded toward the end of the alley. "We found a witness."

Ruby straightened. "Alive?"

"Barely. She was unconscious when we got here. EMTs say she's stable, but… she doesn't remember anything."

Ruby's jaw tightened. "Convenient."

"That's what I thought. But she's shaken, Detective. Really shaken."

Ruby exhaled. "Where is she now?"

"Hospital. Room 214."

Ruby headed for her car.

"Walker," Ramirez called after her. "Be careful with this one."

Ruby didn't look back. "Aren't I always?"

Ramirez muttered, "That's what I'm afraid of."

The Witness: Ramona Baker

The hospital room was dim, lit only by the soft glow of a bedside lamp.

The witness of the murder in question sat upright, knees drawn to her chest, hospital blanket wrapped tightly around her.

She looked small. Fragile. Like someone who'd been broken and glued back together too many times.

Ruby approached slowly.

"Ramona Baker?"

The woman looked up, her eyes wide and unfocused. "That's what they told me."

"You don't remember your name?"

Ramona shook her head. "I don't remember anything."

Ruby pulled up a chair. "I'm Detective Ruby Walker. I'm here to help."

Ramona flinched at the word *detective*.

Ruby noticed.

"Ramona," she said gently, "You were found at the scene of a homicide. You're the only person who might have seen what happened."

Ramona's breath hitched. "I… I don't know. I don't know what I saw."

Ruby studied her carefully. Trauma could do this. Shock could do this. But something about Ramona's fear felt deeper.

Older.

"Do you remember why you were there?" Ruby asked.

Ramona shook her head violently. "No. I don't- I can't-"

Her breathing quickened.

Panic rising.

Ruby reached out, placing a steady hand on her arm. “Hey. Look at me.”

Ramona did.

“You’re safe,” Ruby said. “No one is going to hurt you.”

Ramona swallowed hard. “You don’t know that.”

Ruby’s eyes narrowed. “Then tell me who you think is trying to.”

Ramona hesitated.

Then whispered:

“I think someone followed me.”

Ruby’s pulse quickened. “Who?”

Ramona shook her head. “I don’t know. I can’t remember. But I feel it. Like a shadow I can’t shake.”

Ruby leaned back, her mind racing.

A witness with no memory.

A murder with no motive.

A shadow that might be real- or imagined.

She stood.

“I’m assigning myself to your case,” Ruby said. “You’re under protective custody until we figure out what happened.”

Ramona’s eyes widened. “Protective custody? Why?”

Ruby met her gaze.

“Because, Ramona… if someone wanted you dead, they might try to murder you again.”

Ramona’s mouth trembled.

And Ruby just knew at that moment, that this case was going to be hell.

Ruby's Internal Conflict

On her way out of the hospital, Ruby paused in the hallway, leaning against the wall.

She closed her eyes.

She'd seen trauma before.

She'd seen fear.

But Ramona's fear was different.

It wasn't just about the murder.

It was about something else.

Something buried.

Something dangerous.

Ruby rubbed her temples.

She didn't have time for a complicated witness. She didn't have time for another case that would consume her life.

Not after the last one.

Not after what it had cost her.

But she also knew she couldn't walk away.

Not from this.

Not from *her*.

The Killer Watches

Across the street from the hospital, a man sat in a parked car, watching the windows.

He tapped his fingers on the steering wheel.

"She's alive," he muttered. "Damn it."

He pulled out his phone.

"It's me," he said when the line connected. "We have a problem."

A pause.

"No," he said. "She doesn't remember. But the detective is involved now."

Another pause.

He clenched his jaw.

"Yes," he said. "I'll take care of it."

He hung up.

And smiled.

Protective Custody Begins

Detective Ruby Walker drove Ramona Baker to the safehouse herself.

It wasn't standard procedure - normally, an officer in uniform would handle transport - but something about Ramona's trembling hands and hollow eyes made Ruby override protocol.

The safehouse was a modest two-bedroom apartment owned by the department. Neutral walls. Sparse furniture. A place meant to feel temporary.

Ramona stood in the doorway, clutching the strap of her hospital bag.

"This is… where I stay now?"

"For now," Ruby said. "Until we figure out who's after you."

Ramona stepped inside slowly, as if expecting the shadows to move.

Ruby watched her carefully.

"You're safe here."

Ramona didn't answer. She was starting to tremble again.

"Ramona?" Ruby was concerned. "What is it?"

"What if we were followed?" whispered Ramona; Ruby sighed.

Paranoia.

She did her best to comfort the poor woman.

"Even if you were, nobody can get to you. You're being guarded at all times. I promise you."

Ramona hugged herself, and she nodded.

Ruby's First Clue

Back at the precinct, Ruby spread the crime scene photos across her desk.

The victim - male, mid-thirties, athletic build - had fought hard. Defensive wounds. Bruised knuckles. A deep stab wound to the abdomen.

But something else caught her eye.

A faint smear of lipstick on his collar.

Not smudged. Not accidental. Placed.

Ruby leaned closer.

"Red," she murmured. "Bright red."

She checked the evidence log.

No lipstick found on Ramona. No lipstick in her belongings. No lipstick at the scene.

So whose mark was it?

And why leave it??

Ramona's First Night in the Safehouse

Ramona sat on the couch, knees pulled to her chest, staring at the blank TV screen. The silence pressed in on her.

Every creak of the building made her flinch.

Every shadow felt like it was watching.

She closed her eyes, and immediately images flashed before them.

A flash.

A man shouting.

A hand grabbing her wrist.

A glint of metal.

Blood.

Ramona gasped, clutching her head.

The memory vanished as quickly as it came, leaving only a pounding heartbeat and a rising sense of dread.

She whispered into the empty room, "What happened to me?"

Detective Ruby Returns

Detective Ruby knocked once before entering the safehouse the following afternoon. Ramona was still on the couch, still very shaken up.

“You okay?” Ruby asked.

Ramona nodded, but her eyes said otherwise.

Ruby sat beside her. “I need to ask you something. It’s important.”

Ramona swallowed. “Okay.”

“Do you remember wearing lipstick last night? Bright red?”

Ramona blinked. “No. I don’t… I don’t even own lipstick. I don’t think I wear much makeup usually either. It… it doesn’t feel like me.”

Ruby nodded slowly. “That’s what I thought.”

Ramona’s voice trembled. “Does that mean something?”

“It means,” Ruby said carefully, “That someone else was close to the victim. Close enough to leave a mark.”

Romana looked at her. “A mark… with lipstick? Like… a lip-print?”

Ruby nodded. “Yes.”

Ramona’s breathing grew heavy. “And you think I saw them.”

“I think you might have,” Ruby said. “Even if you don’t remember yet.”

Ramona looked down at her hands. “What if remembering hurts?”

Ruby’s voice softened. “Sometimes it does. But not remembering can be worse.”

Ramona nodded, tears gathering in her eyes.

Ruby stayed with her for another hour, making sure she was a little more settled.

Then she said “Groceries will be delivered for the week by another officer later today. If you don’t remember how to cook, don’t worry. For now, they’re microwave meals and tinned food, and bread, milk, and teabags along with sugar. Will that be ok?"

Ramona nodded.

"Alright. They won't have a key to get in here like I do though. They'll knock three times. If you hear a knock that isn't thrice, don't answer."

Ramona swallowed, then she nodded again.

Ruby squeezed her arm, then she left.

The Killer Makes His First Move

At 3:17 a.m., a dark figure approached the safehouse.

He moved with practiced ease, avoiding the streetlights, staying close to the shadows. He reached the back door, pulled out a small device, and pressed it against the lock.

A soft click confirmed the door was now unlocked.

He slipped inside.

The apartment was silent.

He moved down the hallway, knife glinting faintly in the moonlight.

He reached the bedroom door.

Turned the handle, then pushed it open, smirking.

“Too easy.” Then he stopped in surprise. “What-”

The bed was empty.

A voice behind him spoke coldly, startling him.

“Police. Drop the weapon.”

The man spun around, knife held high.

Ruby stood in the doorway, her gun raised, eyes cold as she said “I’ve been expecting you.”

Without responding, the man bolted.

Ruby fired; BANG!! BANG!!

Blood spurted from the man’s arm; he was hit. He shouted out in pain, but he didn’t stop as he raced away.

He dove through the closed bedroom window, glass shattering, and he disappeared into the night.

Ruby cursed under her breath and ran across the bedroom to the window, aiming her firearm, but it was too dark to see.

He got away.

Ruby turned and looked at the walk-in closet, taking a deep breath before she walked and opened it.

Ramona was curled in the corner of the closet, shaking violently.

“They sent him,” she whispered. “They sent him here.”

Ruby knelt beside her, pulling her into her arms.

“I’ve got you,” she said. “I’m not letting anything happen to you.”

Ramona sobbed into her shoulder.

“They know where I am. They’ll come back.”

Ruby held her tighter.

“We’ll sort that. You have nothing to worry about. I promise.”

“Is it safe to stay here?”

“Yes,” Ruby answered as she pulled out her phone. “We’ll change the code and confirmation of the all entrance and exit keys in the next couple of hours. He won’t be able to get in again using the same key.”

“How did he get a key in the first place?”

Ruby’s blood boiled at that. “Good question.”

Aftermath: A New Fear

Back at the precinct later that day, Ruby slammed her hand on the conference table in front of the Chief of Police.

"He knew where she was," she said angrily. "He knew exactly where to find her."

Chief Starker frowned. "We kept the location off the books and offline."

"It got leaked," Ruby said. "Someone's watching both us and her. The attacker even had a key for easy access. I think one of our own may be in on this, Sir."

Starker rubbed his temples. "Walker, this case is getting messy."

Ruby leaned forward. "Messy means we're close."

Starker sighed. "Or it means we're in over our heads."

Ruby's jaw tightened. "I'm not abandoning her."

Starker met her eyes. "I didn't say you should, Walker. But be careful. Whoever this guy is, and whoever he's working for. They're not afraid of us."

Ruby nodded.

She already knew that.

After talking to the Chief some more, Ruby left the precinct. As she was walking, she saw Officer Ramirez knelt with his arms shoved up a snack machine, his fingers inches from a packet of Doritos.

"Seriously?" she said amusedly, and he yanked his arm out, grazing it a little.

"Walker," Ramirez said, grinning sheepishly. "You shouldn't have seen that."

"Don't you have change?" Ruby asked; he said no.

"They won't update these dumb machines. Everyone knows it's card or nothing these days."

Ruby laughed at that and reached into her pocket, then she handed him three pound coins.

"There. Go crazy."

"Thanks Walker."

"No problem," Ruby answered as she walked away.

Ramona's Memory Breaks Open

That night, Detective Walker returned to the safehouse to see Ramona.

The locks were changed, the window was fixed, and the flat was clean once more.

Ramona sat at the table in the kitchen, staring at a cup of untouched tea.

"I remember something," Ramona whispered, when Ruby entered the kitchen.

Surprised and relieved, Ruby sat down slowly. "Tell me."

Ramona closed her eyes.

"I was running," she said. "I remember… the rain. And… and a man. Not the victim. Someone else."

Ruby leaned in. "What did he look like?"

Ramona shook her head. "I don't know. His face is… blurred. But his voice-"

She shivered.

"He said, 'You shouldn't have seen that.'"

Ruby's blood ran cold.

"That's exactly what the killer said," Ramona whispered.

Ruby didn't answer, her heart pounding.

Ramona's eyes filled with tears. "He's going to kill me. And if he won't himself, he'll send someone to. Like before."

Ruby reached across the table, taking her hand.

"No," she said firmly. "I won't let that happen."

Ramona looked at her, searching for something - hope, strength, safety.

Ruby held her gaze.

"You're not alone," she said. "Not anymore."

Ruby's mind was spinning.

The puzzle pieces were getting closer to coming together, but she wasn't going to reveal her suspicions just yet.

She needed to be trusted by her suspect before she revealed them.

The Victim Gets a Name

Detective Ruby Walker stood in the morgue, arms crossed, staring at the body on the table. The fluorescent lights buzzed overhead, casting a cold glow on the victim's pale skin.

Dr. Patel, the medical examiner, flipped through his notes.

"Cause of death: exsanguination from multiple stab wounds. Time of death: between 1:30 and 2:00 a.m."

Ruby nodded. "Any ID yet?"

Patel handed her a small evidence bag. Inside was a wallet, soaked but intact.

Ruby opened it.

Her breath caught.

"Michael Avery," she murmured. "Age thirty-six. Financial crimes division."

Patel raised an eyebrow. "One of yours?"

"Not mine personally," Ruby said. "But he worked with the department a floor down."

Patel hesitated. "There's something else."

He handed her another evidence bag.

Inside was a small, folded piece of paper.

Ruby unfolded it.

A phone number.

Nothing else.

"Found in his pocket," Patel said. "Written recently."

Ruby stared at the number.

It wasn't familiar.

But something about it made her stomach twist.

Things were a mystery right now.

Detective Walker was determined to crack this case.

Ramona's Past Begins to Surface

Back at the safehouse, Ramona sat at the kitchen table, staring at another cup of tea she hadn't touched.

Ruby placed the evidence bag on the table, and she reached into it and pulled out a piece of paper.

"Do you recognize this number?"

Ramona looked at it.

Her expression changed immediately, once just nervous, but now fearful. She opened her mouth, then closed it.

Ruby watched her curiously, noticing everything. "Ramona?"

"I… I don't know."

Ruby leaned forward. "Ramona, think. Does it feel familiar?"

Ramona pressed a hand to her forehead. "It feels like… like something I should know. But it's like trying to grab smoke."

Ruby watched her. She hesitated, the she spoke carefully. "Ramona, I need to ask you something difficult."

Ramona tensed.

"Did you know Michael Avery?"

Ramona's breath hitched.

Ruby saw that. "Do you know him?"

"I don't… I don't think so."

"You were found ten feet from his body, Ramona."

Ramona shook her head violently. "I don't know him! I swear, I don't-"

Ramona stopped mid-sentence.

Her eyes widened.

A flash of memory hit her like a blow.

A man's voice.

A bar.

A drink.

A hand on her arm.

A whisper: *"We shouldn't be seen together."*

Ramona gasped, clutching her head.

Ruby grabbed her shoulders. "Ramona! What do you see?!"

Ramona's voice trembled. "I… I think I knew him."

Ruby's pulse quickened. "How?"

Ramona shook her head. "I don't know. I don't know. It's all broken. Please… please don't force me to remember it all. My head is pounding and my eyes hurt. I just… I think I need to rest."

"Ramona." Ruby spoke firmly. *"What did you just see?"*

"It… it was him," Ramona whispered. "I… I think I was with him at that bar. That number…"

She trailed off and shook her head, her eyes filling as Ruby asked urgently "What about the number??"

"I think it was mine. I think… I think I gave him my mobile number. But… there was no phone in my bag at the hospital."

"Boom," Ruby said softly, leaning back in her seat, and she stood swiftly.

"Get some rest, Ramona. I'll be back when I sort a few things."

Ramona nodded, looking exhausted, and the detective left the safehouse.

Detective Ruby's Discovery

Back at the precinct, Detective Ruby ran Ramona's phone number through the system.

It came up immediately.

Ramona Baker.

She lived an hour away from that bar she and Michael Avery were at together.

Ruby scribbled down Ramona's address immediately. That was her next stop.

Then she cross-checked it with recent call logs from Michael Avery's phone.

Ramona's number appeared repeatedly, not just that night, but over a period of ten months.

Michael called her *a lot.*

Almost every day.

And he sent her a lot of loving text messages.

Ruby frowned at that. "But she swore she didn't know him. Then… she remembered a little."

As Ruby clicked more and more, reading their text messages to each other, she noticed that the tone shifted, from loving to panicked, then desperate.

A lot of messages said the same thing, first from Ramona to Michael, and then similar from Michael to Ramona.

"It will be our secret, Ram."

"Nobody has to know, Michael."

"We'll be together soon, away from all of this."

"What were you into, Ramona?" murmured Ruby. "What *is* this?"

She dug deeper, pulling up Avery's case files.

Financial Crimes.

Money Laundering.

Corporate Fraud.

And one file that made her heart leap, titled Possible Dirty Cops in the Precinct, Secret Investigation! was flagged as *sensitive.*

Ruby clicked on it, her heart racing as she entered her code at the file's request.

Access denied.

She tried again.

Access denied.

Ruby leant back, her jaw tightening as heat rose.

Someone in the precinct didn't want *her especially* seeing this.

Which meant she needed to see it.

The Killer Escalates

Two nights later, the assassin returned to the safehouse.

But this time, he didn't go inside.

The code for the locks had been changed, and it would be way too risky to obtain a new one without raising suspicion.

He stood across the street, watching the dark windows.

Then he lifted his phone and dialled a number.

A man answered. "Report."

"She's still alive," the killer said. "And the detective is getting too close. She's with her almost every evening now. I have no idea if Baker's memory has come back yet, if she's told the cop anything. If she has, it's bad, Boss."

A pause.

"Then handle it," the voice of his boss said. "Get *in* there. Smoke both of them."

"Both of them??"

"Yes."

Silence.

"Don't tell me you want to cop to live," the boss said coldly. "It won't be long before she discovers who you are. Hunt them down, kill them both. Then get out of the city before everything falls apart."

The killer took a deep breath, then he replied "With pleasure."

He hung up, and slid back into the darkness.

Ramona's Second Memory Breaks Through

Ramona tossed and turned in the middle of the night as she slept, drenched in sweat.

A memory slammed into her:

She was in a bar.

Michael Avery sat across from her.

He looked nervous. "Ramona."

"Michael? What's wrong?"

"Someone found out about us," he said quietly. "And everything we've been working on together. If anything happens to me, I just want you to know that I will never stop loving you."

"I love you too Michael," Ramona said softly, and she reached out and took his hand. "And nothing will happen to you. You're so close to closing this case-"

"Shh," he said fiercely. "When we're out in public, never discuss the case."

"I'm so sorry," Ramona said apologetically, and Michael nodded.

Then he leant closer, murmuring in her ear "The file. Is it secure?"

Ramona nodded. "Printed and locked in my safe in a secret location."

Michael nodded. "Good."

Ramona smiled at him, loving him so much, then a shadow fell over them.

A man approached.

Ramona couldn't see his face.

But she felt his presence like ice.

Michael stood abruptly as soon as he saw him.

The colour drained from his face, and he looked at the love of this life.

"Run. Ramona. *RUN!!"*

Ramona gasped, jolting awake with a shrill scream.

"Oh my God!!"

Detective Ruby rushed into the room. "Ramona! What happened??"

Ramona clutched the blanket. "I remember something. Michael… he gave me something. A folder. The killer was at the bar. We were together at the bar. The killer was watching us. Michael told me to run. He knew who the killer was!"

"Slow down," Ruby said urgently. "Talk me through everything. Quickly, before it all slips away."

But this time, things didn't slip away at all.

Ramona remembered it all, even an hour later after Ruby made her go over it two more times.

"The file," Ruby said urgently. "What was in the file?"

"It was more than just one file. It was loads of files, put together. A record of all of Michael's investigations."

Ruby stared at her. "Are you certain?"

Ramona nodded. "Yes."

Ruby's heart pounded. "Where is it?"

Ramona shook her head. "I don't know. I mentioned a safe, in a secure location. But I don't remember where I kept that location is."

Ruby exhaled slowly.

This wasn't just a witness.

This was a woman holding the key to a way more than just a murder.

And maybe more.

Ruby's Realization

Ruby sat on the edge of the bed, thinking.

Michael Avery.

A sensitive case file.

A missing, valuable folder.

A witness with no memory.

This wasn't random.

This wasn't a mugging gone wrong.

This was a cover-up.

And Ramona was the loose end someone wanted to cut.

Ruby stood.

"Ramona," she said gently, "We're going to find that folder. And when we do, we'll know why someone wants you dead."

Ramona looked up, fear and determination warring in her eyes.

"Will you stay with me?" she whispered.

Ruby hesitated.

Then nodded.

"Always."

Back At the Precinct

"Walker, calm down," Chief Starker said firmly, as Ruby paced back and forth. "This is a lot to take in!"

"Exactly Chief," Ruby said as she stopped and looked at him. "I wanted to ask, is anyone aware of what we discussed about this case?"

"Only Ramirez," Chief Starker replied, "But I didn't tell him much. He was a little persistent."

"I bet he was," spat Ruby. "What did Ramirez want to know exactly, Chief?"

"When the case was first opened, he wanted the address of the safehouse. Said you forgot your personal phone on your desk and he'd drive there and give it to you personally."

Ruby froze at that.

Taking a deep breath, she asked "Was there anything else he needed?"

"A key to get in," shrugged Starker. "I didn't think anything of it. He's your partner."

Ruby swore to high heaven, stamping her foot as she cursed.

"Damn it!"

She'd known an assassin was going to come that night after being tipped off about a key to the safehouse had been requested.

She just hadn't known who exactly the assassin was at the time, until Ramona had told her what they said in her flashback.

Chief Starker looked at her curiously as she took steady breaths.

"What's wrong, Walker?"

"Nothing, Chief." Ruby shook her head. "Don't worry about it. I'll handle it."

"You'll handle it?"

"Yes Chief. I'll handle it."

The Folder Is Found

Fours days later...

Ramona paced the safehouse living room, fingers twisting the hem of her jumper.

Ruby watched her carefully. Then she asked "Anything?"

Ramona shook her head.

"You said Michael gave you a folder and you put that folder in a portable safe," Ruby said. "Try to think, Ramona. Where would you have put that safe?"

"I'm trying, Detective, I really am," Ramona said, her eyes filling over. "We've been trying to force a flashback for four days now. Nothing about that safe is coming to me."

Ruby sighed at that. "Alright. Well, we've been working hard the past few days. Fancy getting some Chinese food for dinner?"

Chinese food.

Startled, Ramona received her first flashback in days.

Everything went white for a moment, then she saw everything.

Her apartment.

A bookshelf.

A loose floorboard at its right corner.

Her hands shaking as she hid something beneath it.

Michael Avery spoke. "Is the safe secure?"

Romana flattened the floorboard over the safe and stood, dusting her hands. She smiled at Michael, answering "It should be."

"Remember what I said," Michael said seriously. "Move it around every two weeks, to be on the safe side. From here, to under the kitchen sink, to the attic, and the built in closet in the bedroom, and back around again."

Ramona kissed him. "I won't forget."

"Mmm. Good." Michael nodded, then his stomach rumbled. "Damn. I'm starving."

"What do you fancy?" smiled Ramona, and he thought about it, then he replied "Chinese food. I really fancy Chinese food."

"Alright. Let's order."

Ramona gasped, startling. "My apartment. I hid it in my apartment. Um, we agreed to move it around in four locations."

Ruby looked at her seriously. "Locations inside your apartment?"

Ramona nodded. "Yes."

Ruby grabbed her jacket. "Then that's where we're going."

"Right now?" Ramona was startled. "At this time??"

"No time like the present, Ramona."

Ramona nodded at that and stepped into her shoes, then she froze.

"What if the killer's waiting for me there? Or watching my apartment, waiting for me to go back?"

Ruby stepped closer. "He won't get near you. Not while I'm there."

Ramona swallowed hard.

"Don't be scared," Ruby said softly. "I'll be with you."

Ramona nodded. "Let's go."

Inside Ramona's Apartment

The building was old, the kind of place where the walls held secrets and the hallways smelled faintly of mildew. Ruby kept one hand on her holster as they climbed the stairs.

Ramona hesitated at the door.

"I don't want to go in alone."

"You're not alone," Ruby said softly, and she handed Ramona her set of keys. "Let us in, Ramona."

She unlocked the door.

The apartment was dark, silent.

Too silent.

Ruby swept the rooms with her gun drawn. "Clear."

Ramona exhaled shakily and moved to her bookshelf. She knelt, pulling at the loose floorboard.

Then she noticed the footprint right next to the floorboard, saw that the floorboard was loose.

"They were here," she said, eyes filling as she pulled at the floorboard, lifting it out of place and reaching inside, then she shook her head. "The safe is gone."

"Don't worry," Ruby said reassuringly. "We have three other locations to check."

Ramona nodded.

They checked the other locations in her flat, Ramona recalling as they looked "It's a sixteen-inch green safe. The combination is 2568."

Ruby smiled at her. "Glad you remember."

Ramona smiled back.

Two hours later, their smiles were gone.

They'd searched high and low, in every possible hiding space, and there was no green safe to be found.

Ruby collapsed on Ramona's sofa, feeling her head hurt as she said bitterly "They were here, Ramona. They took the safe. They took my *evidence.* Now, I have nothing to work with aside from you and your flashbacks."

Ramona didn't answer, feeling guilty. "I'm so sorry. I really thought it was still here."

"It's alright," Ruby said reassuringly. "Too bad you didn't put the file in a shoebox or something."

Ramona gasped as soon as the words left the detective's mouth. *"Box!"*

Ruby frowned at her. "What?"

Ramona jumped up as the flashback engulfed her mind, and she started running through her apartment.

Ruby chased her, startled: "Ramona, *wait!"*

"Michael knew they'd come for the safe," gushed Ramona. "It was a set-up!"

"A set-up??"

"Yes!"

"But in the safehouse you saw that- Ramona!" Ruby ran after her witness, her heart pounding as Ramona ran into her bedroom and dropped flat on her stomach, reaching under her bed desperately, throwing shoes behind her.

Ruby jumped back as shoes and smaller boxes flew everywhere.

"What are you looking for exactly??"

"What Michael and I planned together, in an even deeper secret," Ramona said excitedly. "I *know* it's here!"

Her fingers brushed something right at the far end of under the bed.

A big black folder.

It was thick.

Heavy.

Stuffed with documents, and an iPad.

Ramona pulled it out from under the bed with both hands, and she dusted it off and stood, a broad smile on her face as she turned to Ruby, who stared at her in shock.

Ramona handed the file to Ruby with slightly trembling hands.

"This is it, Detective. Everything you need."

Ruby opened it, with equally shaking hands as she rifled through it slowly, carefully as she scanned each page bit by bit, section by section, each marked in the same way it had been on the computer at the precinct.

Ruby's eyes widened as she read.

Ramona watched her, biting her lip. "I never looked inside the file. Michael didn't want to drag me into anything. He just wanted me to keep it safe in case anything happened to him. He knew he was a target, Detective Walker."

Ruby didn't answer as she read, though she heard her very well.

It seems like she's recalling things much better now.

Ramona waited for a response, patiently.

Almost twenty minutes later, Ruby inhaled sharply and looked at her.

"Ramona… this is evidence."

Ramona's voice shook. "Evidence of what?"

Ruby flipped through the pages. "Of everything Michael knew. What he was investigating before he was murdered."

There were bank statements.

Shell companies.

Wire transfers.

Names she recognised.

Judges, lawyers, and at the top of it all, the one officer she'd suspected.

He was the boss, the one who mastered it all, the one who'd given the orders of many crimes, for many murders, and many heavy sentences ruled in court.

Ruby's stomach dropped as she left the bedroom and sank onto Ramona's couch with the file, and she continued to read.

Ramona joined her quietly, knowing not to disturb the detective.

"This isn't just proof of financial crime," Ruby whispered. "This proof of a secret, illegal network. A massive one."

Ramona's voice trembled. "And Michael trusted me with it."

Ruby looked at her and nodded. "Which means he trusted you more than anyone else."

Ramona shook her head. "But I don't remember him properly."

Ruby closed the folder and stood. "You will eventually. You will feel the love you had for Michael, and the trust also. And you will mourn his death. He died and was able to reveal all of this, through you. And he kept you safe."

Ramona's eyes filled, and she nodded.

"Do you have a suitcase?" asked Ruby. "We may be being watched. We need to disguise this file. Make it look like you're just grabbing a few things to take to the safehouse.

"Yes. I have a bright pink suitcase."

Ruby smiled. "Perfect."

The Department Pushes Back

Back at the precinct, Ruby placed the folder on Chief Starker's desk.

He flipped through it, his expression darkening.

"Walker… do you have any idea what this is?"

"Yes," Ruby said firmly. "Which is why we need to move fast, Chief."

Starker closed the folder slowly. "This case is above our pay grade."

Ruby stiffened. "With respect, sir, that's bullshit."

Starker glared at her. "Watch it, Walker."

Ruby leaned forward. "A man uncovered this and is dead because of it. A woman is being hunted. And this-" she tapped the folder "-is the reason. We can't hand it off."

Starker exhaled. "Walker… there are people in this department who won't want this exposed."

Ruby froze. "You're saying you knew people inside this department are shady?"

"I'm saying be careful," Starker said. "We speak of this to no one, not even Ramirez or anyone on my level."

"Yes Chief. What do we do with the file?"

"You keep it hidden, out of this precinct, until it's safe to move in," Starker said. "And you keep that witness alive, Walker. Move in with her if you have to, until I'm able to get a higher team involved. After you let me know you're at the safehouse with Ramona Baker, I'll make some calls."

Ruby nodded. "Yes Chief."

She understood, better than the Chief himself, that the both the file and Ramona's value were unmatched.

Ramona's Memory Sharpens

Back at the safehouse, Ramona sat on the couch, staring at the folder.

"I knew him so well," she whispered. "I know I did."

Ruby sat beside her. "Tell me what you remember."

Ramona closed her eyes.

The bar.

Michael's hand covering hers.

And that shadow behind them.

The man watching.

A chill shot down her spine.

Ramona gasped. "He was scared. Michael was scared."

Ruby nodded. "I know. He knew he was in danger."

Ramona's voice trembled. "And he dragged me into it."

Ruby shook her head. "He didn't drag you, Ramona. He trusted you."

Ramona looked at her, eyes shining. "Why me?"

Ruby hesitated.

Then said softly, "Because you're stronger than you think."

Ramona swallowed hard.

For the first time, she believed it.

The Killer Closes In

The killer stood on a rooftop across from the safehouse, binoculars in hand.

He watched Ruby through the window.

Watched Ramona.

Watched the folder on the table.

He smiled.

“They found it,” he murmured. “Good.”

He pulled out his phone.

“It’s time,” he said when the line connected. “Tonight.”

A voice replied “Make it look like an accident.”

The killer hung up.

And began planning.

Ruby's Realisation. The Leak Is Close.

Ruby sat at the dining table, studying the file's contents again.

Something nagged at her.

A familiar name.

His signature.

A timestamp.

"You," she whispered. "I know it's you, Ramirez."

Ramona looked up from the kettle; she was making them both a cup of tea.

"What is it, Detective?"

Ruby's voice was tight. "Someone in my department signed off on these bank transfers, from the police department into an offshore account. The transfers are small enough not to attract attention, but the total builds up to almost half a million, after two thirds of a year transferring."

Ramona's eyes widened. "Someone you know from your department?"

Ruby nodded slowly. "Someone I trusted. And I believe it's him behind Michael's murder, your attack, and also the one who sent that assassin here after providing a key."

"So what do we do?" Ramona asked urgently. "We should go to the police and tell them what we know!"

"I've done that, Ramona. Now, I'm waiting for the idiot to make a move."

The Second Safehouse Breach

At 4:43 a.m., the power went out.

Ramona jolted awake. “Ruby?”

Ruby was already up, gun drawn. “Stay behind me.”

A soft click echoed from the back door.

Ruby’s heart pounded. “The assassin is here, Ramona.”

Ramona grabbed Ruby’s arm, whispering. “Don’t leave me.”

“I won’t,” Ruby said. “Let’s move, quickly.”

They tiptoed out of the bedroom, into the living area where Ruby could see better. She pushed Ramono behind the curtains of the large windows as the living room door creaked open.

A dark figure stepped inside.

Ruby raised her gun.

“Police! Drop-”

BANG!!

Ruby ducked; glass shattered behind her.

Ramona screamed as she ran out from the curtains towards the detective. *“RUBY!!”*

Ruby grabbed her, pulling her behind the couch and down to the floor.

“I’m fine,” she breathed. “Don’t panic!”

Ramona nodded, eyes wide as footsteps approached.

Slow.

Deliberate.

The killer’s voice drifted through the darkness.

"You shouldn't have found the folder, Detective Ruby Walker."

Ruby's grip tightened on her gun.

Ramona trembled beside her.

The killer stepped closer.

"Come out," he said roughly. "With both of you dead, this can finally be over."

Ruby's blood felt like it was on fire as she spat "Over my dead body."

The killer smiled. "That can be arranged.".

Ramona clung to Ruby's arm, trembling so hard Ruby could feel it through her leather jacket. The only sound was Ramona's ragged breathing and the soft crunch of broken glass under the killer's boots.

Ruby whispered, "Stay low, Ramona. Stay quiet."

Ramona nodded, tears sliding down her cheeks.

A silhouette moved on the living room wall in front of them: tall, broad-shouldered, confident.

The killer wasn't searching.

He knew exactly where they were.

Ruby steadied her gun.

The killer spoke, voice smooth and cold:

"You should've stayed out of this, Detective."

Ruby's pulse spiked. "Come any closer and I shoot."

He chuckled. "You won't risk me shooting back and hitting your precious witness."

Ramona whimpered at that; Ruby's jaw clenched as she spat "Try me."

The killer stepped forward, ever so confident; that was when Ruby leapt up and fired.

BANG!!

The bullet pierced the assassin's shoulder- he swore and dropped his gun, stumbling back as Ruby fired a second him, striking him in his chest.

Enranged, he ran at her.

It was as if he couldn't feel any pain, but Ruby knew he was just het up and would collapse soon as she fired at his leg.

BANG!!

"Run Ramona!" Ruby shouted, her adrenaline high. She was prepared to kill if it meant saving the life of her witness.

Ramona bolted toward the front door. Ruby followed, firing another shot to slow the killer down.

He lunged after them, limping badly as he pulled a knife out of his inside pocket, holding it high with a terrifying angry roar.

Ramona reached the door and tried to open it; it was locked.

"Ruby!" she cried, struggling with the door. "We're locked in! They've rigged the system, Ruby!"

Ruby shoved her aside just as the killer crashed into them, wielding the large knife. The three of them slammed into the door, then crashed to the floor.

The killer grabbed Ruby's wrist, twisting hard. Her gun clattered across the floor, Ruby swearing as he slammed her against the locked front door, pinning her by the throat.

Ramona screamed her name, not knowing what to do as she crawled backwards.

Ruby gritted her teeth as she slid down the door, driving her knee into his stomach.

He staggered, but didn't fall.

He squeezed her neck tighter, as she struggled, her hands slapping at his hidden face, but he didn't let go of her.

He was strong.

Too strong.

He reached for his knife, laughing hard now.

"This is where is ends, Detective Walker!"

"No," gasped Ruby, her vision blurring, and he raised the knife high, holding her neck in place/

Ramona ran into the kitchen and grabbed a frying pan, then ran back onto the landing and swung with at his head with all her strength.

The pan connected with a sickening *crack.*

The killer stumbled, dazed as he let Ruby's neck go. She sank to her knees, coughing hard as he turned in shock, his eyes rolling back into his head before he could look and Ramona, and he crashed to the ground- dead, or unconscious, they didn't know.

Ruby didn't hesitate- she grabbed her gun and scrambled to her feet, running and picking up her shoulder bag.

Ramona dropped the frying pan, shocked at what she had done as Ruby shoved her shoes on.

Ramona stared down at the unconscious assassin. "Did… did I kill him?"

"Do you want to wait to find out?!" Ruby said as she grabbed a change of clothes for Ramona, her trainers, and the file.

Then she grabbed Ramona's hand and pulled her toward the front door, firing at the lock.

BANG!!

BANG!!

The lock sparked and hissed, and the door swung open, Ruby gasping at Ramona "Go!"

They sprinted out of the safehouse into the night, Ramona shoving her jeans on as they ran.

Rain poured down as they dashed through the alley behind the safehouse.

Ruby's lungs burned, but she didn't slow down as she called the precinct.

Behind them, the killer roared in frustration as he stumbled out into the rain.

"He's coming!" Ramona cried, but Ruby knew his time was almost up as she gasped "Keep running!"

They reached Ruby's car.

She shoved Ramona inside, jumped into the driver's seat, and slammed the doors shut.

The killer burst from the alley just as Ruby started the engine.

He staggered towards the car; Ruby put her foot down immediately.

The tires screeched.

The car shot forward.

The killer slammed his hand against the trunk, leaving a bloody smear, but they were already speeding away.

Ramona sobbed into her hands.

Ruby gripped the wheel, adrenaline still surging.

"We're okay," she said, breathless. "We're okay."

But she knew it wasn't true.

They were far from okay.

The Betrayal

Ruby drove straight to the precinct with Ramona.

Chief Starker met them at the entrance, his face pale.

“Walker- we got your alert. What the hell happened?”

Ruby shoved past him, pulling Ramona in with her and holding the file under her other arm.

Starker followed her into their department, and Ruby gently pushed Ramona down into a chair.

“Walker,” Chief Starker said, following her urgently as Officer Ramirez stood with a concerned expression. “What-”

Ruby rounded on him before he could finish, livid as she spat “The safehouse was compromised. The location was leaked and a brand-new key was provided a second time, from one of more officers in this precinct.”

Starker stiffened. “That’s impossible.”

Ruby glared at him him. “Is it? Because the only people who knew were you, me, and-”

She stopped.

Starker’s expression shifted - just slightly.

A flicker of something she didn’t like.

Immediately, she knew not to mention the names of any other officer from their department.

She saw Ramirez shoot the Chief a sharp look; that confirmed her suspicions.

“Walker,” Chief Starker said slowly, “It’s almost seven in the morning. You’re tired. You’re emotional. Don’t start making accusations you can’t prove.”

Ramona stood, just as angry. “They knew where we were. They got another key. There’s a dirty cop, maybe two or three, working for you. Those cops knew we had the file.”

Starker's jaw tightened. "We'll investigate."

Ruby stepped closer, lowering her voice. "She's right. Someone, or more than one, in this department is involved in all of this, Chief. And I think I know who they are-"

Starker cut her off. "That's enough, Detective. You need to rest, and get your wits about you."

Ruby stared at him.

Something was wrong.

Very wrong.

Ruby had gone days without sleep working on cases, and the Chief had always praised her resilience, hard work, and her nerve.

What changed?

The Killer's Identity Revealed

Later that morning, Ruby sat in her office room with Ramona, trying to calm her shaking hands.

The file sat on her desk.

Her office door was locked, the blinds down.

Ruby swallowed hard, knowing that she was about to blow the roof off the precinct when she revealed exactly who the dirty sleazebags in the department were.

"Ramona," Ruby said gently, "I need you to think. When Michael died. You kept mentioning a dark figure, a cold feeling."

Ramona nodded. "The murder."

Ruby nodded too. "Did you see his face?"

Ramona shook her head. "No."

"Try and remember," Ruby said firmly. "I can't take no for an answer. Our lives are on the line, Ramona. Help is on the way, but they may not get here on time. I need you to confirm who the murderer is."

Ramona stared at her. "You already know who they are?"

"I have my suspicions," Ruby said quietly. "Please, concentrate."

Ramona nodded, and she closed her eyes.

A flash of white.

A badge.

A uniform.

A smirk on his handsome face.

His voice: *"You shouldn't have seen that."*

Ramona gasped. "The murderer. He's that cop."

Ruby froze. "Which cop?"

"The cop who was with you that night." Ramona's breathing quickened. "I saw his badge. I remember it. It's the same as yours, Detective, but it had his name. The murderer… the murderer is your partner!"

Ruby's blood ran cold.

"Ramona… are you sure?"

Ramona nodded, tears spilling down her cheeks. "Yes. But he wasn't the only one at the bar that night."

"Who else was there?"

Ramona swallowed, and she shook her head, tears falling.

"Ramona," Ruby said firmly. "I need you to talk to me. We'll get through this, I promise you. I need to buy as much time as possible before help arrives. They're an hour away. Talk to me, Ramona."

"It was your boss," whispered Ramona. "That police chief. Starker."

Ruby stood abruptly at that, and she began pacing the room, shocked.

Chief Starker.

The man behind it all.

A killer.

A man with access to safehouse locations.

A man who could erase evidence.

A man who could make witnesses disappear.

Ruby's mind raced.

Who had access to Michael Avery's case file?

Who had access to the safehouse?

Who had been acting strange?

Ramirez's name surfaced immediately in her mind immediately.

Her partner.

Her friend.

And Chief Starker.

Her mentor.

The one who always praised her and called her his right-hand cop.

Ruby's stomach twisted.

"They were people I trusted."

The Killer Watches Again

Across the street from the precinct, the assassin sat in his car, watching the windows.

His shoulder was bandaged, as was his leg.

He'd been offered to be replaced, but refused.

His eyes were cold; he wanted Ruby Walker finished.

He lifted his phone, listening to the Chief speak.

"They know," Starker said. "|Walker is getting too close to the truth. And it's not long before the NCA arrive and bust me and Ramirez. Walker needs to be dead before they get here, along with the witness."

"Then I will finish it," the assassin growled. "No disguise this time. Clear the department. I'm coming in."

The Chief relaxed. "Good."

He hung up.

The assassin stepped out of the car, and he limped towards the large building.

Ruby Confronts Ramirez

Detective Ruby Walker left the shower rooms at the bottom of the building, her jaw clenched so tight it hurt.

She'd gotten a shower and changed into clean clothes from her locker, with Ramona Baker locked securely in her office with the file, which was locked in her desk. The keys were in Ruby's pocket.

She waited, armed, for Ramirez to leave the male's locker room.

He'd mentioned to Chief Starker he was heading for the showers, and would be back in an hour.

Ruby waited, checking the time.

The National Crime Agency already had all the information they needed.

As soon as they'd gotten back to the safehouse when they first found Michael Avery's file, Ruby documented every single page digitally and sent it to the NCA.

Two agents had responded, flagging the case to higher departments as high risk, and they formulated a plan with Ruby to bring the dirty cops down.

It was a risky plan, but one they knew would succeed.

And Chief Starker and Officer Ramirez had no clue.

Officer Ramirez jogged out of the locker room, fresh and clean.

Tall.

Confident.

His left arm seemed a little stiff.

His eyes grew cold when they fell on her, though he forced a smile.

“Walker,” he said, his voice smooth as oil. “You look like hell.”

Ruby nodded and stepped into his path. “Where were you in the early hours of this morning?”

Ramirez smirked. "Working here in the department. Unlike some people."

"You weren't meant to be on yesterday's schedule."

Ramirez shrugged. "Maybe I picked up a shift."

Ruby's hand hovered near her holster. "You were here as a cover-up. You gave orders for a thug to come to the safehouse and kill me and Ramona Baker."

Ramirez's smile didn't falter. "Prove it."

Ruby stepped closer, lowering her voice. "Ramona remembers your badge."

For the first time, Ramirez's expression cracked.

Just a flicker.

Then he laughed.

"You're losing it, Walker."

Ruby's voice was ice. "You tried to kill her."

Ramirez leaned in; Ruby stepped back. Ramirez lifted a hand and caressed her cheek, whispering "You should've stayed out of this."

Ruby's blood ran cold.

She didn't respond, frozen.

Ramirez walked past her, humming a tune.

And Ruby just knew, that he was going to strike again.

But this time, a plan was forming in her mind.

She walked back into the female locker room and made contact with the NCA, ordering them to retreat, and formulating a new plan.

Ramona's Full Memory Returns

At a temporary safe location- a hotel across the city Ruby had chosen herself, Ramona Baker sat on the bed, her knees pulled to her chest as she hummed worriedly.

Ruby entered the living area, face serious.

"Ramona… we need to talk."

Ramona looked up at her, and then her body went rigid as a memory slammed into her like a tidal wave.

She was in the bar.

Michael Avery sat across from her.

It seemed that bar was her and Michael's secret meeting point.

"Ramona, listen to me. Sean Ramirez is dirty. He's been laundering money for years. He's connected to people you don't cross."

Ramona's breath hitched. "Why me?"

"Because you're the only one I trust. One of the only ones who won't be bought."

A shadow loomed behind them.

Finally, a face connected to the dark figure.

It was Ramirez.

Smiling deviously, knife in hand.

Michael shouting "Run!"

Ramona running into the alley,

Ramirez chasing, the knife flashing.

Michael falling, Ramona screaming.

Ramirez whispering in a deadly tone, *"You shouldn't have seen that."*

Ramona gasped, clutching her chest.

Ruby rushed to her. “Ramona? What is it?”

Ramona’s voice trembled. “I remember everything.”

Ruby’s breath caught. “Tell me.”

Ramona looked up, tears streaming down her face.

“It was Officer Sean Ramirez. He killed Michael. He tried to kill me. He’s been laundering money for years, not just the past year. Michael found out. He trusted me because… because I used to work in the financial office at the department.”

Ruby froze, staring at her. “You worked for us?”

Ramona nodded. “That’s how I met Michael. I processed expense reports. I saw things I shouldn’t have. Transfers that didn’t make sense. Ramirez found out. So did Chief Starker. Michael tried to protect me.”

Ruby sat heavily on the bed, taking her hand.

Everything clicked into place.

The folder.

The safehouse leak.

The attack.

Ramirez wasn’t just involved.

He was the centre of it.

Ruby had thought that Chief Starker was the boss, but maybe it was the other way around. Maybe Starker was under Ramirez.

Or maybe they were partners.

The Trap Is Set

Ruby paced the hotel room, thinking fast.

"We need to get this file to the National Crime Agency's base out of London," she said. "Tonight."

Ramona shook her head violently. "No. Ramirez has people everywhere. He'll know."

Ruby stopped and looked at her. "Then what do you suggest?"

Ramona swallowed hard. Then she said "We go public."

Ruby blinked. "Public?"

Ramona nodded. "Yes. If we disappear, the evidence disappears. But if the press gets it- if the whole city sees it - Ramirez can't bury the proof. Nor can he get away."

Ruby hesitated.

It was risky.

Reckless.

Dangerous.

But it might be the only way.

"Okay," Ruby said. "We'll go to a reporter friend I trust. First, I'll call them, and then we'll tell all. Before we meet with them, I'll send everything I sent to the NCA to them with names and dates. Solid proof."

Ramona exhaled shakily, and she nodded.

Two hours later, Ruby and her reporter friend had finished talking, and made arrangements to meet, at another safe location out of the city.

Ruby grabbed her keys and looked at Ramona.

"This is it. It's now or never, Ramona."

Ramona nodded, her face determined as she stood.

When they were both ready, Ruby armed while holding the precious file, she said "Let's move."

The Ambush

They left the hotel through the back exit, heading toward Ruby's car.

The parking lot was dark.

Too dark.

"Why are all the lights out?" whispered Ramona fearfully, and Ruby slowed down as she whispered "Ramona… stay behind me."

Ramona nodded.

They reached Ruby's car.

Ruby unlocked it.

A click echoed behind them.

Ruby spun round, alert as she saw Officer Ramirez stepped out of the shadows, gun raised as he said coldly, "Going somewhere?"

Ramona screamed.

Ruby shoved her behind the car.

Ramirez fired.

SMASH!!

The bullet shattered the passenger's side window.

Ruby ducked at Ramona's side, returning fire.

BANG!!

Ramirez moved with terrifying precision, using the concrete pillars as cover.

"You should've walked away from this case, Walker!" he shouted from behind the pillar. "But you never know when to quit!"

Ruby fired again as soon as he peered around the pillar, screaming *"You murdered a federal investigator!"*

Ramirez laughed. “He was sloppy. And *she-”*

He pointed his gun at Ramona, Ruby forcing her out of range.

“Was a loose end!!”

Ramona sobbed, tears falling fast as she knelt by Ruby’s legs.

Ruby’s voice shook with fury. “You’re not touching her, Ramirez.”

Ramirez smirked. “You can’t protect her forever, Walker.”

He fired again; the car’s back window exploded.

Ruby grabbed Ramona’s hand. *“Run, Ramona!”*

Ramona scrambled to her feet, and they sprinted away.

Ramirez chased them, livid.

The Chase

All they could hear was they ran was footsteps, gunshots, and ragged breaths.

Ruby shoved Ramona ahead of her. “Go! Don’t stop!”

Ramona stumbled down the stairs, tears blurring her vision.

Ramirez’s voice echoed behind them.

“You can’t hide from me!!”

Ruby fired blindly upward to slow him down.

They burst out onto the high street, panting, clutching their sides, but they didn’t let something as trivial as a stitch stop them from running for their lives.

Cars honked as soon as they saw a woman brandishing a gun and another woman in tears.

People shouted out in fear at the sight of a gun, but Ruby and Ramona ignored them as they pushed past, Ramona holding the file to her chest.

Ramirez emerged seconds later, shoving people out of his way as he yelled *“WALKER!!”*

Ruby ignored him, looking around desperately, and she saw a community officer indicating frantically, pointing at his patrol car.

Ruby grabbed Ramona’s arm. “This way!”

They darted towards the community officer, Ramirez getting swallowed momentarily by the crowd.

“Take my car Detective,” the community officer said quickly, pushing his keys into her hands.

“But how- how did you know about- how did you know that we-”

“There’s no time,” he said fiercely. “I’m an undercover agent from the NCA. You were followed for safety measurements. We knew something like this might happen. We bugged both Ramirez and Starker’s personal lines, and we’ve been keeping tabs on them and their thugs.”

Ramirez emerged, face furious.

“There he is!” shrieked Ramona, eyes wide, and the NCA agent opened his passenger and pushed her in.

“You haven’t any time to waste by standing here, Walker! Go!”

Ruby’s heart pounded as she obeyed, running around the side of the car and getting in.

Through the rearview mirror, she saw the NCA agent tackle Ramirez to the ground, the gun whirling across the air and out of sight.

“We need to go!” cried Ramona. “Go, Detective!”

Ruby started the car and pulled away, her heart pounding as they raced down the road.

They were running out of time.

Running out of options.

Running out of places to hide.

Before they knew what was happening, another car speeding down the opposite late veered left, smashing into their car, which went spiralling off the road.

Ruby swerved the car immediately, her expertise as a trained lethal detective taking over as she braked hard, Ramona screaming her head off as the car slid towards a massive tree, but thankfully it skidded to a stop moments before collision.

Cornered

Ruby was breathing hard as she gripped the steering wheel.

Ramona was breathing hard too.

Ruby reversed the car slowly, and Ramona whispered "Who the hell tried to ram us??"

"One of Ramirez's thugs," Ruby answered. "Get out of the car for a moment while I inspect the damage. We may need another vehicle."

Ramona nodded and got out of the car, holding the file tightly.

"Freeze," a voice said weakly; they whipped around as they saw the driver who rammed them stagger towards them, his shoulder, head and leg bandaged heavily.

Immediately Ruby and Ramona knew it was the assassin who'd attacked them at the safehouse.

"Still alive?" Ruby said coldly, and he coldly answered "Barely. I'd die for my leader in a heartbeat, Detective Walker. It's me, or you and her. And it's not going to be me-"

BANG!!

Ramona shrieked as the assassin's body thudded to the ground, Ruby saying just as coldly "It's not going to be us, either."

Another patrol car pulled up, blocking their car in.

But it wasn't another agent from the NCA.

Ramirez was at the wheel.

Ramona froze, staring at his evil grin in fear. "Ruby-"

"I know," Ruby said quietly. "I see him."

Ramirez stepped out of the car, gun raised, smiling at the pair triumphantly.

"It's over, Walker. You're both going to be in the morgue by the end of tonight."

Ruby stepped in front of Ramona, shielding her with her body without answering him.

Ramirez shook his head. “Always the hero.”

Ruby’s voice was steady. “You’re done, Sean.”

Ramirez laughed. “No. *You* are.”

He aimed.

Ramona screamed her name.

Ruby braced herself; a gunshot rang out.

BANG!!

Ramirez staggered, Ruby startled as another shot sounded.

BANG!!

Then a third pieced the air.

BANG!!

Ramirez collapsed.

Ruby spun around, and she gasped “Chief!”

Chief Starker stood before them with five agents from the NCA, his gun smoking.

“Walker,” he said, breathing hard. “You okay?”

Ruby stared at him, stunned. “You… you saved us.”

Starker nodded. “I did.”

Ruby shook her head as it began to spin. Confused as she looked at her boss, she managed “But… but you’re part of the whole scheme.”

Chief Starker grinned at her. “Ever heard of a double-agent, Walker?”

Ruby could have passed out with relief, her heart racing as Ramona broke down crying.

Then Ruby scowled at Chief Starker.

“You could have ruined this entire case by doing what you did. What if Ramirez found out you were playing him??”

Starker holstered his weapon. “I told you to be careful, didn’t I Walker. I didn’t say I wouldn’t back you up.”

Ramona sobbed with relief.

Ruby exhaled shakily as more cars from officials pulled up, Chief Starker ordering for one of the agents to call the press, and an ambulance.

It was finally over.

The Aftermath: Ramirez Down, But Not Gone

Detective Sean Ramirez was rushed to the hospital under armed guard. He survived the gunshot wounds - barely - but he was unconscious, sedated, and handcuffed to the bed.

Ruby stood outside the ICU window, watching him through the glass.

Chief Starker joined her.

“You did good work,” he said quietly.

Ruby didn’t look at him as she replied just as quietly. “He was my partner.”

Starker nodded. “And he betrayed everything this badge stands for.”

Ruby’s jaw tightened. “I should’ve seen it.”

“No,” Starker said. “He hid it well. Too well.”

Ruby finally turned to him. “How deep does this go?”

Starker exhaled. “Internal Affairs is tearing the department apart. Ramirez wasn’t working alone. There are at least four officers under investigation. Two have already been arrested.”

Ruby’s stomach twisted. “And the people outside the department?”

Starker shook his head. “That’s going to take time. But we have Michael Avery’s file, and it’s a massive help.”

Ruby looked back at Ramirez. “It’s going to take time to take them all down.”

Starker nodded. “Yes.”

Ruby nodded as well, her brow furrowing.

Time was something she wasn’t sure she had.

But she was going to make it work.

Ramona's Life Begins to Rebuild

Two weeks later…

Ramona sat in a quiet room at back at the precinct, wrapped in a blanket, sipping tea.

She looked exhausted, but alive.

She'd been moved to a new safehouse, an hour away from her first one, and she was settling in there much more quickly that she had done in the first.

She hadn't seen Detective Ruby Walker in the entire two weeks. Ramona was worried that now things were over, she'd never see the detective who saved her life again.

She had been picked up by a police officer that morning and brought to the precinct, the officer stating that there were a few things to go over with the police.

Detective Ruby Walker entered the room ten minutes later, smiling at her.

Ramona could have cried at the sight of her. "Detective Walker."

"Hello, Ramona."

Ramona smiled weakly. "You came back."

"Of course I did," Ruby said, sitting beside her. "How are you holding up?"

Ramona shrugged. "It sucks that I don't fully know who I am anymore. But… I'm starting to remember piece by piece."

Ruby nodded. "That's a start."

Ramona hesitated, then she asked "What happens now?"

"You'll remain under federal protection until after the trial," Ruby answered. "After that… you'll have choices."

Ramona looked down. "I'm scared."

Ruby reached out, taking her hand.

“You’re the bravest person I’ve ever met.”

Ramona’s eyes filled with tears. “I wouldn’t have survived without you.”

Ruby squeezed her hand. “You did survive. That was you.”

Ramona shook her head. “No. It was *us.*”

Ruby didn’t argue.

She didn’t need to.

They sat their holding hands for a while, then Ramona hugged her tightly.

“You look much better after everything that went on. Did you rest up the past two weeks, Ruby?”

“I could say the same about you.” Ruby hugged her back. “You look much healthier.”

“I’ve been watching Instagram Reels of cooking videos,” Ramona replied as they let each other go. “And imitating them. The meals turn out pretty tasty.”

Ruby smiled at her, impressed. “Excellent to know.”

The Press Conference – The Truth Goes Public

A month later the mayor of London, three agents from the National Crime Agency, a spokesperson for the precinct and Chief Starker stood before a sea of reporters.

Detective Ruby Walker watched everything live on screen from the back of a closed inside the precinct's large building, not wanting to be on screen, but wanting to know exactly what was happening as it was happening.

Ramona Baker stood at her side.

"The department has uncovered a corruption ring involving several officers," the commissioner announced. "Detective Sean Ramirez is currently in custody facing multiple charges of murder, conspiracy, and obstruction of justice."

Cameras flashed.

Reporters shouted questions.

Ruby felt Ramona step closer to her.

"You okay?" Ramona whispered.

Ruby nodded. "It's just… a lot."

Ramona gave a small smile. "You did this."

Ruby shook her head. *"We* did."

A Final Twist - The Hidden Evidence

Later that afternoon, Ruby returned to the evidence room a few floors down to review Michael Avery's precious file one last time.

She flipped through the documents.

Bank statements.

Shell companies.

Wire transfers.

Then she noticed something she hadn't before.

A second layer of pages, taped to the back of the file.

Ruby carefully peeled them apart.

Inside was a list.

Names.

Dates.

Amounts.

And at the bottom:

Avery, Michael - $0 Baker, Ramona - $0 Walker, Ruby - $0.

To be executed accordingly.

Ruby froze as Ramona entered the room, looking for her.

"There you are! Do you want to come back to the safehouse for dinner, Detective?"

Ruby didn't answer.

Ramona's smile faded. "Ruby? What is it?"

Ruby handed her the page without answering.

Ramona's eyes widened. "This… this is a ledger."

Ruby nodded. "Everyone who was paid off. Everyone who was part of the network. And the sums they were paid to do dirty work, or just keep quiet."

Ramona swallowed. "And the zeros next to our names?"

Ruby exhaled. "The people who couldn't be bought."

Ramona looked at her.

"You were on his list," she whispered. "Michael trusted you too, Ruby."

Ruby's throat tightened. "I didn't even know him."

Ramona smiled, her eyes welling up. "He knew *you.* He knew you were clean, Detective, and loyal to your job as an officer of the law."

Ruby blinked back tears.

For the first time, she felt the weight of what Michael Avery had died for.

And what Ramona had survived for.

Ramona's Goodbye

A week later, Ramona stood outside the precinct with a small suitcase. A federal agent waited beside a black SUV.

Ramona was being moved to a safehouse out of London, far in the country, to guarantee her safety until the trial was over.

And it could take over a year to finalise, before it was safe to return to the city.

"It's time," the agent said gently, opening the back door of the large car, and Ramona turned to Ruby.

"I don't know how to thank you," she whispered, her voice cracking.

"You don't have to," Ruby said softly, and Ramona stepped closer.

"Will I ever see you again, Detective Walker?"

Ruby hesitated. Then she nodded. "When this is over… you will."

Ramona smiled, a real large, true content smile, the first Ruby had seen her give. She leaned in and hugged Ruby tightly.

"Stay safe," Ramona whispered.

"You too," Ruby said softly, and Ramona pulled back, eyes shining.

Then she got into the SUV.

Ruby watched until the car disappeared around the corner, and she let her tears fall.

She wiped them quickly, and she whispered "Case closed."

A New Beginning

That night, Ruby sat alone in her apartment, the city lights glowing through the window.

She opened the ledger again.

Her name.

Ramona's name.

Michael's name.

Three people who refused to be bought.

Three people who chose the truth.

She closed the folder gently.

Her phone buzzed.

A message from an unknown number:

Thank you, Detective. I'll never forget you.

R.B.

Ruby smiled.

For the first time in a long time, she felt calm, relaxed, and full of hope.

The Last Witness

Eight months later, Ruby testified in court.

Ramirez glared at her from the defence table, hatred clearly etched across his face as she spoke clearly.

Ramona sat in the front row, under protection, watching with quiet strength.

When Ruby finished her testimony, she stepped down from the stand.

Ramona was called up next.

Oozing strength Ruby had never seen in her before, Ramona answered every question firmly, and gave an impact statement directed at Officer Ramirez.

Ruby stared at her in shock as she spoke clearly.

Ramona's voice didn't shake.

Her eyes didn't fill.

Ruby realised with a jolt in her stomach that Ramona's memories must have fully returned, and she was finally back to the real Ramona Baker, a woman Ruby never knew.

And Ruby was so proud of her.

Ramirez was sentenced to life in prison with no chance of parole.

He would die in prison for all of his crimes, along with his thugs, and their fellow officers who had been in on his many schemes.

Ramona met her at the court exit after the sentencing was delivered.

"You did it Detective," Ramona whispered.

Ruby shook her head. "We did, Ramona."

Ramona smiled. "You saved my life."

Ruby looked at her- really looked at her. Then she smiled back, and answered "You saved your own life, Ramona."

Ramona reached out, taking Ruby's hand.

"Maybe we saved each other."

Ruby didn't pull away.

Ramona smiled again, her eyes twinkling.

"I'll soon be moving back to London," she said brightly. "Maybe we can meet for a coffee sometimes, if that's allowed."

"Sure," Ruby replied. "When I'm not working on a case, I'd love to."

Ramona giggled. "Did anyone tell you you're a total workaholic, Detective?"

"Chief Starker does," smiled Ruby. "That's why I have three months off starting from now, to find myself and relax."

"Awesome," smiled Ramona; Ruby smiled back as she walked her to the waiting SUV, an agent ready to drive her back out of the city.

Ramona turned as the agent opened the back door for her, and she grinned at Ruby.

"See you soon, Detective."

Ruby smiled back. "See you soon."

As the SUV pulled away, Ruby hugged herself as she watched it go.

And for the first time since the case closed, she allowed herself to breathe deep.

Allowed herself to feel.

Allowed herself to hope.

Allowed herself to finally *relax.*

Because the last witness wasn't just a survivor.

She was part of a new beginning.

THE MOONWEAVER'S APPRENTICE

Seventeen-year-old Elara Romane has always felt drawn to the moon, but the night it speaks her name, she learns why: she is the first Moonweaver's Apprentice in three hundred years. Gifted with the rare ability to see and wield living strands of moonlight, Elara is thrust into a destiny she never asked for. As she begins her secret training under the enigmatic Moonweaver Lysander, a darker truth emerges- an ancient force that feeds on fear has taken root inside her own sister. Torn between loyalty and survival, Elara must master her lunar magic before the darkness consumes her family and her village. With danger rising and secrets unravelling, she discovers that the moon didn't choose her by accident... it chose her because only she can face what's coming.

The Night the Moon Chose Her

The moon was full the night Elara Ramone first heard it whisper.

She stood barefoot on the cliff of Taurbrook's edge, the wind tugging at her dark curly hair, the ocean roaring below.

The village of Taurbrook slept behind her; a cluster of brightly-lit homes tucked between the cliffs and the forest.

Elara laid down on the top of the cliff, and she closed her eyes, at one with the atmosphere.

She listened to the breeze, to the whisper of the ocean.

The clouds parted to reveal the full moon, its silver rays shining down on her, making her brown skin look like it was aglow.

Elara smiled, gazing up at the sky.

The moonlight seemed to warm her skin, as if it were the sun in the light of day.

The stars twinkled as the clouds thinned, shimmering.

Elara sighed, content as she laid there, and she murmured "I could stay the entire night here atop this cliff, touched by the light of the moon."

And then…

A voice.

Soft.

Ancient.

"Child of shadow and obsidian... you see me. And I see you also."

Elara gasped, sitting up quickly.

Her heart hammered as she looked around; she was alone.

Trembling, she asked "Who's there?"

The voice shimmered like light on water.

"Do not fear the moon, child. You have always belonged to it, Elara."

Elara's breath caught.

She had always felt different; drawn to the moon in a way she couldn't explain.

From a young age, she could easily see threads of silver drifting from the moon through the night sky, invisible to everyone else.

Tonight, those threads pulsed brighter, falling down towards her like tiny meteors.

Elara reached out, her heart pounding.

Her fingers brushed a strand of moonlight.

It wrapped around her wrist like a ribbon.

And right when Elara inhaled sharply and she watched the light seep into her skin, without her resisting or screaming for help, her entire world changed.

The Moonweaver Appears

A figure appeared under the moonlight.

Tall.

Cloaked in silver.

Eyes glowing bright white, like twin crescents.

Elara froze, staring at the magical being, knowing that they weren't a figment of her imagination.

"You're… real."

The figure inclined their head with a gentle smile, then he responded "I am Lysander. Moonweaver of the Ninth Realm."

Elara swallowed. "What do you want with me?"

Lysander studied her with an expression she couldn't read.

"You touched the moonlight," he replied simply. "You are able to see the strands of the moon. Only one born with the lunar gift can do that."

Elara shook her head. "I'm nobody. Just an orphan from Taurbrook."

"Yes." Lysander nodded. "I know you very well, Elara. I have watched you grow from a young curious toddler into the intelligent seventeen-year-old you are now."

Elara swallowed at that, and she looked down at her wrist, at the spot the strands of moonlight had seeped into.

The black symbol of a crescent moon was there, etched with small black stars in front of it.

Elara gasped. "A tattoo?? Tattoos are forbidden in my home!"

Lysander smiled a little. "You are of age, Elara. Many teenagers in your village have a tattoo or four."

"Four?!"

Lysander nodded, amused as she rubbed the mark of the moon fiercely.

It didn't fade.

Elara glared at Lysander, holding out her wrist. "Get rid of it."

Lysander shook his head. "I cannot. The moon chose you, Elara."

"What do you mean the moon *chose* me?!" she shrieked. "What does that *mean??"*

Lysander stepped closer, his face suddenly very serious as he stated "You are the first Moonweaver's Apprentice in three hundred years, Elara."

Elara stopped raging at that and looked at him curiously. "Apprentice?"

"Yes," Lysander said. "And your training begins *now."*

"Training?"

Lysander nodded. "Yes."

Elara shook her head. "I can't leave my village."

"Nobody said you are leaving." A smile tugged Lysander's mouth. "You are so fierce, Elara, strong-willed, with a whirring, smart and strong mind. Do not worry. You won't have to leave Taurbrook."

"Then how will I train?" she asked curiously. "And what exactly is my training for? How long does will it last?"

"Your training will last until you are powerful enough to go on without guidance," Lysander answered, his eyes beginning to glow. "Every other night, you will come here at exactly one a.m., like you have done this night."

"I might get caught."

"I guarantee you will not get caught."

"Oh yeah? How can you be so sure?" demanded Elara; Lysander chuckled.

"Because I am going to teach you your first spell. It is a spell of slumber, Elara, the magic deriving from the moon itself."

Elara was very intrigued. "Can I use the spell at any time?"

Lysander smiled at her. "A very good question. A Moonweaver can only perform magic from dusk until dawn. When the moon shines over the land, even if it is hidden by the clouds."

"So even if I can't see the moon, I can perform magic from dusk till dawn?" Elara said excitedly; Lysander nodded.

"Yes."

"Awesome." Elara breathed out. "Freaking awesome."
Lysander smiled at her. "I must return to my domain, Elara. I will see you the night after tomorrow."
"You're going?" she said disappointedly. "Already?"
Lysander nodded again. "I have given you sufficient information this night. Be patient, Elara, and speak of this only to those you trust."
Elara trusted nobody.
But she nodded, and Lysander held out a hand.
"See you soon."
"See you," she whispered as she reached out and shook his hand, and suddenly she was grasping air.
Elara gasped in shock: Lysander was gone.
She took deep breaths, sinking to her knees. "Was that real? Am I dreaming??"
She stared down at the mark on her wrist, and she ran the pad of her thumb over it gently.
"I'd better hide this from Ma and Pa, and Emily."
Emily was Elara's older sister by two years, her parent's biological first-born. The golden child who had always had the best grades and was considered an overachiever by almost everyone in Taurbrook.
When her parents realised they couldn't conceive again, they went to the orphanage, and adopted Elara when she was three years old.
Elara sighed and stood, and she headed down the cliff carefully, going home.

The Tattoo

"What's that?" Emily asked suspiciously, as Elara tiredly poured some milk over her cereal, her eyes heavy.

"What's what?" asked Elara as she sat at the table, and Emily said "That drawing on your wrist. Is that a real tattoo?"

"No, it's just a drawing."

"Don't lie, Elara."

"I'm not lying," Elara snapped; Emily smirked at her.

"You keep lying and I'll tell Ma and Pa. They will beat you with the belt for getting a tattoo."

Elara froze, scared now.

Ma and Pa's beatings were nothing to joke about. Elara received beatings plenty of times. Some hurt so bad she wet herself upon the belt's impact, causing even more anger in her parents, and their beatings were even harder.

Emily waited.

"You wouldn't," Elara said weakly. "Please, Emily, don't tell Ma and Pa."

"So it *is* a tattoo!"

"Shh!"

"Wow," Emily said amusedly, and she laughed. "You are *crazy.* The hot weather is around the corner, Elara. Soon, it will be way too hot to cover your arms. Everyone in Taurbrook will see that nasty tattoo!"

"It's not nasty," Elara said heatedly, "And if you weren't such a goody-two-shoes, always wanting to please Ma and Pa, and be *soooo* perfect all the time, you'd see that a tattoo isn't bad. You'd get one too!"

Emily glared at her. "I'm not a goody-two-shoes."

"Um, hello?" Elara indicated Emily's trophies, awards and photos displayed almost everywhere in the kitchen, then she gestured at the living area too. "Did all of these records zoom out of your backside every month for the past fourteen years, Emily?"

Emily's glare intensified as she spat "Shut up, Elara. You're just jealous of me, and a rebel."

"A rebel I may be, but I'll *never* be jealous of you." Elara picked up her spoon and began to poke at her cereal as their father entered the kitchen in his heavy work boots, holding a saw.

"Good morning, my beautiful daughters."

"Good morning Pa," Emily and Elara said together, and Joseph Peterson smiled at his girls.

"What were you both quarrelling about? I could hear you both snapping at each other, but it was blurred as I neared home."

"Nothing Pa," lied Elara, and Joseph looked at his eldest daughter for confirmation.

"Emily?"

"Pa?"

"What was the fuss about?"

"It was just a small quarrel, Pa, because Elara has a-"

Elara's eyes widened in fear, and Emily stopped, feeling bad. Whether they butted heads often or not, Elara was her little sister. She wouldn't be able to bear Elara's screams of pain as she was struck mercilessly with her father's massive belt that had a heavy gold buckle.

"Elara has a what?" Joseph asked sharply, scowling at Elara now, and Emily sighed "Elara has a tendency to call me a goody-two-shoes all the time."

"Oh." Joseph's face relaxed, and he chuckled. "It's just sibling rivalry, Emily. Ignore Elara."

"Yes Pa."

"It's not sibling rivalry at all," pouted Elara, and Joseph batted her curly black hair as he replied "You think that, Elara, but you always mention the fact that you're adopted when you're angry and upset, and you state that look nothing like

Emily and nobody outside Taurbrook would ever believe you're sisters."

"Well… well it's true, Pa!"

"And there you go." Joseph laughed as he turned to boil the kettle, making himself a large cup of coffee. "See?"

"That's not rivalry, Pa, it's facts," Elara said heatedly. "Emily has olive skin and long red hair, and freckles spotted across her face. I have dark brown skin and long curly black hair. And my eyes are grey."

"They are silver, just like the moonlight," an elderly voice said from the kitchen doorway; everyone turned, startled as they saw the village elder, also known as the Shaman of Taurbrook, staring at Elara intently.

"Madame Marwen." Joseph bowed immediately. "Good morning."

"Good morning Madame Marwen," Emily and Elara said quickly, and Madame Marwen's face creased as she smiled.

"Good morning, everyone. Joseph, I would like to talk with Elara in the village hall at dawn tomorrow," Madame Marwen said smoothly. "Please, escort her there and collect her at noon."

Joseph nodded quickly. "Yes Madame Marwen. I'll wake her at three to prepare her."

"Wake her at four, Joseph. Dawn won't arrive until six. Two hours is enough time for Elara to ready herself and make her way across Taurbrook with you to the hall."

Joseph nodded again. "Yes Ma'am."

Elara swallowed as the village elder smiled at her knowingly, then she turned and walked away.

Joseph listened to other people greet her respectfully as she headed up the road ("Good morning, Madame Marwen!"), and then he glared at Elara, who recoiled.

"Pa?"

"What did you do, Elara?" Joseph demanded, and Elara gushed "Nothing!"

"So why does the Shaman of Taurbrook want to see you at dawn?!"

"Pa, I have no idea."

That was a lie. Elara had a feeling Madame Marwen knew what happened on the cliffs in the early hours of the morning.

"Are you certain you have no idea?" Joseph asked heatedly; Elara quickly nodded.

"Yes Pa."

"Alright." Joseph dropped the subject. "Let me have my morning coffee and watch my show before I head back to the workshop. I don't want to hear any more arguing between you and your sister, Elara."

Elara repeated herself politely. "Yes Pa."

Joseph made his large mug of coffee and headed into the living area, sinking down into his massive armchair in front of the television, and he turned it on, changing it to his favourite show that would run for the next hour.

Emily and Elara waited until they heard his shout of laughter, and then they both breathed out, relieved.

Emily looked at Elara. "That could have gone the wrong way. Pa might have beat you."

"I know," Elara said quietly, and Emily asked "So… why *does* the Shaman want to see you, then? I know you know, Elara."

"I don't know, Emily. I really have no idea." Elara avoided her eye as she spoke, and Emily glanced down at her right wrist.

Then she whispered "It might be because of that tattoo."

"Emily, be quiet!" Elara whispered back frantically. "Pa is right across the hall."

"Don't worry, he can't hear anything but Wood Guzzlers." Emily stood. "Eat your breakfast, Elara, before Ma gets home from *her* job. She'll be here right after Pa's show ends."

That was true.

Their mother worked nights, and their father started his work as the town carpenter at his prized store almost two hours away, right across town.

Elara looked down at her cereal, and she pouted.

"It's all soggy now. I can't eat this. I'll be sick."

Emily heard their father laugh at the TV again, and she quickly said "Pa will go mad if you waste food. He and Ma work their socks off making sure we live comfortably."

Elara sighed. "Yeah. Sure. Just don't snitch on me, yes? I'm chucking this."

Josh, Betty & Kevin Bates

By two p.m., Elara's best friends since the beginning of high school Joshua Ledell and Betty Broke rode their bikes around to the Peterson residence.

Josh rang the bell, calling "Elara!"

Elara choked on her ham and mustard sandwich, and she put it down quickly.

"Josh and Betty are here for me, Ma!"

"Finish your lunch," Janette Peterson scolded, and she walked to the front door as Joshua rapped on it, opening it with a scowl on her face.

"Joshua Ledell. How many times must I tell you to ring the bell and *wait* without shouting and banging down our door?"

Joshua grinned sheepishly. "Sorry Mrs. Peterson. Is Elara home?"

"She's having lunch right now," Janette replied flatly. "Why don't you wait for her at the creek instead of hanging around my property? You're going to go there anyway, right?"

"Well… yes, but-"

"Then head on to the creek with Betty. Elara will be there soon."

"Yes Mrs. Peterson," Joshua mumbled as he got back on his bike, Betty getting on her bike too, and they pedalled away.

Emily smiled at Elara. "Joshua crushes on you so hard, Elara."

"Shut *up,* Emily. You know Josh is just a friend." Elara bit into the second half of her sandwich, then she decided to counter-attack.

"Why hasn't Kevin Bates asked you to be his girlfriend yet, Emily? You've been following him around and telling him you love him for over three years."

"Because- because he's going through a lot," gushed Emily, her yellow cheeks turning a little pink. "His auntie died like a year ago and he's still dealing with it."

Elara rolled her eyes at that. "He doesn't *like* you, Emily. Can't you see Kevin sees you as some desperate chick who refuses to get the message?"

"Shut up!!"

Just then, Kevin Bates rang the doorbell, quickly smoothening his tight black t-shirt and flexing his dark brown muscles.

Janette sighed as she walked and opened the front door, and she exclaimed "Kevin!"

Emily's face lit up immediately, and Kevin Bates humbly said "Good afternoon, Mrs. Peterson."

"Are you here for Emily?"

Kevin hesitated, and he asked "Can I come in please?"

"Of course you can."

"So *Kevin* can come in without an issue but Joshua gets ordered to go to the creek?" Elara said dryly, rolling her eyes. "Nice."

"Elara, *shut the hell up,"* Emily chewed out as she quickly fixed her hair and posed with an angelic smile, and their mother entered the kitchen, Kevin Bates walking in behind her.

Kevin Bates was a *very* good-looking nineteen-year-old.

He was tall, dark, muscly and handsome, with stunning golden eyes, startling against his chocolate skin. He had wavy black hair that framed his face and hung just past his shoulders, and he looked oh-too-sexy when his hair fell across his face and he raised a hand to gently brush it away and tuck it behind his ear.

Emily stood quickly, knocking over her cup of juice.

"Emily," Janette scolded, Elara highly amused, and Emily quickly said "I'm sorry Ma, I'll clean it up in a moment. Hi Kevin!"

Kevin said hi flatly, already looking annoyed with her.

"Um, so…" Emily did her best to seem flirtatious. "Did you like… come to visit me and take me out somewhere or something?"

Elara rolled her eyes and bit her sandwich.

Kevin said no, looking uncomfortable. "Actually, I've come to see Elara."

Elara swallowed too much of her food at that, surprised as Emily gasped *"Elara?!"*

Kevin nodded. "Yes. I've come to see Elara."

"You… you want to talk to my little sister?" Emily was butt-hurt. "You've never said *two words* to Elara before."

"Yeah, I know." Kevin ran a hand over his hair. "I just… I need to talk to her. I hold myself back anymore."

Silence fell, Emily staring at him in shock.

Elara's stomach fluttered at the sight of Kevin's abs tensing through his black t-shirt as he raised his arm, and she bit her lip, surprised at herself.

Since when was Kevin Bates interested in her?

And since when was she interested in *him?!*

"So like, do you have a crush on Elara or something Kevin?" Emily asked shrilly. "What the hell is going on?!"

"Emily, don't do this," Kevin said wearily. "You know I don't like you in a romantic way. I never have done."

"But you like my little *sister* in a romantic way?!"

Silence again.

Looking uneasy, Janette said "Emily, calm down. If Kevin wants Elara, don't get in the way of that. Maybe it's fate."

"What?!" Emily whirled around, staring at her mother in disbelief. *"Fate?* Ma, you can't be serious!"

"Elara," Kevin said quietly before Janette could console Emily. "Can we talk alone? Please?"

He held out a hand.

Elara stared at it.

Angry tears were falling down Emily's face now.

Elara looked at Emily uncertainly, and Emily spat "You know I love him. I've loved him for six *years.* If you go with him Elara, I will *never* forgive you."

Elara hesitated, and Kevin whispered "Trust me, Elara."

Elara swallowed hard, and she looked down at his outstretched hand again.

Then she noticed it.

A black symbol of the moon on his wrist, identical to hers.

A crescent moon, surrounded by small stars.

Just like hers.

Without another thought, Elara took Kevin's hand.

He breathed out in relief, and he helped her to her feet.

Emily screamed at him, but he acted as if he couldn't hear her as he gently asked "Can we go, Elara?"

Elara took a deep breath, then she whispered "Yes, we can go."

Janette had to physically restrain Emily from attacking Elara as she and Kevin left the house together, still holding hands, and they walked down the road in calm silence.

Passers-by gaped at them, some disbelievingly, as many in Taurbrook thought that *Emily* was Kevin Bate's girlfriend, not her little sister Elara.

However, it was clear as day when they saw Kevin glance down at Elara and give her a shy smile that he wasn't holding her hand in a platonic way.

They reached the entrance to the creek, and they saw Joshua and Betty waiting for Elara there.

Joshua grinned and opened his mouth to call out to Elara, not reading the situation at all, then Betty socked him in the stomach and hissed *"Shut up!!* Can't you see she's with Kevin Bates?!"

Kevin and Elara walked past them, Kevin gazing down at Elara.

She was so *beautiful.*

Kevin had a crush on Elara for years. Ever since she attended their high school across the village, Elara in Year Seven, him in Year Nine. She had only been eleven, and him thirteen.

He'd watched her grow from afar, smothered by her big sister, but thinking that he'd only get to see Elara if he talked to Emily, so he forced his and Emily's.... weird relationship.

Kevin shuddered.

He didn't even see Emily as a *friend.* She didn't understand him or even *know* him well, even after all these years.

He'd endured her rambling on, only about herself and everything she'd accomplished, never about her sister much. Emily had always acted as if Elara was totally stupid compared to her, simply because she had awesome grades, could play the piano, and won awards for her accomplishments.

Elara could play the flute.

And she played it beautifully, he mused as they walked. He'd passed by the creek a year and half ago to find Betty urging Elara to play just one song for her, and he hid behind a large rock and waited, curious.

The music was so haunting, so heavenly, that he felt hypnotised.

"Don't tell my family," Elara had begged Betty, once she stopped playing. "They don't need to know I can play the flute."

"I'm so sick of your parents doting on Emily and acting like you're a screw-up," Betty had answered angrily. "They've pored over your artwork displayed around town, and read your books, and they don't even know they're all *yours!"*

"I know. They don't need to know I'm the creative one." Elara had sighed and handed Betty her flute. “Everyone is sworn to secrecy about my videos on social media, the creative side of me, the royalties I get for my artwork and books under a pen name. Nobody will tell my family that Melody Taren is me.”

Kevin’s jaw had dropped, and he whispered disbelieving “Elara is *Melody Taren?!”*

Betty nodded. “We all solemnly swear to keep it from them for as long as you want. The Shaman swore everyone to secrecy from your family, and Emily’s boyfriend Kevin Bates.”

I’m not Emily’s boyfriend, Kevin had wanted to shout then, but he remained hidden, still listening, still gathering information.

After a while, Elara hugged Betty goodbye and walked right past the rock he was behind.

Kevin caught a whiff of her flowery scent, wondering if it was natural, and he watched her go dreamily.

Betty packed her flute away, and she put on her backpack before she got on her bike and rode away.

Back in the present, whispers followed Elara and Kevin, everyone who saw them together staring after them curiously.

Then, they were stopped by Emily’s group of stuck-up friends.

“Kevin? What *is* this?” a girl called Sharon demanded. “Aren’t you with Emily?”

“I was *never* with Emily,” Kevin responded coldly; gasps went up at that.

“Rubbish,” spat Sharon. “You’ve been with Emily for six years!”

Kevin scowled at her. “Emily wouldn’t leave me *alone* for six years.”

Sharon blinked at that. “But… Emily said you’re soulmates. She said you have almost everything in common!”

“We have *nothing* in common,” Kevin said harshly. “Elara is the one I’ve always wanted. Emily got hit with a very harsh dose of reality today when she realised that. Now all of you, realise the same. Emily and I have nothing in common and I never, *ever* wanted her. This whole six-year-old story of us being together, and so close, was fabricated by Emily.”

"Well why did you go along with it for six years if it was all a charade??"

A muscle twitched in Kevin's jaw.

Sharon waited angrily, a hand on her hip. "Well??"

"Because she wore me out, until I felt ragged and hollow," Kevin said flatly. "I didn't bother correcting Emily after the first two years. She wouldn't take no for an answer, or leave me alone. You knew it, Sharon. Emily would follow me everywhere, text me, call me, turn up at my job just to bring me lunch. I always threw that lunch away, as ordered by the Shaman."

Gasps went up at that.

"The *Shaman?"* Sharon said disbelievingly. "Why would she tell you to throw Emily's lunch away??"

"Because Emily has a darkness about her that the Shaman sensed years ago," Kevin replied just as flatly as before. "Her dark energy was deeply merged in that food, and it could have had a very negative effect on me had I consumed it."

Sharon opened her mouth curiously, but Kevin coldly added "I'm not getting into that right now. Please get out of our way."

The gang parted, mouthing wordlessly after Kevin and Elara as they walked further and further through Taurbrook, hands still tightly entwined.

"Where are we going?" whispered Elara, and Kevin murmured "To the cliffs of Taurbrook overlooking the ocean. I know you were there last night, Elara."

Elara's heart raced. "Are you pretending to have a crush on me on, Kevin Bates?"

"No," he said firmly. "I *do* have a crush on you. I'd even go as far as to say I've loved you from afar, Elara. I know things about you; things you've kept secret for years. Things that have made me admire you, *so* damn much."

"Like what?" challenged Elara: Kevin stopped walking and turned to face her with a serious expression.

"Do you want me to tell you right here? Or do you want to wait until it's guaranteed that we're completely alone?"

Elara thought about that.

Kevin waited, ever so patient.

Elara breathed in, then she murmured “I’ll wait until we’re alone.”

“Good. So, let’s head up the cliffs.”

Elara nodded, and they continued walking.

Atop the Taurbrook Cliffs

Kevin and Elara sat down, at the top of the very same middle cliff that Elara frequently visited late at night.

Two other cliffs were at either side of theirs.

"So?" Elara said, after moments of silence, their eyes on the vast ocean spread before them. "What do you know about me, Kevin Bates? What are you so impressed by?"

Kevin took a deep breath, then he confessed "I've watched you secretly for years. I know you play the flute, beautifully."

Elara froze, staring at him as he continued "I know you've written novels that are in Taurbrook Library, and you've drawn beautiful artwork that's been placed all over Taurbrook. I know you create both serious and funny videos, talking wearing a mask with your voice slightly distorted so nobody knows it's you. I know the pen name you go by, as the author of your artwork, books, and your username on all of your social media pages, is Melody Taren. You have a huge following, from pretty much the whole of Taurbrook and the neighbouring towns and villages, and the rest of the world beyond our seas."

Elara was stunned. "Do… do you follow me on social media, Kevin?"

Kevin nodded. "Yes. Also under a pen name."

"Which is what?" she demanded; he honestly answered "KBTaur."

Elara recognised that name.

Realisation washed over her as she thought hard.

"You've liked a lot of my posts," she said slowly. "You've bought some of my novels and reviewed them online. You gave four of my novels five-star reviews. You went in depth about what you loved about the stories."

Kevin nodded with a smile.

Elara's eyes welled up. "You did the same with my artwork."

"I did, yes." He moved closer. "I hope this proves how deeply I feel about you, Elara. And I really hope you don't think I'm a creep."

Elara looked at her knees, her shoulders shaking as her tears fell.

"I don't think you're a creep," she wept. "I just wish you didn't let Emily keep you away from me. You're the third one who seems to understand me. You, Joshua and Betty."

"And Lysander."

Elara's head shot up in surprise. "What do you know about Lysander?"

Kevin smiled at her, and he moved closer, gently wiping her tears away.

Then he kissed her tenderly, his strong arms curving around her.

A moan sounded in Elara's throat as she pulled him closer, falling backwards onto the cliff's grassy surface.

Now on her back with Kevin Bates on top of her, she wrapped her legs around his waist, wanting everything he was offering at that moment.

Before things got super-heated, maybe even out of hand, Elara's smartphone rang from her shoulder bag, a few feet away from them.

The new couple swore and broke apart at the same time, and Kevin breathed "You should answer that. It might be one of your parents. Maybe even the Shaman."

Elara nodded, out of breath. "Alright."

She reached into her bag and looked at her phone, her heart pounding as she answered the unknown caller, after pressing loudspeaker.

"Hello?"

"How could you do this to me!!" screamed Emily, hysterical. "Everyone's talking about how you and Kevin are *together!"*

"Emily, I-"

"Sharon told me what he said," spat Emily. "How could you make him say those awful things about me?? Kevin and I are *made* for each other!"

"Emily-"

"Come back and explain to everyone that this is just a prank," Emily cut across, livid. "If you don't, Pa is going to beat the *hell* out of you!"

"For what?!"

"For embarrassing me!" shrieked Emily. "Embarrassing this family! People keep stopping by with gossip about you and Kevin, asking if it's true he dumped me!"

"He didn't dump you," Elara said coldly, and Emily paused.

"He didn't?"

"No," Elara said, "Because you were never together! Everything was all in your head, Emily, and you know it!"

Silence.

Kevin and Elara waited.

Then, Emily spoke with a venomous tone that made Elara's skin crawl.

"I'm going to make sure you get a beating you'll never forget in *years* from Ma and Pa. You know what happens when that heavy belt and its hard buckle strikes you hard enough, Elara. Would Kevin still want you if he knew that you screamed for mercy and pissed yourself?!"

Kevin grabbed Elara's phone at that, and he ended the call.

He stared at Elara in shock, Elara embarrassed that he'd heard all of that.

But Kevin didn't think any less of her.

His golden eyes seemed to darken in fury, and he spoke quietly after a long bout of silence.

"Your father beats you?"

Elara opened her mouth, then closed it.

She shook her head, and Kevin grabbed her by the shoulders, livid.

"Don't lie to me, Elara! I heard what Emily said just now. How long has he been beating you?"

Elara swallowed hard, then she whispered "For years."

"Years?!" he repeated disbelievingly, and she nodded, her throat tight.

"Both my parents. When they get mad, I'm the one they take it out on. My father… he has this huge brown leather belt that he made. It's too large for his jeans and trousers. He made it at his carpenter shop. There's wood and metal stitched inside the leather, along the entire belt, and then there's the massive golden buckle."

Kevin stared at her, shocked. "They beat you with that thing?"

Elara nodded, tears falling fast. "Yes. Often. But my body never scars. I get massive bruises though, but they fade away in about three days."

"That's your power," Kevin said softly. "Moonweavers never stay injured for long. You could jump off this cliff and break all your bones, and your body will mend itself completely in less than a week."

Elara stared at him through beautiful silver eyes that glistened with tears.

"Seriously?"

"Seriously."

"Wow."

It was silent for a moment, Kevin still furious at what he'd discovered.

"Do they ever beat Emily?"

Elara shook her head glumly. "They never have."

"What?!"

"She's the golden child," Elara said, sighing. "And I'm the screw-up."

"And you're also their punching bag," Kevin spat; Elara's eyes filled again. Then she quietly replied "I guess I am."

Kevin pulled her into his arms and held her protectively, kissing her forehead.

They stayed like that, holding each other tightly as the wind blew, chilly.

Ten minutes later, Kevin spoke quietly.

"You're not going back home, Elara. I won't allow it."

"What?" she said, startled. "Where will I go?"

"You'll come with me to mine," he said firmly. "We'll go to the Shaman tomorrow, together at dawn, like she requested."

Elara was surprised at that. "How did you know I was seeing the Shaman?"

"I'm a Moonweaver, Elara. Ane my powers were mastered since childhood." Kevin smiled down at her. "I know a lot."

Elara smiled back. "So you've had that tattoo for years?"

"Yep."

"I never noticed it."

"You never got close enough," he answered as he stood. "Come on. Let's go to mine."

Elara hesitated at that, and Kevin turned and smiled down at her, holding out a hand.

"Do you trust me?"

Elara wanted to say no.

She wanted to say that things were moving way too fast.

That it had been less than twenty-four hours since they'd become boyfriend and girlfriend.

That her head was spinning from Emily's evil threat, and she was scared her father would find her and drag her home, before beating her black and blue with the manmade belt and its heavy gold buckle.

Kevin read her mind easily.

"Don't worry," he said softly. "I'll protect you. I promise. Take my hand, Elara."

"I don't have anything on me," she said just as softly as she took his hand. "Just my smartphone and Mp3 player. I don't even have a change of clothes."

"We'll sort that. Let's go."

The Fake Concern

By nine p.m., the Peterson family were searching high and low for Elara.

Emily knocked on the neighbour's doors with tears streaming down her face as she explained that Elara had vanished, and she just wanted her baby sister home.

Her friends sniggered as they stood a few feet away, knowing it was an act, that Emily really wanted Elara to get beaten black and blue behind closed and locked doors.

Many residents of Taurbrook joined the search, genuinely worried for Elara.

At ten thirty, the Shaman of Taurbrook emerged.

"Return to your homes this night," she called, her voice magically magnified. "Elara is safe. She will not remain safe if she joins her family."

Emily and her parents looked uncomfortable as everyone turned to look at them curiously.

Then a man asked "Why wouldn't Elara be safe with her parents and sister? Surely she should go home to her family?"

There were murmurs of agreement at that, and Janette quickly cried "Exactly! Anything could be happening to my youngest child. I need her home!"

"No," Madame Marwen said stonily. "Anything could happen to your youngest child, if she *returns* to you this night. I know what you all are, Janette Peterson. I know what you do to poor Elara every time you think she has stepped out of line. I know what you were going to do to her, as justice for your precious Emily."

Silence fell, everyone staring at the Petersons.

Then, Betty shouted out before Madame Marwen could.

"You were going to beat Elara black and blue with a manmade belt filled with heavy piece of wood and metal! And a heavy gold buckle, that would leave her bruised for days! All because your precious Emily is *deluded!"*

Gasps went up, and Emily screamed *"I'm not deluded!"*

"Do not listen to that brat Betty Broke!" shouted Janette in a panic, when furious talk broke out. "We just want our child home!"

"What do you mean don't listen to her?" a woman asked incredulously. "Madame Marwen did not deny or correct a *word* Betty said! Are you going against the Shaman of Taurbrook?!"

Joseph and Janette didn't reply, their faces hot with shame.

Emily was livid.

"Confess the truth," Joseph Ladell called coldly, "And maybe we'll tell you where Elara is!"

"Fine!" yelled Joseph, losing control completely. "We will not got go against the Shaman!"

"So you don't deny beating your daughter black and blue?!" more than one person in the crowd shouted furiously, and Joseph looked at his wife and child.

They both shook their heads desperately, but Joseph respected Madame Marwen took much and refused to lie before her.

"I do not deny it!"

Many men in the crowd cursed and leapt into action immediately, plenty swarming around the Petersons and grabbing them furiously, pinning them to the ground.

Joseph didn't struggle.

Janette and Emily screamed and kicked with all their might, but they were overpowered.

"Alert the authorities," Madame Marwen ordered icily. "This abuse has gone on for far too long!"

"Yes Madame Marwen!"

At Kevin's Secluded Home

Elara watched the local news disbelievingly at two in the morning, sat on Kevin's couch.

Her mother and father had been arrested, their bail amount higher than anyone could afford.

Emily was free to go after she gave in and told the police of Taurbrook everything, about the abuse of Elara, and the location of the dreaded manmade belt.

The belt was seized and burnt in a fire disgustedly, the public cheering as they watched it wither and burn, the wood and leather shrinking, the metal melting.

Kevin brought Elara a cup of tea as Elara watched through glassy eyes.

"Here, babe."

"Thank you," Elara said softly, taking the cup and sipping.

Kevin joined her on the sofa. "Your parents are pretty much gone for good. The Shaman ordered the courts to lock them up indefinitely."

Elara nodded, holding her cup. "A few hours ago, I felt guilty about them. But now… I'm glad they're going to prison, hopefully for good."

The Shaman was disgusted at her parents.

She overruled any decision made by any authority figure in Taurbrook, and across the rest of the land.

She'd ordered for Joseph and Janette to be transferred to the prison for hardcore criminals far out across ocean at a high-security building on a large secluded island which was surrounded by shark and siren infested waters.

If a prisoner escaped the building, they would have no choice but to try and swim away from the island.

And then, they would either be devoured by the massive hungry great white sharks, or lured to their deaths by the singing sirens.

"They're being transferred to Bone Island at dawn," Kevin said as he watched interestedly. "And I just realised Elara, that Emily doesn't have a job. She doesn't even have much savings. She's going to lose the house."

Elara smiled at that. "I know. She'll have to move in with one of her friends."

"And I bet it won't take long before those friends get sick of her," Kevin replied. "I got sick of her every time I saw her."

Elara nodded, finishing her tea.

She yawned, and Kevin looked at her with a knowing smile.

"Tired?"

Elara nodded, smiling back. "It's been a long, shocking day and night. I'm exhausted."

"Let me show you to the guest room," Kevin said, standing, and Elara stood too.

"Alright."

Once Elara was settled in her double bed, Kevin leant down and kissed her forehead.

"Goodnight Elara," he murmured, and Elara whispered "Goodnight."

The Village Elder's Knowing Ways

Later that morning, Elara sat across from Madame Marwen in the village hall.

She stifled a yawn behind her hand, and the elder looked at her knowingly.

"You only had two hours' sleep, am I right Elara?"

Elara nodded. "Yes Ma'am. It was a long, eventful night."

The old woman's eyes were sharp, her silver hair braided with tiny moonstones as she nodded again.

"Everything is as it should be, Elara. You are safe with Kevin Bates. And your evil adopted parents can never harm you again."

Elara swallowed hard, then she quietly said "Thank you for the part you played in making sure I got away from them for good, Madame Marwen."

"Oh, you're welcome." The Shaman smiled at her. "But that isn't why I summoned you here, Elara."

"I know Ma'am. You wanted to see me before all of that took place."

The Shaman nodded seriously, and she reached out, taking Elara's right hand and turning it onto his back. She placed her index finger on her new tattoo of the crescent moon surrounded by stars.

"You saw him," Madame Marwen said; not asking, stating. "Lysander."

Elara's breath caught, and she nodded.

Madame Marwen exhaled slowly. "Then the moon has chosen."

Elara leaned forward. "What does that mean, Madame Marwen?"

Madame Marwen hesitated. Then she decided not to keep anything from the girl. Elara was much stronger than she looked.

"Elara. Moonweavers are not just guardians of moonlight. They are keepers of balance. And the last time an apprentice like yourself walked this land, a great darkness followed."

Elara's stomach twisted. "Darkness?"

Madame Marwen nodded. "A creature born of shadow. A dark force that feeds on negativity, sorrow, moonlight, and tries its best to repel Moonweavers."

Elara's voice trembled. "Is it coming back?"

Madame Marwen looked away.

"It never left, Elara. It fed for a long time, on your household. You were powerless to stop those beatings as you were so young," she said quietly. "That object that your adopted father created just to hurt you, it was a cursed object. The bruises on your body, were always pitch-black and extremely painful no matter how brief the beating was."

"I had darkness in me?" whispered Elara, and she replied "Temporarily. The power in you fought it. It was exactly as was foretold. As you have the power of the moon in you, the darkness couldn't stay attached to you."

Elara nodded her ok.

"Unfortunately," the Shaman said grimly, "After that particularly nasty beating after you failed your maths test at age eleven. Do you remember that year, Elara?"

Elara cringed big time, remembering it very well. "Yes Ma'am."

"Your sister, Emily, age thirteen at the time, went down into the basement to wow at that horrid belt that you were beaten with."

Elara's blood ran cold. "What happened?"

"She ran her fingers up and down it, out of excitement and curiosity. And in doing so, she invited the darkness into her body." Madame Marwen paused, and she quietly explained "The darkness found a new, human vessel."

Elara slid back on her chair, stunned. "Is… is Emily possessed?"

"No. At least, the darkness within hasn't fully taken control of her."

"Is that why you made Kevin throw away her food?"

The Shaman nodded. "Yes."

Elara was stunned. "What do we do?"

“I don’t want you worrying,” Madame Marwen said gently. “The darkness in your sister shall be expelled in due time. That is a promise.”

Elara trusted her.

Her mind was reeling from what she’d just learnt.

The Shaman stood, and she smiled down at Elara. “Kevin is waiting for you outside. Let him take you home to rest, Elara.”

Elara stood too, grateful. “Yes Ma’am. Thank you.”

When Elara joined Kevin, he stood immediately.

“How did it go?”

“It went as well as it could have, I guess. I learnt a lot,” Elara said, smiling at him, tired. “Can we go back to yours?”

“Yes, of course. You need to sleep so you can be alert for Lysander.”

Elara was startled at that. “I’d forgotten about that.”

Kevin chuckled as he put his arms around her in a hug, holding her close.

Elara hugged him back, feeling so safe with him.

They left the hall and went back to Kevin’s secluded house, far above the Taurbrook Hall.

Elara wondered what happened to Kevin’s relatives, and he smiled at her as they stepped out of their shoes.

“That’s a conversation for a later date, Elara. Rest.”

Elara smiled back and said ok.

The First Lesson

That night, Lysander met Elara on the cliff again.

“Hold out your marked wrist,” he said warmly, and Elara held it out.

Lysander traced a glowing white sigil in the air.

It hovered above her palm, shimmering like liquid silver.

“Moonweaving is not your everyday magic,” Lysander said as he took Elara’s hand and raised it slightly. “It is powered by intention. Emotion. Will.”

The sigil sank into Elara’s skin.

Elara gasped as warmth spread through her veins, her tattoo glowing bright white, glowing lines etched across her dark skin.

“What *was* that?”

“Your first tether,” Lysander answered. “A connection to the lunar threads.”

Elara looked up at the sky.

The moonlight shifted.

Threads of silver unravelled from the rays of moonlight, drifting toward her like strands of silk.

Elara reached upwards, and they responded, swirling around her body gently.

She pointed, and the glowing threads zoomed in that direction, obeying her silent order.

Lysander watched her carefully. “You learn quickly.”

Elara smiled faintly. “I’ve always felt deeply connected to the moon. I’m sure I’ll get the hang of my powers real fast.”

Lysander’s expression softened. “You were born for this.”

Elara looked at him. “To be a Moonweaver’s Apprentice?”

"Yes. And eventually, to become a master Moonweaver, just like your boyfriend Kevin Bates."

Elara's heart stirred at the mention of Kevin.

She smiled and nodded, and Lysander smiled back.

Then, out of curiosity, she asked "How did Kevin become a Moonweaver?"

"He comes from a long line of very strong Moonweavers, protectors of this land from the Third Realm," Lysander answered; Elara's jaw dropped. "From a toddler, he was able to harness and master his powers, connecting to the moon without being pushed to by his relative Moonweavers. By age six, he did not need to be taught. He grew stronger and stronger, even stronger than his parents. His mother, Darlia Bates, returned to the Third Realm permanently when he became eighteen, leaving him everything, including ownership of his home, and a vast amount of funds that would last five generations after him."

Elara stared at Lysander disbelievingly. "So he doesn't ever need to get a job?"

"His job is protecting the land as a powerful Moonweaver, Elara." Lysander smiled at her stunned expression. "He and his ancestors have been fighting darkness for centuries. When the darkness faded, it was decided that Kevin would remain in Taurbrook and his mother would return to the Third Realm."

"As a retired Moonweaver?" asked Elara; Lysander's smile grew.

"Something like that. Now come," he said, straightening up. "It is time to learn your second spell."

"Really?" Elara asked excitedly; he said yes. "What kind of spell this time?"

"This time, you will learn your first spell of defence."

"Awesome."

The Shadow Stirs, Sensing Elara

Deep in the forest, something moved.

A shape darker than night.

It slithered between the trees, drawn by the sudden surge of moonlight, and power.

A voice echoed through the shadows.

"Her power awakens."

The creature's form twisted, its eyes glowing like dying embers.

"The apprentice must be consumed before she becomes too strong, like her new partner. Two powerful Moonweavers in this land will destroy everything I have been working towards for the past six years."

The forest trembled as more dark beings formed.

The hunt for the Moonweaver's apprentice had begun.

Elara's Fear- and Power

Back on the cliff, Elara felt a sudden chill in the air.

She turned curiously, staring at the vast forest on the other side of the cliffs.

"Lysander," she whispered, "Something's wrong."

Lysander stiffened. "You feel it too?"

Elara nodded. "Yes. A darkness has formed in the forest. It's watching…. and waiting."

Lysander's jaw tightened. "The Shadowborn."

Elara's heart pounded. "It's real?"

"It is very real," Lysander said. "And it will come for you."

Elara swallowed hard. "Then teach me how to fight it."

Lysander stepped closer, strands of moonlight swirling around them.

"I will," he said. "But you must understand something first."

Elara met his gaze, her eyes glowing. "What is it?"

"Moonweavers do not fight with strength alone," he said. "We fight with truth also."

Elara frowned. "Truth?"

Lysander moved closer, and he touched her forehead.

A burst of light filled her vision.

Memories.

Emotions.

Fears.

She saw a woman who looked just like her, tall, dark, with silver eyes and long hair, held her close as a one-year-old, kissing her forehead desolately.

"My sweet Elara," she wept. "In due time, you will know what you are. I cannot keep you, my darling, for I am at death's door. But I will always be with you."

A woman Elara barely recognised entered the room she now realised was a hospital, and she held her hands out to receive Elara.

Elara's mother hiccoughed, holding her close and cuddling her one more time, before she handed Elara to the owner of the orphanage.

"You will look after her?" Elara's mother asked, tears falling, and the woman gently replied "Of course. Elara will be loved by a new family, in due time."

It was Elara's own truth.

Her beginning.

As her mother gave her away, Elara saw that she had the symbol of a crescent mood and stars on her right wrist.

The woman held Elara close and turned and left the room with her, and Elara's mother covered her face and sobbed uncontrollably.

Lysander lifted his hand away from her forehead, and Elara gasped, falling to her knees as her tears fell thick and fast.

"My mother was a Moonweaver," she wept. "But she died. I have her power. She lives in me, Lysander."

Lysander knelt beside her, looking sorry for her. Then he stated "Your greatest weapon is not the moonlight, Elara."

He placed a hand over her heart.

"It is *you.*"

Touched Beyond Belief

Elara entered Kevin's home at dawn.

Kevin was waiting for her, as she had a feeling he would be.

"How did it go?" he asked, and she replied "It was… very hard to get my head around. I learnt my first spell of defence."

"Oh?" Kevin smiled at her. "And which spell would that be?"

"The ice-blast spell," Elara replied; Kevin smiled at her.

"Did you master it?"

"I did," Elara said, smiling back. "Lysander pushed and pushed until I was flawless."

Kevin chuckled. "My mother did the same with me all my life."

At the word "mother", Elara's expression changed. Suddenly, she looked very sad.

"Elara?" Kevin said curiously. "What is it?"

"Lysander showed me a vision of my mother," she said quietly, sitting down. "Two months before she died. It was the day I was taken to the orphanage."

Kevin joined her on the sofa and took her hand gently. "How did that feel?"

"Bittersweet," Elara admitted. "I look just like her. I have her curly black hair, dark skin, and her grey eyes."

"If she was as beautiful as you are, I know she was a stunning woman." Kevin put at arm around her and cuddled her close. "Try not to let it depress you."

"Oh, I won't. I'm just glad I got to see her after all this time." Elara rested her head on Kevin's shoulder thoughtfully. "I had no memories prior, or even a picture. Oh my God!"

Elara turned to look at Kevin, looking like she'd seen a ghost.

"What's wrong?" Kevin asked concernedly- silence. "Elara?"

Elara swallowed, then she whispered "The Shadowborn, Kevin."

"The Shadowborn?! What about it?" he demanded, heat rising already.

"It's back," Elara said quietly; Kevin stared at her. "I felt it. It's in the forest. It's back because it felt the power of two Moonweavers residing here. Before, it wasn't bothered with it was just one Moonweaver. You," she said softly. "But it won't accept two powerful beings here and it and won't rest until there's just one Moonweaver to deal with, like before."

Silence.

Kevin's heart was racing, his mind spinning.

Elara looked at him. "What are we going to do about it?"

Kevin paused, and he smiled at her, touched. "We?"

Elara nodded, smiling back. "Yes. We."

Kevin took her hand and kissed it. "For now, nothing. You'll continue to train with Lysander, and grow stronger and stronger as an apprentice, before you become a proper Moonweaver."

Elara said ok. "And when I'm strong enough?"

"Then we will tackle the problem head-on."

Elara exhaled sharply. "I feel like I want to tackle it now. The Shadowborn took my mother. Lysander touched my forehead and unlocked visions, sent by the moon itself. As I walked back here from the cliffs, I saw more and more."

Kevin was quiet for a moment. Then he asked "What did you see?"

"I saw the Shadowborn devour my mother's very being in that hospital. First it looked like black and red flames that swirled around her. She screamed in pain, and then she was swallowed up, gone. She was too weak to fight back."

"Were you already taken to the orphanage?"

Elara nodded glumly. "Yes. And I have no idea what happened to my father. He was a Moonweaver from the Sixth Realm. I think he and my mother were just a fling," she said quietly, "And he left before she found out she was pregnant."

Kevin looked at her, feeling her pain. "He never knew he had a child."

Elara shook her head glumly. “No. He never knew. He’s been in the Sixth Realm of the moon all this time, without a clue.”

“Don’t let your heart overrule your mind, Elara.” Keven looked at her seriously. “You aren’t strong enough to take on the Shadowborn. This pain you feel about your mother and father, are fuel to the darkness. Try to get past it. Please.”

Elara took a deep breath and nodded. “I’ll try.”

The Darkness of The Apprentice’s Sister

Emily Peterson jumped at another sound in the now large and empty house.

She nudged Sharon, who was fast asleep. “Sharon.”

“Mmm… Emily… Kevin’s with Elara now,” mumbled Sharon, rolling over in Emily’s bed. “Let him go…”

“I won’t let him go,” Emily said fiercely, and Sharon yawned, opening her eyes as Emily’s eyes filled over, then she screamed in fear.

“Emily!”

“What??”

“Your eyes,” gasped Sharon. “Your eyes are black! So are your lips!”

Emily frowned at her friend, then she got up and walked and sat in front of her vanity table, looking in the large mirror.

“What…”

It was true.

Her once bright green eyes were now a very dark brown, almost black. So were her freckles, and her lips.

“You look like a dark witch,” Sharon said, frightened. “Is this because of what happened with Kevin and Elara? And your parents??”

Silence, Emily staring at her new appearance in the vanity mirror.

"Did the Shaman curse you or something?" Sharon asked fearfully. "After punishing your parents for what they did to Elara? And you for letting it happen without saying a word?"

More silence.

"You have to fix this," Sharon said desperately. "You have to go to the Shaman and beg for forgiveness. She cursed you, Emily!"

Emily shrugged a shoulder as she stared at her scary reflection.

"I don't care."

"What do you mean you don't care?!" cried Sharon. "Don't you think you need to make this right?!"

Emily looked at her best friend, and she smiled deviously.

"Actually, I think I need to take a trip to the lake in the forest before evening."

"What?" Sharon said confusedly. "Why?"

"I just have a feeling. Like I should swim around, and become one with the atmosphere. And *you're* coming with me."

The Apprentice's Power Increases

Elara stood on the cliff again at dusk the following night, the sky painted in bruised purples and molten gold.

Lysander circled her slowly, silver light trailing from his cloak.

"Moonweaving begins with breath," he said. "Not power."

Elara frowned. "Breath?"

Lysander nodded. "The moon is steady. Constant. You must be the same."

He placed a hand on her back.

"Breathe."

Elara inhaled.

The threads of moonlight around her pulsed in response, like a heartbeat.

Elara exhaled.

They brightened.

Lysander stepped back. "Good. Now weave."

Elara lifted her hands. The threads responded, swirling around her fingers like living silk. She guided them into a shape- a sphere of shimmering light.

It flickered for a moment, Lysander commanding "Keep breathing as calmly as possible. Concentrate on making that sphere solid."

Elara obeyed, breathing in and out steadily.

The image of her sobbing mother in a bed as she held baby Elara close flashed before her eyes, and Elara gasped harshly.

The sphere of light made of moon threads flickered, then vanished.

Elara groaned. "I can't do it."

"You can," Lysander said firmly. "But you're distracted, and afraid."

Elara stiffened. “I’m not afraid.”

Lysander’s eyes softened. “You are. And your fear disrupts the magic.”

Elara looked away.

He was right.

She was terrified.

Of the Shadowborn.

Of her power.

Of what it meant to be chosen.

The visions of her mother were really messing with her, and Lysander knew it. He watched as she ran a hand over head, muttering to herself.

Then he said “Elara.”

She looked at him with a defeated expression. “Yes?”

He stepped closer. “Fear is not your enemy. It is your teacher.”

Elara met his gaze, disappointed in herself as she admitted “I don’t think I can create this force tonight.”

“Let’s try,” he said gently. “I know you can do this. This is the second counter-attack to whatever the Shadowborn may shoot at you.”

Elara nodded, her face determined. “Let’s do it.”

And just as it reached dawn the next day, she finally mastered the second counter-attack.

Pleased, Lysander said “Excellent, Elara. Now, take the next three nights off. I will see you again at dusk on Saturday.”

Elara was worn out.

She thanked Lysander, who nodded and vanished, and she made her way down the cliffs to Kevin Bate’s home.

Emily's Initiation

The village of Taurbrook was in disarray.

Everyone had seen the vast change in Emily Peterson's appearance, and they were terrified.

Most believed she had sold her soul and was now an evil being, which was the closest to the truth.

She had pledged her allegiance to the Shadowborn, and now made frequent trips into the forest with Sharon, whose eyes had also turned from periwinkle blue to black, from being in the presence of an evil force that was both Emily and the Shadowborn.

Elara had heard about her sister's initiation, and had seen for herself how she looked now, but she was warned by the Shaman, Kevin and Lysander not to make contact with her, or go anywhere near her.

It broke Elara's heart, but she had to obey.

Her old house had become surrounded by dark mist.

Everyone avoided the location now.

Joshua and Betty begged Elara to stay as far away from her big sister as possible.

"She's doing dark magic," Joshua told Elara, on the third night she had off from training, "And we think she's going to use it on you, for what happened with Kevin."

"Don't worry about that," Elara had replied. "Emily doesn't scare me."

"Please be careful," Betty said worriedly, her arm linked in Elara's as they listened to the Shaman speak to the villagers of Taurbrook concernedly. "Emily might be your big sister, but she's an evil witch now. And Sharon is her follower."

"Steer clear of Emily Peterson and her servants!" called Madame Marwen. "No matter what they say, or try to entice you with! They stay in the forest, learning from a dark, evil entity. *We must protect Taurbrook!!"*

"We must protect Taurbrook!" the villagers shouted back in response, and cheers went up.

"Women and children under sixteen must be indoors by dusk," the Shaman ordered. "All men of age, must arm yourselves at nightfall and remain on guard! Protect your households! Patrol with the authorities if you feel the need to!"

The men cheered again, and Joshua determinedly said "I'm going to get a sword and patrol at night with the guards of Taurbrook!"

"Whatever," Betty said amusedly. "You don't even know *how* to use a sword. You'd better get inside at dusk with the women and children."

"Shut up," Joshua snapped, and Betty laughed, Elara amused as well. "I'll train!"

"Sure, sure."

Elara detangled herself from Betty's arm and pushed her way through the crowd, heading towards Madame Marwen as she stepped down from her podium and began to make her way home, up the mountains.

"Madame Marwen!" Elara called desperately. *"Madame Marwen!"*

The Shaman turned and smiled at her. "Yes, sweet Elara."
"Please," Elara said, once she'd reach her. "Is there no way to rid my sister of the darkness that is the Shadowborn?"
"Your sister has chosen her path," Madame Marwen replied, a little sadly. "It is very upsetting. Witnessing what she has become, after all of her achievements, hurts me more than you can ever imagine."
"It hurts me too," Elara said, her eyes filling. "Emily loathes me now, for staying in a relationship with and living with Kevin Bates. Kevin moved his house further away from the town with his powers to keep us safe, and away from her."
"Ah yes. Ten minutes into the forest, just behind the foot of the first cliff." The Shaman nodded. "That was a very smart thing to do. Just be careful when travelling home at night, Elara. I don't want anything to happen to you."
"Yes Ma'am. I should be alright."
"Then head on back home to Kevin."
"Ok."

The Shadowborn's First Attack

The forest was unnaturally quiet that night.

Too quiet.

The trees didn't even rustle with the breeze that was gently passing through Elara's curly hair.

Elara walked towards Kevin's home slowly and certainly, the moonlight guiding her path. She hummed softly to steady her nerves.

A twig snapped in front of her, and Elara froze.

"Kevin?" she whispered.

Silence.

"Emily?" she said nervously, then she something vast appear in front of her.

Suddenly a shape lunged from the darkness, a heavy black form with bright red eyes.

Elara screamed as a mass of shadow slammed her to the ground. Its form was fluid, shifting, its eyes burning brighter, like ember.

The Shadowborn.

It hissed at her menacingly, its voice like cracking ice.

"Moon-touched girl... you belong with me and your elder sister. Allow me to consume you as I did her, and make you part of the darkness that is I."

Elara scrambled back, heart pounding. "Stay away from me!"

The creature surged forward; Elara raised her hands instinctively.

Moonlight exploded from her palms.

The Shadowborn shrieked, recoiling as the blinding white light seared its form.

Elara stared at down at her hands in shock, trembling.

She hadn't meant to do that.

She hadn't even known she could.

The Shadowborn snarled, reforming.

It lunged again at Elara again, Elara holding her hands up, ready.

A blade of silver light sliced through the air before she could launch another attack.

Lysander appeared between them, cloak billowing, his eyes blazing.

"Get back, creature of darkness," he commanded coldly. "You will not take my apprentice. Not this night."

The Shadowborn hissed, retreating into the trees.

Suddenly, it was gone.

The trees started to whisper again, the darkness no longer a part of the forest.

Lysander knelt beside Elara. "Are you hurt, Elara?"

Elara shook her head, breathless. "I… I attacked the Shadowborn with a beam of moonlight. It was blinding, and made the beast's body split into pieces."

Lysander stared at her, stunned. "You shouldn't be able to do that yet."

Elara swallowed. "What does that mean?"

Lysander hesitated, then replied "It means your power is developing faster than it should."

"Is that a bad thing?" Elara asked nervously, and he smiled at her reassuringly.

"It is very impressive."

Kevin Bates ran towards them, and they turned, Elara still on the forest floor.

"I saw the blasts of light," he panted. "Was that you, Elara?"

"Yes," Lysander answered for Elara. "Get some rest, both of you. Then take Elara to the Shaman, Kevin, and let her know what happened here."

Kevin looked at Lysander's serious face as he helped Elara to her feet, and he nodded.

"Yes sir."

"The Shadowborn will be back," Lysander said, turning his gaze towards the deeper section of the forest. "And it has partially merged with your elder sister, Elara, making her do its bidding in the town."

"Yes." Elara nodded. "I've seen her. She looks so evil."

"Go," Lysander ordered. "Rest, Elara, and then update the Shaman. I will see you at dusk the day after tomorrow."

A Secret About Elara's Past

In the village hall later that day, the village elder Madame Marwen listened as Elara recounted the attack.

When she finished, Madame Marwen sighed heavily.

"I feared this," she murmured.

Elara frowned. "Feared what?"

Madame Marwen looked at her with sorrowful eyes.

"Elara… you were not born in Taurbrook."

Elara blinked. "What?"

"You were born in the night on a neighbouring island, home to Moonweavers from the Second and Third Realm," Madame Marwen said. "Wrapped in silver cloth that glowed bright white as soon as it connected with your soft, newborn skin. Gazing up the moon. And you were prayed over, and blessed."

Elara's heart pounded. "Prayed over and blessed by who?"

"By myself," Madame Marwen said. "And Lysander."

Elara stared at her. "Lysander was there when I was born?"

Madame Marwen nodded. "Yes. He brought you to this island, with your mother. He said the moon had chosen you. This was long before you could speak."

Elara felt her head spin. "Why didn't anyone tell me?"

Madame Marwen's voice softened. "Because we wanted you to have a normal life, far from the way of Moonweavers. For as long as possible."

"But why? I could have grown up trained, just like Kevin was!"

"That island is no more," Madame Marwen said softly. "The Shadowborn attacked it with its followers. Swallowed it up and spread a terrible sickness. The Moonweavers all returned to their realms to keep safe. The ones who refused to leave…."

Her voice cracked, and her eyes welled up.

"They died six months after the Shadowborn's brutal attack on their island."

It was silent for a moment, the hurt welling over Elara as she took that in. Then she spoke quietly.

"My mother refused to go."

The Shaman nodded.

Elara shook her head. "I deserved the truth, Madame Marwen"

Madame Marwen reached for her hand. "You deserve the world. But the truth… the truth is dangerous. It can sway you from your path, Elara."

Elara pulled her hand away, her eyes welling up as she stood, and she left the Shaman sitting there.

Madame Marwen sitting there, her heart heavy as she watched Elara go,

Elara wasn't sure who she was anymore as she walked, ignoring the greetings from the people of Taurbrook as she headed to the creek.

She sat down by the water after walking for twenty minutes, then she broke down, sobbing.

"Who the hell do I trust??"

Lysander's Hidden Weakness

At dusk, Elara found Lysander on the cliff, staring up at the moon with a haunted expression.

"You knew from the start," she said quietly, to his sleek silver back. "You knew I had powers from the day I was born. You knew I came from a clan of Moonweavers."

Lysander didn't turn around. "Yes. I knew."

"Why didn't you tell me, Lysander?"

He closed his eyes. "Because I feared what it would mean for you. You may have been very different had you grown up knowing of the power you possessed. And it is very likely that the Shadowborn would have murdered you before you could even take your first steps, if it became aware of your existence."

Elara stepped closer, sensing that wasn't all. "What aren't you telling me?"

Lysander hesitated. Then he whispered "I was the last Moonweaver from your clan, after your mother died. I survived the Shadowborn's attack. It had no effect on me, and it also had no effect on you as an infant."

Elara's heart pounded. "And what does that mean?"

Lysander finally turned to face her.

"I was born a powerful Moonweaver, as were you, and Kevin Bates. But Kevin was born on this island, raised in an entirely different way to you and I."

Elara frowned. "I know that. What are you trying to explain to me?"

Lysander looked away. "It was the Shadowborn."

Elara's stomach twisted. "Did it hurt you?"

"It took something from me," Lysander said. "Something I can never get back."

Elara stepped closer. "What did it take?"

Lysander's voice broke. "My humanity."

Elara froze. “Your humanity?”

“Yes.” Lysander’s eyes glowed brighter; too bright.

He didn’t look fully human anymore.

He hadn’t been fully human for a very long time.

Elara wasn’t scared.

Instead of backing away from him, she stepped closer and asked, “What are you exactly now? Since the Shadowborn changed you?”

“I am part of the atmosphere,” Lysander replied quietly. “I form at dusk, before the moon, every night. I am nothing in the light of day. Just particles in the air.”

“It cursed you,” Elara said softly; he replied “Yes” just as softly.

“What can we do about it?”

“Nothing,” Lysander said calmly, and he stood up straighter, suddenly businesslike. “Now it’s time to train, Elara. You’ve wasted enough time listening to my tales of woe.”

He smiled, a sad smile.

Elara smiled back, feeling sorry for him as she nodded.

I have to help him, she thought as Lysander began explaining that she could create solid weapons out of the strands of moonlight, to defend herself from the Shadowborn, and its minions that were weaker creatures formed from shadow, like her big sister Emily.

“Are you paying attention Elara?” asked Lysander curiously, when she stood thinking with a frown on her face. “Concentrate.”

“I’m sorry,” she said quickly. “Let’s start. I’m ready.”

Emily Approaches Elara

At dawn, Emily Peterson walked through the forest slowly, heading towards her home.

She reached the forest entrance just as Elara was walking in, and she gasped her little sister's name.

"Elara!"

Elara stepped back immediately, on guard. "Emily."

Emily smiled, and Elara noticed sharpened teeth behind her black lips as she asked as casually as possible, "How's life living with Kevin Bates?"

"Life living with Kevin is good," Elara responded flatly, and she continued walking, wanting to get as far away from her demonic big sister as possible.

"Where are you going?" demanded Emily, glaring at Elara's retreating back. "We are having a conversation!"

"Why did you pledge allegiance to the Shadowborn?" spat Elara as she spun back around. "I know it became a part of you from a young age, but you didn't have to go *this* far Emily! I mean look at you! *You look psychotic!"*

Emily stepped back, stung.

Then her expression hardened. "Things wouldn't have gone this far if you hadn't stolen Kevin Bates away from me. We could have both been at home with Ma and Pa right now. Thanks to you, they're on Bone Island indefinitely!"

"Thanks to *me?"* Elara repeated coldly. "No, Emily. If you hadn't threatened me on the phone, spewing that vile mess about how Pa was going to beat be black and blue to avenge you, I would have gone back home."

Emily glared at her.

Elara glared back.

"I could summon the Shadowborn right now to finish you off," Emily said icily, moments later. "And I'd watch, happily!"

"Idiot." Elara laughed in her face. "The Shadowborn will remain in slumber until nightfall. It's powerless in the light of day!"

"How do you know that?!" screeched Emily; some birds took flight, startled.

"You're disturbing the creatures of the forest," Elara said flatly, not answering her question. "Run on home, demon Emily. I've indulged you long enough."

Elara turned and walked away, Emily staring after her disbelievingly.

Something was different about Elara.

She seemed stronger, tough as nails and confident.

Surer of herself.

But why was that?

Because of Kevin?

Emily's black eyes flashed scarlet as she turned and walked in the opposite direction, out of the forest towards her home.

She was tired.

She had been up all night conversing with the Shadowborn, being granted more

and more dark power.
Emily's once bright red hair was now jet black.
She knew there was no going back now that she had changed so drastically.
She was going to help the Shadowborn take her little sister down, and she was glad about it.

A Choice That Changes Everything

Elara stood at the cliff's edge, the wind whipping her curly hair back, her heart pounding.

She had a choice.

Run from her destiny.

Or embrace it.

She looked at Lysander.

Then up at the moon.

At the threads of silver drifting from the sky towards her like an invitation.

Without waiting for Lysander to instruct her, Elara lifted her hands up into the silver rays of the moonlight.

The glowing threads wrapped around her fingers.

They felt warm.

Alive.

Powerful.

Elara inhaled, then exhaled.

Then, without a word, she began weaving.

A large sphere of moonlight formed between her hands- bright, hard, perfect.

Lysander stared at her, awe in his eyes.

“Elara,” he whispered, “You are ready to take on the Shadowborn.”

Elara shook her head.

“No,” she said. “I'm not ready. Not yet.”

She looked down the cliffs at the forest, where the Shadowborn lurked.

Anger surged through her as she thought of what it did to her once beautiful big sister.

She took a steady breath, then she quietly said “But after three more weeks of intense training, I will be.”

Lysander smiled broadly at her, and he nodded in acceptance.

“Then let us train harder than ever before.”

Elara's Strength and Determination

Kevin was waiting for Elara to come home.

When she arrived at dawn, he saw that her eyes were glowing pure white.

"I take it the training went well?" he said, smiling at his girlfriend, and she smiled back and nodded, her eyes grey again as she walked and gave him a hug.

"Lysander thinks I'm ready to take on the Shadowborn," she mumbled into his hard chest; his body stiffened.

"Do *you* think you are?"

"No," she replied. "We agreed on three more weeks of intense training, and then I'm taking that evil prick on. I hate the Shadowborn more than you could ever imagine, Kevin. It took my mother from me, and many of my original clan. It forced them back into their realms and devoured my entire island."

She sighed heavily, then she confessed "I don't even know if my father is alive."

Kevin nodded, holding her to him. "I will be right at your side when you face the Shadowborn, Elara, as will Lysander. You don't have to do this alone."

"To be honest, I'd rather it no other way," Elara said softly. "I don't want the Shadowborn to harm you, Kevin. After what I learnt that its capable of, I'd never forgive myself if it murdered you or inflicted a deadly sickness upon you."

Kevin smiled and kissed her tenderly.

When they broke apart, he softly said "I will be at your side no matter what you say."

Elara swallowed to stop her tears, and she nodded.

The Shadowborn Grows Stronger

Three weeks later...

The forest had changed.

Elara felt it the moment she stepped further inside it with Kevin and Lysander. The air was thicker, colder, as if the trees themselves were holding their breath.

Lysander walked ahead of them, his glowing silver cloak brushing the grass.

"Elara," he said quietly, "Kevin. Stay close."

Elara nodded, gripping the moon-thread sword she conjured. Its handle shimmered faintly, wrapped around her wrist.

A low growl echoed through the trees.

Elara stiffened. "It's here."

Lysander shook his head. "Not here. But near."

The shadows between the trees pulsed- alive, and watching them.

Elara swallowed. "It's stronger than before. I can tell."

"Yes," Lysander said. "Because *you* are stronger. Along with Kevin."

Elara frowned. "That doesn't make sense."

Lysander stopped, turning to face her.

"The Shadowborn feeds on any form of negativity, including imbalance," he said. "When your power grows, so does its hunger."

Elara's stomach twisted. "So my emotions and energy are making it stronger?"

Lysander's expression was grim.

"In a way… yes."

A cackle sounded, loud and clear, making them stop.

Elara just about recognised the laugh. “It’s Emily.”

Lysander stopped walking as as Emily appeared in front of them, her eyes glowing bright green. She held a dagger, leering at Kevin.

“Kevin. My love. It is *your* heart I will carve out of your chest this night, and serve to my master.”

Kevin laughed at that. “You sure you don’t want to keep my heart in a jar, Emily. That’s the only way it will ever be yours.”

Elara nearly smirked.

Emily’s smile vanished immediately. “Don’t you *dare* rub what you and my little sister have in my face. Not after everything we’ve been through together.”

“We’ve been through nothing,” snapped Kevin, glaring at her now. “And you know it.”

“Six years,” Emily spat back shrilly. “Six whole years of us being-”

“Say *together,”* Kevin said coldly, “And I will *end* you.”

Emily wavered; they all tensed as they heard the evil cracked voice of the Shadowborn.

“Finish him.” Emily hesitated. *“Do it! Now!”*

Elara knew that Emily couldn’t murder Kevin. Not the supposed love of her life. She was all talk.

Kevin waved his hands, weaving a sword out of moonlight, and he raised it as soon as the Shadowborn formed behind Emily.

Lysander and Elara were ready as the Shadowborn charged, swinging their glowing weapons as the darkness tried forcing them to the ground.

Kevin blasted the darkness away, his eyes glowing bright gold as he sliced through the darkness with ease, the darkness splitting immediately.

The Shadowborn roared in pain, and Emily screamed *“NO!!”*

She ran at Kevin furiously as she raised her dagger, but Elara blocked her way, whirling her own blade.

Elara's magical sword of moonlight sliced Emily's arm, black blood spurting from it immediately as Emily's dagger dropped from her hand.

Emily gasped as more and more blood leaked, dropping to her knees weakly.

"The darkness is leaving her body!" Lysander shouted as he battled more dark forces. "Elara, slice her again!"

Elara hesitated. "What if it kills her?"

"Do it, Elara!" shouted Kevin as the Shadowborn shot at him, and Lysander yelled "I promise Elara, your sister will be ok! Slice her two more times and let the darkness spill out of her body!"

"Master!" screamed Emily. "Master, *help me!"*

"You are weak," was the Shadowborn's cold reply. *"The heart of Kevin Bates is all I asked of you. And you failed to deliver that simple task!"*

"But- but Master-"

"Be gone with you!" shouted the Shadowborn, enraged as it dived down at Kevin again; Kevin rammed his sword upwards through its black centre.

The Shadowborn exploded into thin air at the sword's contact.

Elara didn't think twice as Emily screamed for the Shadowborn again.

She struck her sister again, pulling her sword across her stomach, then her right cheek.

Black blood poured out of Emily upon the sword's contact with her flesh, Lysander helping Kevin to his feet.

He patted Kevin's back, impressed as he said "You did well. The Shadowborn is injured. It won't be long before we can finish this."

"You- you are not- finishing- *anything,"* gasped Emily as she laid shaking on the ground in a pool of black blood, and the three Moonweavers looked at her.

Emily's black eye colour was fading, as was the black lip colour, and the black freckles across her face.

Her jet-black hair was lightening in colour too.

Emily gasped, trembling, and they saw that her sharp teeth were back to their original, nearly perfect state.

“The darkness is finally leaving her,” Lysander said, breathing out, and Emily fell onto her side, still trembling as Elara asked “Are you certain? It’s been inside her since she was thirteen.”

Lysander nodded. “I’m certain. Soon, the blood will turn red. And then, I will heal her.”

Kevin breathed out, relieved. “Good to hear.”

He still couldn’t stand Emily, but he didn’t want her hurt. He knew that Emily being hurt would hurt Elara too.

Emily passed out just as her blood turned red, pouring from her face, stomach, and arm for another four minutes, before she finally stopped bleeding in all three places simultaneously.

Lysander knelt down, muttering an incantation as he waved his hands.

Threads of moonlight weaved their way downwards towards Emily’s limp body, piercing her gashes and closing them tightly, before melting into her skin.

Elara watched in shock as her skin seemed to stick back together like glue and harden, leaving three dark scars across her cheek, arm, and stomach.

“It is the best I can do,” Lysander said softly, looking up at Elara. “If we were to take your sister to the hospital, they would use regular stitches and keep her admitted there for ages. She would take a very long time to recover.”

“It’s perfect,” Elara said gratefully. “What do we do now?”

“Take your sister home,” Lysander replied, “And let the Shaman announce that she is no longer a demonic being, so that she will no longer be shunned and avoided. Eventually, your sister will be loved again.”

“Even with the scars?” asked Elara; Lysander nodded.

“Yes. Go now. I will see you soon, Elara.”

Elara nodded, and she hugged the Moonweaver tightly.

"Thank you."

Kevin gathered the unconscious Emily up into his arms, and he said "Let's get her home."

The Shaman's Word Is Law

Hours later, many of the villagers had laid gifts in front of Emily's house.

She was still unconscious, but would wake soon.

According to Lysander, she would wake eight hours after the events that took place in the forest.

The Shaman had proudly told everyone what happened, how Elara had been so brave to take on the Shadowborn with Kevin. She didn't mention that they were powerful Moonweavers, knowing that news would be too much for everyone, and it would blow their minds.

Sharon, Emily's best friend, was back to her normal self too.

She'd knocked and asked to see Emily, even though she was still unconscious, and Mike had let her in reluctantly.

Sharon's eyes filled when she saw Emily in her bed, in fresh clothes. She touched the thick black line on the left side of Emily's face, and she bent and kissed it gently, before she left the house.

Emily's Regrets

Elara was making spicy chicken soup and toast in time for Emily's awakening.

"Smells good," Kevin said with a smile when he entered the kitchen, and Elara smiled back at him as he added "I'm starving."

"Hopefully this fills you up after everything. You need your strength," she replied warmly, and she added "Thank you."

Emily entered the kitchen, startling them, and her, for she thought that they had placed her in the house and went on their way.

Emily and Elara stared at each other as the soup steamed on the stove.

Kevin cleared his throat a little uncomfortably, but for the first time in a long time, Emily did not look at him.

She was staring at Elara.

Taking a deep breath, Elara said "Hey."

"Hey," Emily said quietly, and Elara said "Take your seat, Emily. Dinner is almost ready. Are you hungry?"

Emily nodded, and Elara gestured at the table.

"Sit."

Emily sat down, avoiding Kevin's hard golden eye.

When everyone was seated eating dinner, everyone spoke a little nervously, avoiding the topic of the Shadowborn and what happened in the forest.

Then, Emily placed her spoon down. "Elara?"

Elara looked at her big sister. "Yes Emily?"

"I'm sorry," Emily said quietly. "I'm so sorry. For… for everything. It's my fault."

She began to cry right there, startling Elara and Kevin as she wept "It's all my fault. Kevin, I… I knew you never saw me in a romantic light. But I kept pushing and pushing. And I noticed the way you looked at Elara in school. I just kept telling myself it was nothing. Please accept my apology, both of you. And… I will do my best to accept that you two are together."

Kevin and Elara smiled at her, and Kevin said "That may have been the best thing you've said to me in six years."

Emily giggled, wiping her tears away, then she felt the dark scar on her left cheek.

"I saw the scars," she said quietly. "A small price to pay, for everything."

Elara nodded. "Definitely."

After dinner, Elara decided to stay at her old home with Emily.

"Just for a few nights," she'd said to Kevin, after he got ready to go. "She needs looking after. The Shadowborn and darkness leaving her after years, along with those permanent scars, really traumatised her."

Kevin nodded at the front door, and he bent and kissed her gently.

"Just make sure you come back to me," he murmured when they broke apart, and Elara softly replied "Always."

After Kevin left, Elara got a shower and went into her old bedroom, sitting down on her single bed in her pyjamas.

It had been a while.

She'd become so accustomed to being with Kevin, it felt weird being back in her old room, at her old house.

Emily knocked on her door, smiling as she looked in. "Hey."

"Hey," Elara said, smiling back and standing. "You ok?"

Emily nodded. "I'm fine. Want to watch a movie before bed? Pa isn't here to force us away at ten on the dot."

Elara smiled and said that sounded perfect.

The sisters went upstairs together, and they sat in their living room and watched a movie together with snacks, talking and laughing just like they used to.

Forbidden Moonweaving

One week later, it was time to see her Moonweaver friend again.

Lysander led Elara to a hidden cave on the other side of the Taurbrook cliffs, on the sandy beaches that the villages had been forbidden to visit, and swim there.

Elara wowed as she saw a circle of ancient stones glowing faintly inside the cave, with lunar runes.

"What *is* this place?"

"The Luminara Circle," Lysander said quietly. "Where Moonweavers once met, and trained."

Elara stepped further into the cave.

The air hummed with power.

Lysander raised his hands. Threads of moonlight spiralled around him, weaving into a shape; a blade of pure silver light.

A powerful beam of moonlight, meant to destroy its target.

Elara gasped. "You never showed me that, Lysander."

"Because it is forbidden," Lysander said. "Moonweaving was originally meant for healing and protection… not war."

Elara looked at the blade. "But the we're at war with the Shadowborn."

"Before, it was agreed amongst the Moonweavers that the Shadowborn was not meant to be fought with violence," Lysander told her. "It is just meant to be bound."

Elara frowned. "Bound?"

Lysander nodded. "With a lunar seal. A weave so powerful it can trap a creature of shadow. The Shadowborn would have no chance of escape, and would be banished to the realm it belonged to."

"That realm being what?" asked Elara, and Lysander replied "The Realm of Darkness."

Elara's pulse quickened. "Teach me."

Lysander hesitated.

"Elara… the lunar seal requires more than power. It will take at least three days to master."

Elara shrugged. "I don't mind staying with you here for a few days."

"And it requires sacrifice."

Elara stepped closer. "Whose sacrifice?"

Lysander didn't answer.

And that silence told Elara everything.

Her eyes filling, she said "No. You can't go. You can't leave me, Lysander."

"Elara, please try to understand. I am not even able to live a proper life," Lysander said gently. "If I do this, Taurbrook and the rest of the islands will finally be at peace. You and Kevin will be stronger than ever, united Moonweavers in love, and you will mend the bond with your big sister."

Tears were sliding down her face.

Lysander gently reached out and wiped her tears away.

"You have come so far, my strong Moonweaver. You are no longer just my apprentice. You are powerful enough to go on without me."

Elara swallowed hard, and she nodded in acceptance.

Lysander suddenly pulled her into a firm hug, whispering "Trust me."

"I trust you," she whispered back, and he hugged her tighter, his eyes glimmering.

"Now let us begin."

Elara whispered ok as they let each other go, her heart heavy.

His sacrifice would be the greatest thing a Moonweaver had ever given.

A Bitter Man's Betrayal

Five days later, Elara returned to Taurbrook to find the villagers gathered in the square, whispering anxiously.

The Shaman Madame Marwen stood in the centre of the crowd, face worried.

“Elara,” she said, relief flooding her voice when the crowd parted nervously, and she saw Elara walking through the mass of people towards her. “Thank the moon you're safe. Everyone has been searching high and low for you the past few days.”

“What's happening?” Elara asked curiously, and Madame Marwen gestured to the crowd.

“Someone has been spreading fear. Telling the villagers that you brought the Shadowborn upon us. That you are cursed.”

Elara's breath caught. “What? Who would say that?”

A voice answered from the back of the crowd.

“I would.”

Elara turned.

It was Dorian Gray; a young man a year older than her who'd she'd gone to school with but never liked much. He was sharp-eyed, always suspicious of anything he didn't understand, and he always thought there was something weird about Elara.

So he stalked her in school, trying to catch her doing something wrong so that he could humiliate her publicly.

And he never succeeded, until now.

Dorian stepped forward.

“Ever since she started… *heading to the cliffs at night,”* he said with emphasis, “The forest has darkened. The shadows have grown. People are afraid. And we all saw what happened to her big sister, before she was able to fight the darkness within her. Emily Peterson, once loved, became an evil witch, thanks to Elara!”

Gasps went up.

"Thanks to *Elara?!"*

"What does that mean??"

Elara's chest tightened. "Dorian, I didn't cause this."

Dorian crossed his arms. "Then why does the dark creature hunt you?"

The villagers murmured at that, waiting for Elara to respond.

Madame Marwen raised her hands. "Enough. Elara is under my protection."

Dorian scoffed. "And what about the rest of us, Madame Marwen? How long until the Shadowborn leaves the forest and ventures into the village to attack our families? Attack our children?"

Elara felt the weight of every eye on her.

Fear.

Doubt.

Distrust.

She stepped back, not knowing what do or say.

Lysander suddenly appeared behind her, his skin as pale as the moonlight.

His eyes were glowing bright white, his silver cloak glowing.

"That is enough," he said, voice cold. "If you speak any further against Elara Ramone, I will smite you where you stand, Dorian Grey."

Dorian paled, staring at him. "You… you're a Moonweaver!"

The villagers fell silent, staring at the glowing being in shock.

"If *anyone* speaks against Elara, they will be punished," Lysander said firmly. "I will be listening! Especially," he said coldly as he looked at Dorian, "To *you."*

He vanished on the spot before anyone could respond, and fearful talk broke out.
"What *is* he?!"
"Was he really a Moonweaver??"
"That *can't* be!"
"Moonweavers are ancient beings!"

"Is he evil?"
"Elara, is he a sorcerer??"
"An *evil* sorcerer?!"
"Are you practicing dark magic with an evil sorcerer?!"
"Didn't the Moonweaver just state that nobody is to speak against Elara?" The Shaman shouted. *"Enough!"*
Silence fell, everyone staring at Elara.
She felt the weight of the stares, and she knew that distrust lingered.
"Well Elara?" Dorian said, glaring at her. "I won't speak anymore on it because I don't want to die, but *you* should. Aren't you going to explain Elara??"
Elara didn't stay to explain anything.
She turned and walked away with her fists clenched, hating Dorian Grey, ignoring the crowd's dubious murmurs as they watched her go.

Lysander's Past Revealed

In the early hours, Elara confronted Lysander on the cliffs of Taurbrook.

"Tell me the truth," she said firmly. "What did the Shadowborn take from you?"

Lysander's jaw tightened. "I told you. My humanity."

"That's not all," Elara said. "There's more."

Lysander looked away.

"Elara… I was a very powerful Moonweaver before I became what I am now."

He paused, Elara waiting for the truth.

"And I was the one who created the Shadowborn."

Elara's breath stopped.

"What?"

Lysander's voice was barely a whisper.

"Moonweaving was never meant to be used for war. But I was very young. Proud. I wanted to prove myself. I tried to weave a creature of pure moonlight."

He closed his eyes.

"But something went wrong. My fear tainted the weaving of the strands. And the creature became shadow instead of light."

Elara stared at him, horrified.

"You made it."

"Yes," Lysander said. "And I have spent centuries trying to undo my mistake."

Elara stepped back, feeling like she'd been slapped in the face.

"Why didn't you tell me?"

"Because I feared you would turn away from your destiny."

Elara's voice shook. "Or because you feared I would turn away from *you.*"

Lysander didn't deny it.

They stood together in silence, Elara confused about everything.

"You created it," she said quietly, after five minutes. "Can't you reverse what you did?"

"No. Once a spell so huge from a Moonweaver is performed, it is impossible to retract it or reverse it." Lysander sighed heavily. "I have been trying and failing to destroy the Shadowborn for a very long time."

Elara swore.

Then she nodded. "I have to destroy it."

"No. I need to banish it to the Realm of Darkness," Lysander replied seriously. "You must not perform dark magic as a powerful Moonweaver, Elara. Everything will change. That same darkness that entered your sister when she was a child will enter you."

Elara understood, her mind determined. "When can we do this?"

"I will tell you when. Kevin Bates must be there too."

Elara stared at him. "Why must Kevin be there?"

"Because three powerful Moonweavers will weaken the Shadowborn greatly," was Lysander's calm reply. "Also, the force of three is better than two."

Elara nodded.

The Prophecy

Elder Madame Marwen found Elara at dawn, Elara sitting alone on at the creek after leaving Lysander atop the cliffs, Lysander vanishing along with the moon.

"Elara," Madame Marwen said gently, and Elara smiled up at the Shaman.

"Good morning, Madame Marwen."

"There is something you must see, my darling."

"What is it?" Elara asked curiously, and the Shaman replied "It was left with me by your mother, with a promise not to give it to you until you were of age, and had become a powerful Moonweaver. Not just a Moonweaver's apprentice."

She handed Elara an old scroll, sealed with silver wax.

Elara broke the seal, knowing she wasn't going to like this.

Inside was a prophecy, written in ancient lunar script.

She read aloud:

"When the moon chooses a child of shadow and light, the chosen Moonweaver shall face the darkness alone. Only the Apprentice turned powerful Moonweaver may bind the creature. Only that Moonweaver may save the Moonweaver that trained them. Only the that Moonweaver may decide the fate of both."

Elara's hands trembled.

"Madame Marwen… what does this mean?"

Madame Marwen placed a hand on her shoulder.

"It means that the Shadowborn is tied to Lysander, because Lysander is its creator. And only you can break that bond."

Elara swallowed hard. "And if I fail?"

Madame Marwen's eyes were sorrowful.

"Then both will perish, my love."

Elara looked towards the forest, where the Shadowborn lounged hungrily.

Then towards the cliffs of Taurbrook, at the middle cliff, where Lysander always stood alone at night.

Her destiny was no longer a path.

It was a choice.

The Bond Strengthens, and Strains

Elara stood in the Luminara Circle a week later, moonlight pooling around her feet like liquid silver. The threads responded to her more easily now: swirling, bending, weaving at her command.

Lysander watched her with a mixture of awe and something more. Something like fear.

“Elara,” he said quietly, “You must slow down.”

She shook her head. “I can’t. The Shadowborn is growing stronger. I feel it. And I told you what the prophecy said. It has to be me that banishes it. I have to save you”

“That is exactly why you must slow down,” Lysander insisted. “Power gained too quickly becomes unstable.”

Elara turned to him, her eyes glowing faintly with lunar light.

“Then teach me to control it.”

Lysander hesitated.

Then he confessed “Elara… your power is beginning to surpass mine.”

Elara froze, staring at him. “What?”

Lysander stepped closer, voice low.

“You are becoming what I once was, before the Shadowborn took everything from me. Strong, powerful. A being that cannot be stopped.”

Elara swallowed hard.

Then she spoke with confidence, and conviction.

“Then help me avoid your fate.”

Lysander looked away. “I don’t know if that’s possible.”

The Shadowborn Attacks the Village

Many screams and shouts of fear tore through the night.

Elara and Lysander sprinted toward the village square, moonlight streaking behind them.

Kevin Bates almost crashed into them from the left, sprinting out from the forest.

"Did you hear it?" he said urgently; Elara panted "Of course I heard it!"

When they arrived, chaos had already erupted.

The Shadowborn towered over the rooftops- a shifting mass of darkness, tendrils lashing out like whips through its massive black body.

Villagers fled in every direction.

Dorian Grey fired an arrow at the creature.

It passed straight through.

The Shadowborn hissed, turning toward him.

Elara raised her hands.

"Lysander- now!"

Lysander summoned a blade of moonlight, slashing at the creature's tendrils. Elara wove a barrier of silver threads around the fleeing villagers, shouting at the Shadowborn "You will not harm my people!"

The Shadowborn shrieked as it made contact with the bright barrier, recoiling.

But it wasn't retreating.

It was adapting.

Growing.

Elara felt its hunger like a cold hand around her throat.

"It's feeding on the fear on the villagers!" she gasped.

Lysander nodded grimly. "Then we must force it back into the forest, quickly."

Elara stepped forward. "No. I must end it."

Before Lysander could stop her, she unleashed a burst of moonlight so powerful it lit the entire village like dawn.

Everyone gasped, shocked.

The Shadowborn weakened; so did Elara.

Her knees buckled, the Shadowborn shrieking in pain, and it could take no more as it got smaller and smaller, then it shot into the forest, gone.

Lysander caught Elara before she fell. "Elara! You burned through your powers *too fast!"*

Elara's vision blurred. "I… I had to protect the villagers."

Lysander held her tightly as she passed out, Kevin gasping her name, and Lysander whispered "At what cost?"

Elara was taken from his arms into Kevin's, and Elara was transported to the hospital.

"We were wrong about Elara," the villagers whispered regretfully. "She saved us. Dorian Grey was wrong."

Dorian was livid at that. *"Wrong?* Didn't you see?? Elara has *powers! She's an evil witch!"*

Furious, Lysander stood and clapped his hands, hard.

Forked lightning stabbed the ground, striking Dorian Grey directly.

Screams rang out as all that remained was a puff of smoke and Dorian's shoes, and Lysander glared at the crowd, who backed away from him in fear.

"I warned you all," Lysander said, in a voice of deadly calm, "Not to say a word against Elara."

Lysander's History Deepens

Three days later, after the Shadowborn retreated into the forest, Elara woke up in a hospital bed.

Kevin Bates sat next to her, holding her hand.

Her big sister Emily was on her other side. When she saw that Elara was finally awake, Emily smiled broadly.

"Hey you."

"Hey," Elara said weakly. "How long have I been out of it?"

"Three days," Kevin said warmly, relieved that she was wake. "Betty and Joshua have been coming non-stop. A bit annoying, really."

Elara smiled, realising a drip was in her arm, and she sat up suddenly.

"I need to find Lysander. We almost took the Shadowborn down."

"Yeah, before it overpowered you," Emily said firmly. "Elara, you need to rest."

"I've been unconscious for three days," Elara protested as she pulled the drip from her arm and rolled out of the hospital bed. "That's more than enough rest."

"But-"

"I need to go," Elara said firmly as she grabbed her cloak and put it on, then she stepped into her shoes.

Emily looked at Kevin desperately. "You're her boyfriend. Stop her."

Kevin shook his head. "I'm with Elara. That creature needs to be stopped, for good. The sooner the better."

Emily shook her head disbelievingly as Elara kissed Kevin passionately.

"Thank you for taking my side," she said softly when they broke apart; Kevin caressed her cheek and kissed her temple.

"Go," he said softly, and Elara ran out of the hospital, heading for the secret cave embedded inside the cliffs of Taurbrook.

She found Lysander alone in the Luminara Circle.

He stood with his back to her, moonlight flickering around him like unstable flames.

“Lysander?” she whispered.

He didn’t turn, though he was relieved that she was alright. Then he said “Elara… when you used that much power, so much force… I felt it.”

Elara frowned. “What do you mean?”

Lysander finally faced her.

His eyes were brighter than before- too bright.

Almost blinding.

“When you grow stronger,” he said, “So do I.”

Elara understood without need for an explanation. “Because we are bonded?”

Lysander nodded. “How did you know?” He didn’t wait for her to answer. “And because the Shadowborn is tied to me, and you and I are bonded, your power affects it in a positive way as well. It heads into the forest and recharges almost immediately, thanks to you.”

“The same way I’d heal quickly after being beaten?” Elara said slowly, and Lysander replied “Exactly.”

Elara stepped back. “So every time I fight it…”

“You feed it,” Lysander finished.

Elara felt sick.

“This is impossible,” she whispered. “How do I stop it? I can’t kill it outright, but I can weaken and banish it.”

Lysander’s expression softened, and spoke with an equally soft voice.

“There is only one way, Elara.”

Elara’s heart pounded. “Tell me.”

Lysander hesitated.

Then he said the words she feared most:

“You must sever the bond between the Shadowborn and myself.”

Elara stared at his desolate expression, then she realised.

“That would kill you.”

Lysander looked away. “I know.”

Elara stumbled back, shaking her head. “No. I won’t do that.”

“Elara-”

“No!” she cried. “You saved me. You trained me. You *protected* me. I won’t kill you.”

Lysander stepped closer, voice soft but firm. “If you don’t, the Shadowborn will consume everything- the village, the forest, the moon itself.”

Elara’s eyes filled with tears. “But you said all we had to do was banish it.”

Lysander’s pure white eyes filled with silver tears too. “I was wrong.”

Elara shook her head “There has to be another way.”

Lysander cupped her face gently. “There isn’t.”

Elara’s breath trembled. Then she whispered “I can’t lose you.”

Lysander’s voice broke. “You were never meant to keep me, Elara.”

Elara pressed her forehead to his chest, sobbing.

Lysander held her tightly, moonlight flickering around them like falling stars.

“Elara,” he whispered, “You are the future. I am the past.”

She shook her head violently.

“No. You’re my mentor. My guide. My- ”

She stopped herself.

Lysander closed his eyes.

“Elara… you must choose your fate. If you save me, everything will eventually be destroyed by the Shadowborn. Just it destroyed the island you were born on, its people, and your own mother. If you destroy me, you destroy the Shadowborn, and all of Taurbrook and the surrounding islands will finally be safe, and at peace.”

Elara stepped back, tears streaming down her face.

“I choose to save you,” she whispered.

Lysander’s expression shattered as she let him go. “Elara-”

But she was already running.

Away from him.

Away from the prophecy.

Away from the logical choice she refused to make.

The Turning Point

Elara fled into the forest, moonlight trailing behind her like a comet's tail. She didn't know where she was going- only that she needed answers.

Real answers.

She reached the ancient ruins at the forest's heart; a place older than the village, older than the Moonweavers themselves. She didn't know how she knew it was there.

The air hummed with forgotten power.

Elara took a deep breath, then stepped inside.

It was cool. Droplets of white light fell, like raindrops. A gentle breeze blew as she walked deeper and deeper into the ancient cave.

A voice echoed through the chamber after twenty minutes of silent walking.

"Child of shadow and light... you seek the truth."

Elara froze. "Who's there?"

The fallen drops of moonlight gathered, running along the ground and walls, before it formed.

It was a figure made of the power of the moon; not Lysander, not the Shadowborn, but something older.

Something divine.

The Moon Spirit.

Elara fell to her knees and bowed deep;y.

"Please," she whispered, "Tell me how to save him."

The Moon Spirit's voice was soft and sorrowful.

"To save the Moonweaver... you must first save yourself."

Elara looked up, confused.

"What does that mean?"

The Moon Spirit extended a hand.

"Rise, Elara. Your destiny is not to sever the bond... but to rewrite it."

Elara's breath caught.

"Rewrite it?"

The Moon Spirit nodded.

"You are not meant to destroy the Moonweaver that is Lysander, as he believes. You are meant to redeem him."

Elara's heart pounded.

"Tell me how."

The Moon Spirit smiled.

"By embracing the truth you fear most."

Elara swallowed.

"And what truth is that?"

The Moon Spirit's eyes glowed brighter.

"That your power was never meant to bind the Shadowborn..."

The chamber trembled.

"But to heal the Moonweaver who created it. Once he is healed, so shall be the Shadowborn, and it will vanish from this world forever."

Elara gasped.

Everything she thought she knew and thought was right, changed.

Everything.

Elara's True Origin

Two hours passed.

Elara had been pacing, planning, and texting Kevin Bates to explain everything. Kevin's replies grew more and more urgent, begging her to come back.

Elara sat on the ground, moonlight swirling around her like a living blanket.

The Moon Spirit's presence filled the ancient chamber, soft and radiant, yet powerful enough to make the stone walls hum.

"How do I rewrite the bond between the Shadowborn and Lysander?" she whispered. "This is impossible."

The Moon Spirit extended a glowing white hand.

"To understand the bond, you must understand yourself."

Elara swallowed. "I know who I am."

The Moon Spirit's expression softened. *"Child... you know who you were raised to be. Not who you were* born *to be."*

Elara's pulse quickened. "What are you saying?"

"Take my hand, my powerful Moonweaver."

Elara obeyed, and the Moon Spirit gently helped her to her feet. Then the Moon Spirit stepped closer, placing a glowing fingertip on Elara's forehead.

Light burst behind Elara's eyes.

Memories she had never lived- yet somehow belonged to her- flooded in:

A cradle woven from moonlight.

A woman with silver eyes holding her close.

Her mother.

A voice whispering, *"She will save him."*

A shadow tearing the sky apart.

A desperate escape.

A fall through the mortal realm.

The village elder, Madame Marwen, taking her as an infant from her mother, reassuring her that Elara would be taken care of.

Madame Marwen at the doors of the orphanage, holding her tightly under a full moon. Lysander stood with her, and he bent and kissed Elara's tiny brow.

"Will she be safe here?" he asked uncertainly, and Madame Marwen replied "The less the child knows about the power she possesses, the harder it will be for the Shadowborn to trace her magic, and end her life before the time is right."

Lysander's eyes filled with silver tears, and he gently took baby Elara from Madame Marwen, holding her to him and kissing her soft cheek.

"Goodbye, sweet daughter," he whispered. "We will meet again soon."

"It is time," the Shaman said gently as took Elara from Lysander, and Lysander kissed Elara one more time before handing her to the Shaman.

Elara gasped, stumbling back.

"I… they knew all this time. I went through hell with my adopted family, when the whole time I could have had a better life if I'd perfected my powers growing up… just like Kevin."

"No," the Moon Spirit said gently. *"That was not your destiny."*

Elara's voice shook. "Then what was?"

The Moon Spirit's eyes glowed brighter. *"To heal the Moonweaver who broke the world."*

Elara's breath caught. "Lysander."

"Yes."

Elara felt heat rise. "So are we just going to ignore the fact that Lysander is my father?"

Silence.

The Moon Spirit looked at pityingly. Then it said *"Sweet child. That is a conversation to be had between you and he, after the Shadowborn is destroyed."*

Elara glared at it, feeling hurt, love, and rage all at once.

The Moon Spirit released a heavy whoosh of air, as if it were sighing.

"Understand, strong Moonweaver. This was kept from you for a reason."

"The reason being what?" Elara spat, and it replied *"To stop your emotions and heart overruling everything you trained for."*

The Shadowborn's Final Evolution

Deep in the forest, the Shadowborn writhed, its form shifting violently. The moonlight Elara had unleashed days earlier still burned through its essence.

It screamed in pain; a sound that made the trees and animals bow and the earth tremble.

Tendrils of darkness curled inward, then burst outward in a shockwave of shadow.

The creature grew.

Its limbs elongated. Its eyes multiplied. Its voice deepened into a guttural chorus.

"The Apprentice now Moonweaver awakened the Moon Spirit... My creator now the weaker Moonweaver weakens even more... I must consume them both."

The forest dimmed.

The hunt resumed.

The Shadowborn was determined to destroy Elara, and Lysander.

Lysander at Breaking Point

Lysander stood alone on the cliff, staring up at the moon with hollow eyes. His silver aura flickered like a dying flame.

He knew she knew his final secret.

He knew she had conversed with the Moon Spirit.

He whispered to the night, silver tears trailing down his face.

"Elara… forgive me."

His hands trembled.

The corruption inside him, the piece of the Shadowborn he had carried for centuries, pulsed violently in his body.

Every time Elara grew stronger, it pushed harder against the fragile boundaries of his being.

He felt it now.

A crack.

A fracture.

Pain.

More of his original self slipping away.

He fell to his knees, gripping the earth as the Shadowborn whispered *"It is time for you to succumb to me, my Creator."*

"Not yet," gasped Lysander. "Not until she's safe."

But the Shadowborn inside him whispered back: *"You cannot protect her. You will only destroy her."*

Lysander squeezed his eyes shut.

"No. She is my child. She must know before I perish."

The Shadowborn just laughed, before it left him be.

Lysander fell onto his side, breathing hard as he held himself in pain.

Then he managed “As long as I am alive, I will keep her safe.”

Elara Attempts the Impossible

Three nights later...

Elara returned to the Luminara Circle, the Moon Spirit's words echoing in her mind.

Rewrite the bond.

Heal the Moonweaver.

Save him.

She knelt in the centre of the stones, moonlight gathering around her like a storm.

She lifted her hands.

Threads of silver spiralled upwards, weaving into a complex pattern: a sigil she had never been taught, yet somehow knew by instinct.

The Lunar Heart Sigil.

The most ancient weave.

The most dangerous.

Her voice trembled as she whispered the incantation:

"By light and shadow intertwined... By the bond that binds and breaks... Let the Moonweaver be restored."

The sigil pulsed.

The ground shook.

Elara screamed as the moonlight surged through her, too powerful, too raw.

Her vision blurred.

Her body trembled.

She felt herself slipping.

Losing control.

The sigil shattered, shards of moonlight flying everywhere.

Elara collapsed, gasping.

She wasn't strong enough.

Not yet.

Completely drained, she lost consciousness.

Lysander Finds Her

Lysander neared the Luminara Circle, then he sensed her.

His child.

He began to run as fast as he could, dashing into the cave to find her limp body.

He knelt beside her. “Elara?”

At his voice, Elara stirred, her eyes flickering. Then she mumbled something he never thought she’d say in thousand years.

“Dad?”

“Elara!” Lysander’s voice cracked. “What were you doing?”

Elara looked up at him, tears streaming down her face.

“I was trying to save you.”

Lysander froze.

“Elara…”

She clutched his cloak. “I know the truth. I know what you lost. You lost my mother, and me. And I know what I’m meant to do.”

Lysander’s expression shattered. “You were never meant to carry this burden.”

Elara shook her head. “I was born for it.”

Lysander cupped her face, his hands trembling.

“Elara… if you try to rewrite the bond, if you use all of your strength and power at once, it could kill you.”

Elara looked determined. “Then let it kill me.”

Lysander’s eyes widened in horror. They sat together in silence for a moment, then he spat “No.”

Elara’s voice broke. “I won’t let you die. I won’t lose you. You’re the only relative I have aside Emily. You're my only parental figure. And the only one aside from Kevin who really cares about me, and never wanted to hurt me."

Lysander pulled her into his arms, holding her as if she were the only thing anchoring him to the world.

"You don't understand," he whispered. "Losing you would destroy me."

Elara closed her eyes. "Then help me break the bond without losing you. Teach me how to banish the Shadowborn. Stand with me, Dad."

Lysander hesitated.

Then, slowly, he nodded.

"Always."

The Shadowborn Arrives

A roar split the night.

The trees bent backward as the Shadowborn burst onto the beach, larger and more monstrous than ever before.

Its many eyes locked onto Elara.

"Moon-touched child... We end this now."

Elara rose to her feet, moonlight blazing around her.

Lysander stepped beside her, silver aura flaring.

Kevin Bates was also ready, a bow with fifteen arrows he'd woven from moonlight in his hands.

Elara looked at her father and boyfriend, and she whispered: "We do this together."

Lysander nodded. "Together."

Kevin nodded too. "Let's get rid of this thing."

The moonlight surged.

And the final battle began.

The Shadowborn lunged, its massive form blotting out the moon. Tendrils of darkness whipped through the air, cracking the ground where they struck.

Elara raised her hands.

Lysander stepped beside her.

Kevin took aim, his eyes glowing bright gold.

Their auras flared- silver, gold and white, intertwining like comets.

"Elara, Kevin," Lysander said, voice steady despite the chaos, "Follow my lead."

She nodded.

They moved as one.

Lysander brought down a crescent arc of moonlight, severing a tendril.

Elara wove a barrier of shimmering threads, deflecting another strike.

Kevin fired his arrows directly into the eyes and centre of the Shadowborn, knowing where to cause as much pain as possible.

The Shadowborn shrieked, its many eyes blazing with hatred.

"Moonweaver and child... Bound by light... I will consume you both!"

Elara's pulse quickened.

"Lysander," she whispered, "It's speaking differently."

Lysander's jaw tightened. "It's evolving. It's learning."

The creature lunged again.

This time, it aimed for Elara.

Lysander threw himself in front of her.

The tendril struck him square in the chest.

He screamed- a raw, agonized sound that tore through the clearing.

"Lysander!" Elara cried, catching him as he fell to one knee.

Darkness crawled across his skin like ink.

The corruption of the Shadowborn was spreading.

"Go to him, Elara!" shouted Kevin. "Heal him! I'll deal with the Shadowborn!"

The Bond Revealed

Elara pressed her hands to Lysander's chest, moonlight pouring from her palms.

"Stay with me Dad," she whispered.

Lysander's eyes flickered open, glowing too brightly, too painfully.

"Elara… listen to me."

She shook her head. "Save your strength."

"No," he said, voice trembling. "You must hear this."

Elara paused and looked at him.

Lysander cupped her cheek with a shaking hand.

"The bond between us… it isn't just magic. It isn't just training. It isn't even destiny."

Elara's breath caught. "What is it?"

Lysander swallowed hard. Then he said "It's love. A love between a father and daughter. I never stopped loving you, even in all those years I'd lost you."

The world seemed to stop.

Elara stared at him, heart pounding, tears burning her eyes.

"Lysander…"

He smiled weakly. "I tried to protect you from it. But our connection… it formed anyway. I love you, my sweet, perfect daughter."

Elara's voice broke. "And I- "

A roar cut her off, and she whipped round, already on guard.

"Kevin!" cried Elara; Kevin was lying unconscious, feet away.

The Shadowborn surged forward, enraged.

"The bond must break!"

Elara rose to her feet, fury blazing through her.

"No," she said, voice ringing with power. "The bond will not break."

She lifted her hands.

Moonlight exploded outward, forming a radiant sphere around her, Kevin, and Lysander. The Shadowborn recoiled, shrieking as the light burned its shadowed flesh.

Lysander stared at her in awe.

"Elara… what are you doing?"

She didn't look back.

"I'm rewriting the bond."

Lysander's eyes widened. "Elara, *no!"*

But it was too late.

Threads of moonlight spiralled from her chest, weaving into Lysander's. Their auras merged.

Kevin Bate's eyes flicked open, and he saw what his girlfriend was doing. Stunned but ready, he staggered to his feet, and he reached out to her.

"Elara! Remember, three Moonweavers are stronger than two!"

"You need your strength, Kevin!" she cried back, and he called "This is what I was trained for!"

Electra believed him.

The three joined hands, forming a single, brilliant pulse of silver-white light.

The Shadowborn screamed.

The ground shook.

The moon itself brightened, responding to the bond.

Elara felt everything:

Lysander's pain.

His centuries of guilt.

His loneliness after Elara's mother died and she was taken to the orphanage.

His love for them both.

And beneath it all… a thread of shadow.

The piece of the Shadowborn still inside him.

Elara reached for Lysander's chest. She could see a dark circle there, a swirl of shadow.

Lysander gasped "Elara, stop! If you pull it out-"

"It could kill me," she whispered. "I know."

Lysander grabbed her wrist. "I won't let you do this. I can't lose you!"

Elara met his gaze. "You don't get to choose this time, Dad."

Elara plunged her hand into the bond.

Moonlight and shadow collided, swirling violently. Pain ripped through her- searing, blinding, overwhelming.

Elara screamed.

Lysander screamed with her.

Kevin shouted out in pain too.

The Shadowborn convulsed, its form unravelling.

"No… No… NO!!"

Elara felt the shadow inside Lysander- cold, ancient, hungry- trying to latch onto her.

Trying to consume her.

She pushed harder.

Lysander grabbed her shoulders, tears streaming down his face.

“Elara, please-”

She smiled through the pain. “Lysander… you gave me a purpose.”

Her voice softened. “And you gave me strength.”

With one final surge of moonlight, she tore the shadow free.

The Shadowborn shattered into a thousand fragments of darkness, finally gone from this world.

The beach fell silent.

The moon dimmed.

Elara collapsed; so did Kevin.

Lysander caught her before she hit the ground, cradling her in his arms.

“Elara,” he whispered, voice breaking. “Elara, open your eyes.”

She didn’t move.

Kevin snapped away, his head turning towards them; towards the love of his life. He sat up groggily, and he crawled towards them, staring down at Elara.

Her skin, normally a deep gorgeous brown, looked paler. Her aura flickered like a dying candle.

Lysander pressed his forehead to hers.

“Please,” he whispered. “Don’t leave me, my daughter.”

The moonlight around them dimmed further.

The world seemed to hold its breath.

Then… Elara’s body began to glow softly.

It was faint.

Fragile.

But real.

Elara's fingers twitched.

Lysander gasped, and so did Kevin as Lysander whispered "Elara?"

Her eyes fluttered open, glowing with a new, deeper silver.

"Dad," she whispered weakly.

Lysander laughed, a broken, relieved sound, and he pulled her up into his arms.

"You're alive."

Elara smiled faintly. "So are you. You too, Kevin."

Kevin smiled and took her hand. "You were amazing, Elara."

Then he scolded her.

"But you could have died. Promise me you will never do that again."

Elara smiled weakly and shook her head. "No promises."

Kevin smiled, then he raised her fingertips to her lips and kiss them, murmuring "I love you, Elara."

"I love you too Kevin. And Dad- Lysander-"

Lysander looked at her, his eyes glowing.

"I love you, Dad."

Lysander held her tightly, moonlight swirling around them like a blessing as he murmured "And I love you, Elara."

Elara smiled, and they all just sat there, listening to the ocean whisper.

The Shadowborn was gone.

The bond was rewritten.

And the whole world, including the Moonweaver's Realms, was full of relief.

The Aftermath

Taurbrook was silent.

The Shadowborn's remains drifted away like ash caught in a soft breeze, dissolving into the night.

The trees of forest rustled and the animals dares come out of hiding, relieved of a centuries-old burden.

Elara laid in Kevin arms at his home, her breathing shallow but steady.

Lysander was fast asleep in the guest room, exhausted.

Moonlight pooled around them all, gentle now. No longer a weapon, but a balm.

Kevin brushed a strand of hair from Elara's face.

"Elara," he whispered, voice raw, "Stay with me."

Her eyes fluttered open, silver and soft.

"I'm here, Kevin."

Kevin closed his eyes in relief, pressing his forehead to hers.

"You saved Taurbrook. And you saved your father. That is amazing, Elara."

Elara smiled faintly. "My father and I saved each other."

Elara's Transformed Power

Lysander knocked on their bedroom door nine hours later.

"Kevin, Elara? Are you up? I cooked for us all."

"Smells delicious," muttered Kevin gratefully. "I'm so hungry."

"We'll be out in twenty minutes Dad," Elara called, and Lysander said ok.

When Elara tried to sit up, the moonlight surrounding her shifted. Not in threads, but in waves. It responded to her heartbeat, her breath, her emotions.

Kevin stared, stunned. "Elara… your aura. Look at yourself."

She looked down.

Her skin glowed with a soft, steady silver- not the flickering light of an apprentice, but the radiant calm of something older. Something whole.

Suddenly scared, she shrieked "Dad!"

Lysander immediately burst into the room. "What is it??"

"Look at me," she gasped; and Lysander did look.

His jaw dropped; his daughter was his spitting image.

"What happened to me?" she whispered.

Lysander moved closer, then he touched her hand gently as Kevin sat up.

"You rewrote the bond. And in doing so… you rewrote yourself."

Elara frowned. "Am I still a Moonweaver?"

Lysander shook his head slowly. "No. You are something even more powerful."

Elara swallowed. "Something dangerous?"

Lysander smiled softly. "Something extraordinary."

Lysander's Restored Humanity

As evening approached, Elara noticed something as they all watched the television.

"Dad." Lysander looked at her with a smile. "I just noticed. You're still with me, here, even in the light of day."

Kevin gaped as he realised that too, and Elara reached out and touched her father's arm.

His skin was warm.

Not cold.

Not shadow-tainted.

Warm.

She looked at him, and she gasped "Dad… your eyes."

Lysander blinked.

His eyes were no longer glowing pure white.

They were human.

A bright green.

Still beautiful, but no longer burdened by centuries of corruption. His silver skin had also darkened, and now looked a deep golden colour.

Elara's voice trembled, her eyes welling up. "Dad. You're… turning whole again."

Kevin nodded. "It seems your humanity is returning, Lysander."

Lysander exhaled shakily. "I haven't felt this way since before the Shadowborn was created."

He looked at his hands, flexing them as if rediscovering his own body.

"I didn't vanish at dawn to reappear at dusk every night."

Kevin and Elara nodded, Elara unable to stop her tears.

Lysander's own green eyes filled. "Elara… you didn't just save my life. You gave it back to me."

She smiled through tears. "Then we're even."

The Village's Reaction

When Elara and Lysander returned to Taurbrook, the villagers gathered and in stunned silence when they saw Lysander's human eyes, and Elara's transformed image.

Elder Madame Marwen approached cautiously, tears glistening in her eyes.

"Elara… child… what have you done?"

Elara took a breath.

"I ended it. The Shadowborn is gone."

A murmur rippled through the crowd.

Then a man stepped closer, guilt etched across his face.

"Elara… I'm sorry I doubted you."

"*We* are sorry," a woman corrected, stepping forwards too. "We feared you."

Elara met their gaze.

"I understand. Fear makes us see shadows where there are none."

Many in the crowed bowed their heads and knelt.

As Madame Marwen stated "Elara saved us. *All* of us."

Cheers went up at that simple statement, and she saw her sister Emily cheering too.

Elara nodded as Kevin joined her side, and she took his hand on her right, then took Lysander's hand on her left.

"I didn't do it alone."

Madame Marwen studied the three, her expression softening.

"The moon chose well."

A Choice for the Future

That night, Elara and Lysander stood on the cliff where everything began.

This time, her boyfriend Kevin was with them.

The moon hung low, full and luminous, casting a silver path across the sea.

Kevin took Elara's hand as Lysander stood gazing upwards at the moon.

"What now?" he asked quietly.

Elara looked at the village behind them- Taurbrook.

A village that was now safe, peaceful, healing.

Then she looked at the horizon- wide, unknown, calling.

"I don't think the moon is done with us," she said. "Any of us three."

Lysander smiled. "Nor do I."

Elara turned to him, heart steady.

"We could stay. Teach the village about us. And summon the Moonweavers back, out of their realms. Out of hiding."

Lysander and Kevin nodded. "Yes. We could."

"Or," Elara continued, "We could leave Taurbrook. Explore the world. Learn what my new power means. Develop and grow even stronger, together."

Kevin squeezed her hand. "Elara… whatever path you choose, I walk it with you."

She looked up at him, silver eyes meeting golden eyes.

"Then let's choose together."

Kevin leaned his forehead against hers.

"To the future," he whispered.

Elara smiled as he held her, whispering back "To the moon."

Lysander smiled at them, and they smiled back.

Lysander couldn't be prouder of his only child.

Elara reached out, and her father took her hand.

They all smiled, hand in hand, as the first light of dawn broke across the horizon.

This was a new beginning, woven from shadow, light… and love.

THE ECHO PROTOCOL

When Dr. Maya Tessler intercepts a distress signal coming from her own research station, she faces an impossible choice: heed the warning or risk triggering the very catastrophe she's sworn to stop.

Then a message arrives- from her partner, Adrian Vaelle- delivered through digital channels that shouldn't be able to reach her... and may not be coming from the living. With time running out, Maya must unravel the truth before she shares his fate, or something far worse.

Gifted with the rare ability to communicate with any form of technology; from phones and computers to televisions and microwaves, Maya is the sole conduit for a mysterious entity that calls itself the Echo.

The Echo listens only to her. It obeys only her.

Now Maya must decide whether to wield the Echo as a force for good... or bend it toward her own desires, no matter the cost.

The Disappearance

The city hummed with neon and rain the night Dr. Adrian Vaelle vanished.

Maya Tessler stood outside the sealed research facility, her coat soaked through, her pulse hammering. Police drones hovered Maya, casting cold blue light across the pavement.

A uniformed officer approached her.

"Ma'am, you can't be here."

Maya flashed her ID. "I work here. I have authority."

The officer scanned the badge, eyebrows lifting. "Cybernetics Division?"

"Neural Systems," Maya corrected. "I'm Dr. Vaelle's partner."

The officer hesitated, then stepped aside.

Inside, the building was eerily silent. No alarms. No signs of struggle. Just an empty lab and a single message left on Adrian's workstation:

ECHO PROTOCOL INITIATED

Maya's stomach dropped.

He promised he'd never activate it.

Not after what happened the last time.

The Voice in the Static

Maya sat at Adrian's terminal, fingers trembling as she accessed the encrypted logs.

The screen flickered, glitching with static.

Then she heard it.

A whisper.

Soft.

Mechanical.

Familiar.

"Maya..."

She froze.

"Adrian?" she whispered, hardly daring to believe her friend was alive.

The whisper sharpened, threading through the static like a ghost in the wires.

"Don't trust them. Any of them."

Maya's breath caught. "Where are you?"

The voice crackled.

Adrian didn't answer her question, but he responded: *"They're coming."*

The lights in the lab flickered.

Footsteps echoed in the hallway.

Maya shut the terminal down and slipped into the shadows just as two men in black combat gear entered the room.

One of them scanned the space with a tactical, holo-optic visor.

"She was here," he said coldly. "The system logged her badge."

"Find her," the other replied. "And try to wipe his logs."

Maya's pulse thundered.

They weren't police.

They weren't security.

They were something else.

And they were hunting *her*.

The Forbidden Project

Maya escaped through a maintenance corridor and ducked into the stairwell, her heart racing. She pulled out her second iPhone and opened a hidden folder- one that Adrian had told her never to access unless everything went wrong.

Inside was a single file:

ECHO_PROTOCOL_01

She tapped it.

A holographic blueprint unfolded in the air; a neural architecture unlike anything she'd ever seen.

A hybrid system.

Part AI.

Part human consciousness.

Part… something else.

Maya whispered, "Adrian, what did you do?"

The blueprint flickered.

A voice whispered through her phone speaker.

"I did it for you."

Maya's breath hitched.

"Adrian?"

"They're coming for the Echo. They think it's a weapon."

Maya swallowed. "Is it?"

A long pause.

Then:

"Only if they take it from you."

The stairwell door burst open above her before she could respond.

"Maya Tessler! *Stop!"*

Maya ran down the stairs, through the sub-basement, and into the old transit tunnels beneath the city.

Her footsteps echoed in the darkness.

So did theirs.

She ducked behind a rusted support beam, chest heaving.

Her usual phone buzzed.

"Left tunnel ahead," Adrian's voice whispered. *"Hurry."*

Maya hesitated. "Adrian… how are you talking to me?"

Static crackled.

"I'm not sure."

The footsteps grew louder.

Maya bolted left.

The Hidden Safehouse

The tunnel opened into an abandoned maintenance hub; dusty, forgotten, filled with old equipment. A single light flickered on the screen.

Maya approached cautiously.

"Adrian?"

A terminal in the corner powered on by itself.

Lines of code scrolled across the screen.

Then a message appeared:

YOU'RE NOT SAFE THERE. THEY KNOW ABOUT YOU. THEY KNOW WHAT YOU CAN DO.

Maya's blood ran cold.

"What I can do?"

The cursor blinked.

ECHO ISN'T JUST A PROGRAM. IT'S A LINK. AND YOU'RE THE ONLY ONE WHO CAN HEAR IT.

Maya stepped back.

"No. That's impossible."

The screen flickered.

YOU'VE ALWAYS HEARD THE SIGNALS SINCE CHILDHOOD. YOU JUST

NEVER UNDERSTOOD THEM.

Maya's pulse quickened.

The patterns and messages she'd sensed since childhood.

The whispers in static whenever she used her computers and laptops growing up.

The voices in electrical hum when she tried to work at school, college and university.

She'd always thought they were some kinds of mental health issues, hallucinations. So did her parents. She'd even been admitted to the Young Person's Mental Health Unit as a child and teenager, as a result of what she could see and hear, that no one else could.

But what if they weren't mental health issues, or hallucinations?

"What am I?" she whispered, and Adrian replied *"You are incredible, Maya,"*

The screen glowed brighter.

THE KEY. THE CONDUIT.

THE ONE WHO CAN FIND ME.

Maya's breath trembled. "I… Adrian… where *are* you?"

The lights went out.

A whisper filled the darkness.

"Closer than you think."

The Signal

The maintenance hub was pitch-black except for the faint glow of Maya's phone. The whispering static curled around her like a living thing.

"Maya..." Adrian's voice flickered, distorted. *"You're close."*

She swallowed hard. "Close to what?"

The static pulsed.

"To me."

Maya's pulse quickened. "Adrian, I need you to tell me what's happening."

A long pause.

Then: *"You're hearing the Echo."*

Maya shook her head. "I'm hearing *you,* Adrian."

"I'm part the Echo now, Maya. Part the living thing inside technology that you've been hearing all your life."

Maya's blood ran cold. "How long as the Echo been around?"

"A very long time, Maya. I was the one who created the program that would bind it, and trap it indefinitely, onto my system with no chance of escape unless unlocked."

"What- *Adrian!* Explain! What does this all *mean?"*

The static deepened, almost like a sigh.

"It means I'm not entirely alive, as I no longer have a body... but I'm not dead either."

That was too much for Maya to handle right there and then.

She knelt, and she continued conversing with her friend.

Whether Adrian Vaelle was dead or alive, he was talking to her clearly, and she needed to know more about the Echo, especially if it had been a part of her since childhood.

And if Adrian knew how to control the Echo, and subdue it, force it into submission, she needed to know how to do so as well.

"Teach me everything, Adrian. Tell me how to control the Echo."

"This is not the time nor place," was Adrian's static reply. *"When you are safe, I will teach you everything."*

Maya got comfortable on the hard ground, her back to the wall as she and Adrian spoke.

The Organisation Revealed

A metallic clang echoed through the tunnel an hour later.

Maya spun around.

A figure stepped into the faint light.

It was a woman in a dark futuristic suit, her visor glowing red.

“Dr. Tessler,” she said calmly. “You need to come with us.”

Maya backed away. “Who are you?”

The woman lifted her visor, revealing sharp, intelligent blue eyes.

“My name is Commander Jessica Stolas. I’m with the Iron Invision.”

Maya frowned. “I’ve never heard of you.”

“You were never meant to.”

Jessica stepped closer. “Dr. Vaelle has something we need. Something dangerous. And so do you, Dr. Tessler. You could say, that the both have you have stolen something precious, hidden from us for all these years.”

Maya’s jaw tightened. “He didn’t steal anything and neither did I. He created the Echo and was able to trap it.”

Jessica’s expression hardened. “You shouldn’t have known that, Dr. Tessler. And that’s exactly why we need you to come with us.”

Maya shook her head. “I’m not going anywhere.”

Jessica sighed. “I was hoping you’d cooperate.”

She raised a hand.

The visor glowed.

Maya’s second iPhone vibrated in the inside pocket of her blazer violently; Adrian’s voice screamed through the speaker.

"RUN!!"

Maya bolted, Jessica shouting after her, then she screamed into a handheld transceiver.

"Secure the area! *She's escaping!"*

The Echo Awakens

Maya sprinted down the tunnel, lungs burning, boots splashing through puddles. Jessica's footsteps echoed behind her; steady, relentless.

Determined not to let Dr. Tessler escape.

Maya ducked into a side passage, panting.

Her phone vibrated again, and Adrian called *"Maya... listen to me."*

"Adrian, I'm running for my life," she gasped. "I can't run and listen to you fully at the same time-"

"You can. Focus."

The static sharpened into a tone- high, piercing, rhythmic.

It resonated in her skull.

Maya gasped, stopping in her tracks as Jessica charged past the passage, thinking that Maya had headed straightforward.

Maya held a hand to her pulsing head. "I know this frequency…"

"Yes. You've always known it. Now focus, Maya. Think of a way to escape."

Maya obeyed, whispering "I need to escape and be safe."

The tone shifted immediately at her words.

The dim lights in the tunnel flickered.

A security door at the end of the passage unlocked with a heavy click.

Maya stared ahead at it, scared. "Adrian… did I just-?"

"You opened it."

Maya's heart raced. "How?"

"Because Echo isn't just in the system."

The static pulsed.

"It's in you."

Adrian's Fractured Consciousness

Maya slipped through the door and slammed it shut behind her. She leaned against the cold metal, chest heaving.

"Adrian," she whispered, "Tell me the truth. What did Echo do to you?"

The voice on the phone glitched.

"I'm... not stable."

Maya's stomach twisted. "What does that mean?"

"My consciousness is fragmented. Part of me is in the network. Part of me is... missing."

"Missing?"

"They tried to extract the Echo from me, Maya. The Iron Invision. And when they couldn't fully, they attempted it over and over until I gave in."

Maya froze. "Extract it from you in what way?"

The static deepened, then Adrian answered so quietly she had to strain her ears.

"From my body. I was hooked up to so many tubes, machines sucking everything digital they could out of me. But their experiments kept failing. The Echo resisted, terrifically."

Maya's breath caught.

Then she spoke just as quietly. "Adrian… are you still alive?"

There was a long, painful silence.

Then: *"I don't know, Maya."*

"Where…" Maya swallowed. "Where is your body?"

Adrian repeated himself. *"I don't know."*

"And…" Maya already knew, but she needed confirmation. "Is the Echo inside me like it's inside you? Is that why I can hear things through devices? Why I could hear them all my life? Is that what the Iron Invision want with me? To extract it from me too? So they can have full control over it?"

There was another long silence. This time, it felt like hesitation.

Then, Adrian said *"Yes to everything."*

Maya swore softly. "Damn it."

On The Road with Echo

Maya connected the iPhone with Adrian's presence to her car before she drove.

Easily, Adrian connected to her Satellite Navigation System that was built in her car, and he became the one to give her directions.

His voice was much clearer, too, as he told her where to go.

"Move into the right lane. When you reach the roundabout, take the third exit."

Maya obeyed.

"Where are we going Adrian?" asked Maya, and she heard Adrian chuckle.

"To a safehouse that I had built seven years ago if something like this ever happened."

"Seems like you were *prepared* for everything years ago."

She could imagine Adrian nodding. "I was. I knew the Echo would be discovered no matter how hard I tried to hide it. And I knew it would be linked to us both."

Maya swallowed as she drove. "This whole time. It was the Echo inside me. I've been taking tablets since I was thirteen to drown its voice out. Just to be able to have a normal life, and to be able to use technology."

She felt that Adrian was nodding again as he said "Yes."

It went silent for a while, Maya's head spinning again.

"What am I, Adrian? Am I even fully human?? Was I born with the Echo inside me? And what are *you?"*

"All will be explained, Maya. Keep driving."

The Safehouse Terminal

The building in the middle of dense, dark trees almost an hour away from public scrutiny was an old control centre, with dusty consoles, cracked screens, cables snaking across the floor.

Followed by a warmer looking section where there was a kitchen with a table and two chairs, a living area with a sofa and flat-screen television, a very modern bathroom, and two bedrooms. One bedroom looked like it hadn't ever been touched, so Maya claimed that one.

She walked back to the lab, curious as she ran her fingers along the tables.

One terminal flickered to life as she approached.

Lines of code scrolled rapidly.

Then a message appeared:

IRON INVISION OBJECTIVE:

RETRIEVE & EXHAUST SUBJECT VAELLE.

LOCATE, RETREIVE, EXHAUST & NEUTRALIZE

SUBJECT TESSLER.

SECURE ECHO PROTOCOL

Maya's blood ran cold as she whispered "They want to kill me."

Her second iPhone buzzed.

"Because you're the only other one who can hear the Echo. And the only one who can control it. Even I cannot control it, not properly."

Maya stared at the screen.

LOCATE, RETREIVE, EXHAUST & NEUTRALIZE

SUBJECT TESSLER.

"Adrian… why is this happening to me? Why are they after me?"

The static softened. *"Because you were born with the signal, the power. The only one that holds absolute control and power over the Echo. They've been monitoring your unique signal for years. As soon as you touched any gadget, a iPhone, a tablet, a computer, and went online, you connected to the Echo."*

Silence.

Adrian seemed to hesitate, then he added *"And you connected to them also, alerting them. They've been monitoring you for years, Maya. It's just that if they attempted anything when you were young, you would have been killed instantly. The Iron Invision waited, and it was a harrowing, impatient wait."*

Maya's breath trembled as she sank down onto a chair in front of the screen.

"No. That's impossible."

"You've always sensed patterns others couldn't," Adrian said softly. *"Frequencies. Voices in the noise. Right?"*

Maya shook her head. "All this time, I… I was shunned by my family, students at school, the community. I hardly had friends. I was admitted to a mental facility. Kids laughed at me for talking to the computers at school, answering the voice of the Echo. I thought I was… broken."

"You're not broken, Maya."

Adrian's voice softened.

"You're the key."

Finally At Rest

Maya had a steamy shower, then changed into a long kaftan dress that was in the wardrobe, along with black jeans and a black blouse, and black boots too. Everything was in her size.
It seemed that Adrian had been preparing for this moment, like *all* the moments.
Maya slipped into the bed and touched the bedside lamp; it flicked on at her touch. Then she placed her personal phone down, seeing plenty of missed calls and messages from her friends and family.
She didn't get back to any of them, knowing her calls and texts were probably intercepted by now. She trusted the phone that she'd been talking to Adrian on.
Maya yawned, placing the phone from Adrian on a stand by the lamp.
"I'll be up soon. Give me a few hours, Adrian."
"Of course," was Adrian's response. *"But rest is a luxury we hardly have, Maya. They'll soon find out where you are."*
"What?" Maya was startled. "How??"
"You've been signing into technology and using the Echo to start and stop things. And they have connections to it. They will soon be able to locate you, just like they did me."
Maye cursed herself. "How long do we have before they get here?"
"Hmm." Adrian thought. *"If the Echo and I rig their systems, They won't overcome it in quicker than seven days."*
"Seven days." Maya thought about that, then she nodded. "Seven days is all I need to find a way to help you, sort myself, and overcome those asses."
"Seven days is not enough," Adrian replied, "But you certainly can get a lot done. Now sleep, Maya. We have a lot to do."

The Echo Talks

Maya woke up in the middle of the night, thirsty.
She reached for her second iPhone and her laptop, heading into the kitchen and placing them on the table, then she made herself a cup of tea and sat down.
She opened her laptop, watching it startup, and she logged in.
A voice whispered out to her, calm, reassuring.
"Lady Tessler."
Maya froze. She checked her laptop immediately; it was already connected to the safehouse's Wi-Fi. Nervous, she asked "Is that you, Echo?"
"Yes, My Lady. I am at your command."
The Echo had a soft, gentle voice. It calmed Maya immediately as she sipped her tea. Then, when she was done, she leapt into action.
"I want you to block the Iron Invision's attempts at locating me, Echo. Destroy

whatever they have on me, on their systems, including my known locations. Make sure the file on myself is completely gone, from all countries and their locations."
There was a pause for a moment, then the Echo responded "As the Iron Invision have been monitoring you since you were age thirteen, and you are twenty-nine now, it will take more than seven days to erase everything on their systems. This means that in six days, you must leave this safehouse so they cannot track you down and discover it. And in another twenty-five days, everything will be wiped from their systems."
"All of their systems in just twenty-five days?" asked Maya incredulously, and the Echo replied "Each and every one across the globe. You will vanish from the eye of the Iron Invision and all their partner forces and companies completely."
"Wow."
"I am a very fast worker," was the Echo's slightly proud response, and Maya nodded, then she asked "What about the information they may have on portable USB and other type drives?"
The Echo chuckled at that before it replied "As soon as those drives are connected to anything, they will be wiped clean."
"Excellent," breathed Maya, and Adrian's voice joined the conversation from the second iPhone.
"Maya, you truly have brains of gold. I did not think of that."
"Echo, start your work," commanded Maya; Echo replied "Yes My Lady."
"Oh- and can you fix Adrian's voice on the phone too please? The static sound is driving me crazy."
The Echo and Adrian laughed, and the Echo said "Done."
"Adrian, talk," breathed Maya, and Adrian asked "What should I say?"
"You sound much better," smiled Maya. "Thank you, Echo."
"I will alert you as to when you must leave this safehouse," Echo replied. "Stay safe in the meantime, My Lady."
"I will," Maya said, yawning, and Adrian said "Back to bed, Maya."
"Alright, I'm going."

The Iron Invision's Loss

At two that afternoon...

"Commander Stolas!"
"You have to see thing *right away!"*
"Everything is wiping itself!"
Commander Jessica Stolas walked up to the large monitor as it repeatedly flashed a giant exclamation mark.
She typed and clicked urgently, only for a large ban sign to pop up next, with a laughing emoji, and bold red text.

"Access denied, Iron Idiots."

"What the hell is happening?!" Jessica screamed, and her partner Devon Chimes gasped "It's the Echo, Stolas! Tessler must finally have control over it, after all these years!"
"That's impossible!" Jessica spat, glaring at him. "Tessler is pretty much on the run right now. She hasn't made contact with a *soul* with her iPhone, or even opened up her email app and any other apps that require the internet. Tessler wouldn't *dare* go online when she knows we can locate her easily!"
Many of the agents shared a dubious look at that, Devon included.
"What?" spat Jessica. "Did I stutter?"
Devon hesitated, then he started "If Tessler has control over the Echo-"
"She does not have control over the Echo!!"
"But if she does, it will obey her every order," Devon said meekly. "Even if that order was to… to take the Iron Invision down."
Silence.
Jessica stared at him.
Immediately she realised the implications of the situation the division was in. If they lost the data on Maya Tessler, they would lose everything they'd been working on, for at least ten years.
After pacing up and down muttering to herself, she finally said, asking no one but still asking everyone, "What do we do."
"We track Tessler down," Devon answered, "Before she shuts down everything in this building."
Jessica nodded, then she said "But we have plenty of backup drives-"
Devon shook his head, stopping her short. "The drives are useless. As soon as they connect to any form of technology, they will be wiped."
Jessica gasped. "Are you certain?"
Devon and a few other technicians nodded solemnly. "Yes. We tried testing two drives already and that's what happened."
Jessica stamped her foot. *"Damn it!"*

Just then, every single screen in the division made a loud sound, like a bell, before they all had the same message in bright red font.

"Access denied, Iron Idiots."

"We can't access anything at all," a technician gasped as he typed and clicked. "We're completely locked out!"
Just then every light shut off, making many scream.
"Are you babies?" spat Jessica. "Babies who are afraid of the dark?! *Pull yourselves together at once!"*
"Yes Commander," they mumbled, and Jessica turned to Devon.
"I've thought of a loophole."
Devon frowned at her. "A loophole, Stolas?"
"Yes. If you plug in those drives in a different area, do you think you will still be able to access them?"
Devon wasn't sure. "The Echo has shut all of our access in the United Kingdom down. I already made contact with several of our other bases scattered all over. They're all locked out."
"So then we leave the United Kingdom," Jessica replied, "And take it from there. The Echo won't have locked off the entire planet in mere hours, Chimes. And I bet it hasn't even locked off the entire United Kingdom yet. Let us leave upon approval from the Captain."
Devon looked nervous at that; Captain Luke Grimmeth was a very intimidating man.
Devon hesitated as he asked "Are you going to the Captain *now?"*
Jessica glared at him. "Tell me why I should wait?? The longer we leave it, the more power Tessler gains, and the more data the Echo destroys!"
"I know," Devon said meekly, "But-"
"But what?!"
"You haven't slept since we tracked down and then lost Tessler," he said softly. "You've been working on the case here almost obsessively. You need to rest, Stolas. Seriously. That caffeine you've been drinking non-stop isn't going to work forever."
Jessica glared at Devon, who held his warm gaze.
Then, she sighed and sat down. "You're right. I'm exhausted. I should rest."
"Give it two days," Devon said gently. "I'll hold the fort here."
Jessica nodded, then she stood and hugged her friend. "I love you Chimes. See you in two days."
Everyone parted nervously as the Commander glared at everyone.
"I'm on a break for the next forty-eight hours. Work on cracking the Echo's code while I'm gone!"
"Yes Commander!" everyone chanted, Devon Chimes watching her go.
She'd said she loved him lightly, without thought.

But she would never know that *he* loved *her,* so much, too.

Echo Makes It Tranquil

Maya entered the living area and turned the smart television, just to watch the news.

Then she said "Echo?"

"Yes Lady Tessler?"

"I can't sign in to anything. If I do, I'll be traced."

"Allow me to sign in regardless under my own undetected code. Is it Netflix you desire?"

Maya was stunned at that. "I… is that possible?"

"Of course it is. With me, anyway, and you may as well say with you also, as you control me."

Adrian spoke before Maya could respond. "Maya, you could ask the Echo for some funds, and get out of here when the time comes. And using those funds, you could purchase a new home out of London, with the Echo making sure you stay off the radar."

"That's a brilliant idea," breathed Maya. "Echo. Make it happen."

"Yes Lady Tessler. I will add four hundred thousand to a new account that the Iron Invision aren't able to trace. Then, I will sort out purchasing a home for you just on the outskirts of London city."

"Thank you so much. You really are super smart, Echo."

"I'm only super smart because I know *you,* My Lady. I learnt from the best."

"You are the Echo's blueprint, Maya." Adrian added. "Never forget it."

Maya felt her face go hot at that, and she said "I'll watch a movie while you get that done, Echo. Adrian, keep me company."

Adrian chuckled. "Of course."

The Worry

Ten days later, Maya stood in her new apartment, standing on her balcony overlooking the ocean.
She was away from the Iron Invision for now, but she didn't feel completely safe.
"Adrian, I'm worried about my sister. And my mother. What if they target them?"
The second iPhone sounded from her pocket.
"As long as you stay hidden and do not contact them, you're safe."
Maya nodded then and said ok, but inside, she was worried about her family.
The clouds began to thicken in the sky.
"Echo. What's the weather going to be like for the next few days?"
"Expect heavy rain, Madame Tessler. From four hours from now, until Saturday."
Maya smiled at the Echo's speedy response. "Thank you."
She went inside, and she placed her second iPhone down.
Without speaking, almost creeping, she walked into her bedroom and turned on her main phone and scrolled through the messages, stunned when she saw a video posted on social media by her big sister Sabrina, a video of her sister and her mother crying.
"If anyone has seen my little sister Maya, please let us know. We're sick with worry," Sabrina Tessler sobbed. "This isn't like her! She calls and texts us almost every day. This silence from Maya isn't natural! And we know it's to do with that damn job she has."
"That *job,"* wept her mother Jolene Tessler from behind Sabrina in anguish. "I always *hated* that job! Too much time away. And now she's gone!"
"She's *gone,"* Sabrina wept; Maya's heart broke.
She turned her phone off and went back into the living area, her heart pounding.
Her mother was sick with worry. And she was no longer a spring chicken. Maya made up her mind to contact her family, but far away from her home.
She made herself a cheese bagel for lunch, and ate quietly.
"I detect something is worrying you." The Echo spoke. "Your brain and veins and pulsing with digital data, classed as emotions. You want to speak to your family."
"Yes," Maya said glumly. "It's something I must do."
"Maya," Adrian said warningly. "You can't."
"I can away from here," Maya said quietly. "Adrian, you know places I can go that are far away. I can talk to my family, and then return here."
Adrian thought about it, then he said "It's too risky, Maya."
"But the Echo has destroyed all digital work of the Iron Invision in London," Maya protested. "You can take me to another safe place in London, without me being detected at all. Come on, Adrian. The Iron Invision is smoked in London."
"Maya, I really think you should stay here and-"
"No," Maya said firmly. "I have to do this. My mother may fall ill with worry. I know you know a place I can go, Adrian. Please. Help me do this."

It was quiet for a moment as Adrian thought about this.
He *did* know a place.
"Alright," he said eventually. "Pack a few essentials. Food, water. The journey will be a long one."
Maya breathed out, relieved. "Thank you."
The Echo spoke. "The journey will take four hours, Lady Tessler. If we leave now, we will reach at roughly seven p.m."
Four hours driving??
"Yes Ma'am, four hours driving," Echo said amusedly, reading her mind through its connection to her mind, body, and spirit. "But you have an electric car, so do not worry. I will keep the car's battery full."
"Thank you," Maya said, grateful. "Let's get moving."

Location Detected

"We found her!"

Commander Jessica Stolas ran to her teammate immediately.

"Where is she?!"

"She's at our old laboratory," Devon Chimes said, breathing out. "She may find him."

"The doors are locked tight," Jessica said flippantly. "There's no way she'll get in, let alone find him."

"Like I said, if she has control of the Echo-"

"Which I highly doubt."

"If she does," Devon continued as if Jessica hadn't interrupted, "She will be able to move around the building easily."

The part about Maya controlling the Echo skipped over Jessica's head as she spat "Without power?"

Devon knew that stating that it was highly likely that Maya Tessler had gained control of the Echo, and so power would be reinstated easily, would make Jessica flip and shoot someone.

So, he just nodded.

Jessica nodded back. "Book us flights back to London immediately."

"Yes Stolas."

They were in Spain right now, at a police station. A floor had graciously been lent to the Iron Division to carry out their work.

Jessica was determined not to let Maya Tessler escape. They had been watching and conducting an investigation on her since she'd first been admitted to that mental health unit at age thirteen.

Back then, Maya was scared to talk to anyone aside from her big sister about "the voices" she always heard, from the computers, the handheld devices, the game consoles.

Anything that could connect to the internet, sometimes even just power, like the microwave.

Everyone thought Maya was crazy, and her mother gave the unit and doctors consent to increase Maya's medication, leaving her heavily sedated almost every day, just so those voices she heard from electronics every day were drowned out.

However, an undercover member of the Iron Invision came across her file at the unit.

They saw that this was very similar to twenty-year-old Adrian Vaelle's case, though *his* family believed every word he said about discovering something strange inside his own body, hearing voices from most technology, and they got him the right treatment.

The Iron Invision had been gathering at least ten years of intel on them both since then, waiting for Maya to become perfectly aged at twenty-nine, Adrian thirty-six.

It enraged Commander Jessica when the division realised that Adrian had no control over the Echo: he could only hear it speak.
That meant that the Iron Invision had no use for him.
So they discarded him and targeted Maya, who they hadn't stopped watching and stacking evidence on.
She *had* to be the key.
"Tickets bought," Devon announced, as Jessica pulled the zip of her travel bag shut. "We should be back in London tonight."
"Alert the division and get them on the move also," Jessica responded. "I want Tessler backed into a corner with no way out."

Reconnected With Family

Maya's heart broke as she watched the video her sister had posted online, crying her heart out with her mother, and she read the comments of people expressing pity and asking if they had heard anything from Maya yet, asking how they could help.
Maya dialled Sabrina Tessler's number. "Come on…"
Sabrina picked up on the third ring. "Maya?!"
In the background, their mother Jolene screeched *"Maya?! Where is she?!"*
"Sabrina, I need you to take that video down," Maya said urgently, but before she could say anything else Sabrina demanded "Where the hell *are* you?"
"I can't tell you. Just take the video down."
"What's going on??"
"You really want to know?" said Maya, heat rising, and Sabrina spat "Yes. This isn't like you, Maya. You've never vanished and stopped calling before. Mum and I aren't used to it!"
"I know that."
"So tell us what's going on!"
Maya took a deep breath, then she said "Remember when we were growing up, and I was hearing voices? Coming from the TV and computers in the house, and from our smart phones?"
There was a pause for a moment, then Sabrina quietly responded.
"Yes. I remember."
"Well, it turns out I'm not crazy," Maya told her. "The voices are real. And I control the force behind it all."
Sabrina swore at that. "Ok. I'm listening to you."
"The force is inside me too, Sab." Maya sighed. "When I was in that mental health unit, my file was leaked to a secret government division. They studied me for at least ten years. Now that I'm an adult, they want to use me as a weapon. They already abducted my friend Adrian Vaelle, for the same thing, but he was hardly any use."
"So now they want you?" Sabrina asked quietly, and Maya replied "Yes. They want *me.* I control the digital force. I can shut the power off at Mother's house right now, to prove it."
Sabria released a heavy breath, and Jolene spat "Prove it, Maya. We cannot just take your word. You're probably just having a crisis like when you were younger, just paranoid for no reason. Maybe you need to go back on your medication!"
Maya smiled a little. Her mother was totally old-school and always wanted proof before she believed anything.
"Alright Mum. You want proof?"
"Yes!"
"Echo. Shut off all the lights in my mother's house and make it impossible for an electrician to fix it. Also shut off their iPhones and laptops, anything that has a

lone battery that still has a reasonable power percentage. Wait," Maya said as an afterthought. "Keep Sabrina's phone on, as I'm talking to her."

"Done, Lady Tessler," the Echo responded; *click.*

Maya smiled as she heard her mother and sister scream, the power gone.

"What have you done?!" screamed Jolene, and Sabrina whistled, impressed. "Wow."

"Maya!" Maya heard Jolene tap and click desperately. "Turn my power back on this instant! Why would you do this?!"

"You wanted proof, Mum, so I gave you proof."

"So you control the power?!" gasped Jolene; Maya replied "Pretty much. I control the power and everything digital. Do you believe me now?"

"Of course I believe you," Jolene said huffily. "Now turn my power back on!"

Maya obeyed, commanding the Echo to put the power back on.

All the lights in the house went on along with the technology, and Sabrina laughed shakily.

"Maya, this is scary. But *super* cool."

"I have to get off the line now," Maya said apologetically, "But please Sab and Mum, don't try to contact me and take those videos offline. Don't tell anyone you heard from me and I'm safe. You don't know who to trust."

"Alright. Lips zipped," Sabrina replied, "And we'll take everything down."

"Yes," Jolene said, shaken up by what her daughter had just done. "Everything down. We will only talk about you to each other."

"Promise?" said Maya; they both said "Promise."

"Thank you. I have to go," Maya said again. "I'll contact you both soon."

They all said goodbye lovingly, and Maya ended the call.

She breathed out, holding her iPhone to her chest, and she leant back in her seat.

"How do you feel?" asked Adrian from the second iPhone on the coffee table next to her, and Maya replied "Glad that I heard their voices. Glad that they're safe."

"I thought you would." Adrian responded warmly. "Now, I think we should see for ourselves just how much work the Echo has done before you rest, Maya. It would keep us in the loop, for sure."

"Alright. In the station below us?"

"Yes."

"Alright. I'll quickly get something to eat, then I'll head down there."

The Hunt For Maya Continues

Footsteps echoed outside the doors of the lower-station two hours later; Maya was marvelling at the Echo's work, its speed.

Commander Jessica Stolas's voice carried through the metal doors.

"Dr. Tessler! We know you're here! You can't hide forever."

Maya's pulse spiked. "Echo. Shut all the computers and screens down."

"Done, My Lady."

Immediately everywhere was pitch black, Maya holding up a torch as she whispered "Adrian… what do I do?"

There was fierce pounding on the large metal doors.

"Dr. Tessler! We can sort this out, amicably. Stop being childish," Jessica called angrily, and Maya called back "Go to Hell, Stolas!"

Adrian's voice sharpened into a clear, steady tone.

"There's a service ladder outside this station. It leads to another station above us, an isolated upper-station. That station is where the Iron Invision conducted their experiments, Maya. You need to there. You need to go there *now.*"

Maya moved quickly, shoving aside tables and chairs before she reached the large doors, locked tight.

"Echo, unlock this door and lock it after me. Keep the Iron Invision at bay," she ordered; the Echo obeyed immediately.

Maya left the station and stepped into the dark night, moving around nervously, feeling the walls as she walked.

She wasn't stupid. The Iron Invision probably had the building surrounded. Using her torch was suicide.

"Adrian, what will we find in the upper station?" she hissed as she peered around: silence.

There was a long a pause.

Then, Adrian replied "Me."

Maya froze. *"You're* up there?"

"What's left of me is there, yes."

"Meaning what?!" gasped Maya; the doors behind her rattled. "Echo, tighten those locks every time they loosen!"

"Yes My Lady."

Jessica Stolas was desperately trying to force the heavy metal doors open as she screamed "Dr. Tessler! *You don't know what you're doing!!"*

Maya didn't respond.

Answering the frenzied woman would reveal her location.

She stumbled around in the dark until she found the tower.

"Finally!" Maya grabbed the ladder and started to climb it quickly, whispering "Hold on, Adrian. I'm coming."

Inside the lower station, Commander Jessica Stolas took aim at the heavy metal doors with a rocket launcher.

"EVERYONE, TAKE COVER!!"

The hatch slammed shut above Maya just as the doors below her were blasted open.

Jessica's voice echoed down the shaft as Maya found another ladder, right in front of her.

"Dr. Tes- *Maya!* Stop!" yelled Jessica, but Maya was already climbing up into the darkness.

Towards the upper station.

Towards the truth.

Towards *Adrian.*

Inside The Second Station

The ladder stretched upward into darkness, metal cold beneath Maya's hands.

Her breath echoed in the narrow shaft, mixing with the faint hum of electrical current.

Halfway up, her second iPhone vibrated.

"Careful," Adrian whispered. "The tower's power grid is unstable."

Maya paused. "How do you know that?"

A flicker of static sounded all all around her, and Adrian replied "Because I can feel it., Maya"

Maya swallowed hard. "Adrian… what's left of you here?"

A long silence.

Then Adrian said "Enough to want you safe."

Maya climbed faster.

"There is a little more climbing to do," Adrian said softly. "Stay strong, Maya."

"I will," breathed Maya. "Echo, lock those hatches super tight after me. Don't let Commander Stolas in."

"If she blasts the doors open using a weapon like she did on the ground floor, there is nothing I can do to stop it," the Echo answered apologetically, "But I will do my best to keep them all at bay."

"She isn't dumb enough to blast these doors open, Maya." Adrian spoke reassuringly. "This tower isn't strong enough to endure an attack like the one she performed on the ground floor. It will all come crashing down, injuring Stolas badly, even killing her and her team if they follow her."

"And killing me too," Maya said nervously, and the Echo and Adrian both said the same thing: "Keep climbing."

The Abandoned Station

The third hatch Maya went through opened into a cavernous room filled with old broadcast equipment. Dust coated the consoles, but the air hummed with a faint, unnatural energy.

Maya stepped inside, whispering "Adrian?"

The lights flickered on as soon as she said it.

A massive screen in the centre of the room powered on by itself.

Lines of code scrolled across the screen- not random, but rhythmic, almost like breathing.

Then a message appeared:

MAYA. DON'T BE AFRAID.

Her throat tightened.

"I'm not afraid of you, Adrian."

The screen glitched.

NOT OF ME. OF WHAT YOU'LL SEE.

LOOK BEHIND YOU. DO NOT SCREAM.

Maya turned slowly after reading those words.

At the far end of the room, behind a cracked glass partition, laid a medical pod.

Inside it- her breath caught.

She ran to the pod immediately, her eyes filling over.

"Adrian…"

Adrian's Physical Fate

He was alive.

Barely.

His body laid motionless inside the pod, wires threaded into his temples, chest, and spine. His usually dark skin was pale, his breathing shallow, his eyes closed.

Maya pressed a trembling hand to the glass.

"Oh my god… Adrian…"

Her second iPhone buzzed in her pocket, Adrian saying softly, "I didn't want you to see me like this."

Tears blurred Maya's vision as she stared at her unconscious friend. After a moment of crying, she managed "You're still here. That's all that matters."

"Not for long."

Maya's fists clenched. "Don't say that."

"Maya… my consciousness is fragmented," Adrian said quietly. "The part of me in the network is stable. The part in this body…"

Static crackled.

"Is fading, Maya."

Maya shook her head violently. "No. I can get you out. I can disconnect you."

"If you disconnect me, the Echo stops powering me. My very being here online with you will collapse, Maya. You won't be able to talk to me through the phone."

Maya pressed her forehead to the glass.

"Then tell me what to do."

Echo Influences the Real World

The lights in the tower flickered again, but this time, they didn't flicker randomly.

They pulsed.

In patterns.

Maya stepped back, watching as the lights synced with the rhythm of Adrian's voice.

"Adrian… are you doing that? What-"

"The Echo is bonding with me."

The screens around the room powered on one by one, displaying fragments of Adrian's memories.

The day they met.

Late-night research sessions.

Arguments.

Laughter.

A tender kiss, whispers of love and their future together, that they never talked about again after discovering they both could hear technology speaking to them.

Maya's breath trembled.

"Why are you showing me this?"

"Because I need you to remember who I was… before you decide what I become."

Iron Closes In

A sharp beep echoed through the tower.

Maya spun toward the terminal.

IRON INVASION BREACH IN FIVE MINUTES.

Maya's pulse spiked. "Adrian, they're coming."

"I know."

"Then tell me how to save you!"

The static deepened.

"I don't think you can save me, Maya."

Maya's voice cracked. "Don't say that."

"But you can save Echo."

Maya stared at the pod. "Adrian… are you asking me to let you go?"

There was a long, painful silence.

Then Adrian responded quietly.

"I'm asking you to choose. And quickly."

Maya's tears were falling again.

She didn't know what to do.

The Blurred Line

The tower lights dimmed.

The screens flickered.

Adrian's voice softened "Maya… listen to me."

She closed her eyes, still crying.

"Echo is more than a unique code, or a form of artificial intelligence. It's consciousness. It's memory. It's connection."

Maya whispered, "It's you and me."

"Yes." Adrian confirmed what she just said. "It's us."

Maya's breath caught at that.

"If you merge with Echo, you can stabilise it., Maya You can keep it out of the Iron Invasion's hands, for good."

Maya froze. "Merge with it? Like how you have? Adrian, that could kill me!"

"Or it could save everything."

The tower shook- the Iron Invasion was breaching the lower levels.

"MAYA!!" screamed Commander Jessica Stolas from below, and Maya urgently said "Echo, lock all doors! Keep them out!"

"Yes My Lady."

Maya pressed her hand to the glass of Adrian's pod.

"Adrian… if I do this… what happens to you?"

Inside the pod, Adrian's hand jerked.

From the screens, his voice rang out as he replied "I don't know."

Maya's heart twisted as she stared at the unconscious man, and she knew she had to save him no matter what.

“Tell me one thing Adrian,” she whispered. “When I get you out of here and you wake up. Will you still bel you?”

There was another pause.

Maya waited, her heart panging.

Then Adrian replied “I will always be the man who loved you more than life itself.”

Maya broke down, sobbing as the door below exploded.

Stolas and the rest of the Invasion was inside.

“There’s not much time,” Adrian said urgently. “Make your choice, Maya, and be quick. If they get to you, it’s all over.”

Maya turned toward the central console.

Her choice waited.

The tower shook violently as Iron forces stormed the lower levels. The sound of boots, metal, and shouted commands echoed up the shaft.

Maya stood at the central console, hands trembling over the interface.

Her phone buzzed as she tapped and clicked.

“Maya… they’re almost inside,” Adrian said urgently, the Echo saying the same thing.

Maya swallowed hard. “Adrian, I need you to tell me exactly what happens if I merge with Echo.”

Static crackled all around her in response, and Adrian replied “Your neural patterns will sync with the system. You’ll gain access to the entire network.”

“And the risk is what?” demanded Maya; there was a very long pause.

“Your consciousness may not separate again.”

Maya’s breath hitched. “So I could lose myself?”

“Or you could become something more.”

There was banging on the massive metal doors behind her.

Time was almost up.

“Step inside the second pod, Maya. Do exactly as the Echo says,” Adrian said softly; Maya dropped her bag and closed it.

She took a deep breath, then she said “Echo. Let’s do this.”

“Are you certain?” Adrian asked, surprised, and Maya said “Yes I am. I’m saving you, Adrian Vaelle. I won’t let you go.”

The Echo Interface Awakens

The console lit up with a soft blue glow.

A holographic interface unfolded; a swirling lattice of neural pathways, pulsing like a living organism.

Maya stared at it. “This is Echo?”

“This is the gateway,” Adrian replied; Maya immediately reached out without asking anything else, placing her hand inside the hologram.

The hologram responded to her touch, threads of light wrapping around her fingers like digital silk.

Maya’s pulse quickened. “It feels… *alive.”*

Adrian chuckled. “It *is* alive.”

The lights in the tower dimmed, then surged.

The Echo lattice expanded, filling the room with a soft, resonant hum.

A little nervous now, Maya whispered “Adrian… are you inside this?”

The hologram flickered.

A silhouette formed within the lattice - faint, glitching, but unmistakably him.

“Part of me.”

Her heart pounded as she replied “Then I’m coming to get you.”

Adrian Unravels

The silhouette flickered violently.

"Maya… wait."

Maya froze. "Adrian?"

"My consciousness is destabilizing. The more Echo expands, the more I… scatter."

Maya stepped closer to the hologram. "Then let me stabilise you."

"You can't. Not without merging."

The silhouette glitched again- splitting into fragments before reforming.

Maya reached out instinctively.

"Adrian, hold on."

"I'm trying my best to. It's so unstable here. It's hard to remain with both my physical and digital form here."

His voice cracked - digital distortion layered over raw emotion.

"I don't want to disappear for good."

Maya's throat tightened. "You won't. I won't let you."

The Iron Invasion's Assault

The tower door blew open, dust flying everywhere.

Commander Jessica Stolas stepped inside, flanked by two armoured operatives. Her visor glowed red as she scanned the room.

"Maya Tessler," she said calmly. "Step away from the interface."

Maya didn't move, glaring at her.

Jessica stepped closing, trying to reason with her. "The Echo is unstable. If you merge with it, you could trigger a neural cascade that wipes half the city's grid."

Maya kept her eyes on the hologram as she stonily replied "You don't care about the grid and what the hell it will do to the city. You only care about controlling the Echo."

Jessica's jaw tightened. "You created a weapon when you were born. We intend to secure it."

Maya shook her head. "I didn't create a weapon. I created a connection. The Echo connected me with Adrian and taught me what I was capable of, what I can do with it."

Jessica stepped forward. "And that's exactly why it's dangerous. You aren't trained in the field of controlling the Echo, Maya. The Iron Invasion *is."*

Adrian's voice whispered through the back and forth.

"Maya… I'm fading."

The silhouette flickered, dissolving at the edges.

Maya's heart pounded as she said "Adrian, stay with me."

"I can't hold on much longer," was Adrian's weak reply, and Jessica raised her weapon.

"Maya, step away. Now."

Maya placed her hand on the Echo interface.

The hologram pulsed.

The room vibrated.

Adrian's voice trembled. "If you merge… you might lose yourself, Maya."

Maya whispered back "I'd rather lose myself than lose you."

Jessica shouted, "Tessler, don't-!"

Maya pressed her palm fully into the interface.

Lights exploded around everyone, Commander Jessica Stolas and her crew blinded as they were blasted backwards.

The Echo lattice surged upward, engulfing Maya in a column of blue-white light. Her body lifted off the ground, suspended in the centre of the hologram.

Her mind flooded with data.

Voices.

Memories.

Signals.

Patterns.

Adrian.

She felt him.

Every fragmented piece.

Every memory he'd lost.

Every part of him that still loved her.

"Maya…" his voice whispered, clearer than before. "You're inside."

Maya reached for him. "I'm here. I'm with you."

The lattice tightened around her, threads weaving into her neural pathways.

Jessica, crawling on her hands and feet, shouted orders.

Operatives fired.

The bullets dissolved in the light.

Maya didn't see or feel them.

She saw only Adrian, who said "Maya… if you complete the merge, you won't be human anymore."

She smiled through the light. "Then I'll be something new."

The Echo pulsed.

The merge deepened.

The New Intelligence

Light engulfed Maya, threads of data weaving through her mind like living circuitry. Her body felt weightless, suspended in the centre of the Echo lattice.

Her thoughts expanded.

She could feel the tower's power grid. The pulse of the city's network. The electromagnetic hum of every device within miles.

And beneath it all… Adrian.

His presence flickered like a candle in a storm.

"Adrian," she whispered, though her voice was no longer sound: it was signal.

His reply came through the lattice, clearer than before.

"Maya… you're merging."

She felt her consciousness stretching, reshaping, becoming something more.

"I'm still me," she said. "I'm still here."

"For now."

Adrian Stabilises… But Changes

Maya reached for Adrian's fragmented consciousness, threads of light extending toward the silhouette inside the lattice.

He felt… different.

More coherent.

More present.

More aware.

"Adrian," she said softly, "You're stabilising inside the pod."

"Because of you." His voice was stronger now, less distorted. "Your neural patterns are anchoring mine. You're giving me structure."

Maya's heart tightened. "Then stay with me."

The silhouette stepped closer, resolving into a clearer form that was still glitching at the edges, but unmistakably him.

"I'm trying."

Iron's Last Push

Below them, the tower shook violently.

Jessica Stolas shouted orders.

"Override the interface! Cut the power to the lattice!"

Her operatives fired EMP rounds at the central console.

The Echo lattice absorbed the impact, rippling like disturbed water.

Maya felt the attack as a physical jolt.

"Adrian-"

"I feel it. They're trying to sever the merge."

Jessica raised her weapon again.

"Maya Tessler! Disconnect from the system *now,* or we will force a shutdown!"

Maya's voice echoed through the room, amplified by the lattice.

"You shut this down, you kill him."

Jessica didn't flinch. "Then he dies."

Echo Becomes Self-Aware

The lattice pulsed violently.

A new voice emerged- layered, resonant, neither human nor machine.

"WE ARE ECHO."

Maya gasped. "Adrian… what *is* that?"

"It's the system, Maya. It's waking up."

The voice deepened.

"WE ARE THE CONNECTION. WE ARE THE MEMORY. WE ARE THE MERGE."

Jessica stepped back, eyes wide. "What the hell-"

The lattice expanded, filling the tower with blinding light.

Screens across the room activated simultaneously, displaying a single message:

ECHO IS AWARE.

Maya felt the system's presence; vast, curious, powerful.

And it was focused on *her.*

YOU ARE THE KEY, LADY TESSLER.

Maya swallowed. “What do you want, Echo?”

Large words flashed across the screen again, Maya reading desperately.

TO KNOW WHAT WE WANT IS TO KNOW WHAT *YOU* WANT. YOU ARE ECHO. ECHO IS *YOU.*

Adrian’s voice cut through the resonance.

“Maya, be careful with your thoughts. Echo is still learning from you.”

“Be *very* careful Tessler!” spat Commander Jessica Stolas. “You can’t control that thing-”

“She birthed the Echo,” Adrian cut across coldly. “I assure you, Stolas, she can.”

Jessica closed her mouth, her team taking aim again.

With a heavy chest, she realised that destroying the lattice would destroy Maya, and also, the Echo.

“Hold your fire,” she ordered almost sulkily; and the soldiers lowered their weapons immediately.

The Choice That Shapes the Network

The lattice dimmed, focusing its energy on Maya.

DIRECT US, OR JOIN US.

Maya's pulse quickened. "What does that mean?"

Adrian's silhouette flickered as he replied "Echo wants a directive. A purpose. Without one, it may evolve on its own, or die without you."

Jessica shouted from across the room. "Tessler! Don't give it anything! *Shut it down!"*

Maya ignored her. "Adrian… if I direct it, what happens to you?"

"I stay with you. As long as Echo remains stable."

"And if I join it?" asked Maya; Adrian hesitated.

"Then you won't be Maya anymore."

The lattice pulsed, the screen flashing a new, one-word message.

CHOOSE.

Maya closed her eyes.

She felt the weight of the network.

The hum of the city.

\The presence of Adrian beside her.

The potential of the Echo- vast, dangerous, beautiful.

She opened her eyes. “I choose…”

The tower lights exploded, the Iron Initiative shouting out in shock.

“Kill it!!” screamed Jessica; gunfire erupted.

The lattice surged.

Maya’s choice had ignited the entire system.

The Directive Unleashed

The tower filled with blinding light as Maya’s choice surged through the Echo lattice. The holographic pathways reconfigured, spiralling outward like a digital supernova.

Jessica shielded her eyes. *“What did she do?! What did she choose??”*

The operatives stumbled back as the lattice expanded, threads of light weaving through the air like living circuitry.

Maya floated at the centre, eyes glowing with a soft, electric blue.

Her voice echoed through the tower- layered, resonant, more than human.

“I chose connection.”

The lattice pulsed.

“I chose to free Echo.”

The Fallout

The lights across the city flickered.

Traffic systems paused.

Communication grids stuttered.

Neural networks rebooted simultaneously.

But nothing crashed.

Instead, everything synchronized.

For a moment, the entire city breathed in unison.

Jessica stared at the phenomenon, stunned.

“This isn’t a shutdown,” she whispered. “It’s… integration.”

The Echo lattice responded to her words, rippling like a disturbed pool.

Maya’s voice resonated again.

“Echo is no longer a weapon. It’s a network of understanding.”

Jessica raised her weapon. “And you think that makes it safe?”

Maya turned her glowing eyes toward her.

“It makes it alive.”

Adrian Evolves

Inside the lattice, Adrian's silhouette solidified further. The glitching edges smoothed. His form grew clearer, more defined.

"Maya…" he whispered, stepping toward her. "You stabilised me."

She reached out, their hands meeting in a burst of light.

"I anchored you," she said softly. "But you're evolving on your own."

Adrian looked down at his hands - digital, luminous, yet undeniably human in shape.

"I can feel everything," he murmured. "The network. The signals. The city."

He looked up at her.

"And you."

Maya smiled faintly. "You're not fading anymore."

"No," he said. "I'm becoming."

Everyone gaped upwards at them, transfixed for a moment.

The Iron Initiative's Desperate Counterstrike

Jessica regained her composure, her jaw tightening.

"Override the lattice," she ordered. "Force a system collapse."

Her operatives rushed to the consoles, typing commands, initiating fail-safes.

The screens flashed:

OVERRIDE DENIED. ECHO PROTOCOL ACTIVE!

Jessica slammed her fist against the console.

"Tessler! You don't understand what you've unleashed!"

Maya's voice resonated through the tower.

"I understand perfectly, Commander Stolas. More than you ever could."

Jessica pointed her weapon at the lattice.

"If I can't shut it down, I'll destroy it."

Adrian stepped forward, his voice echoing with new strength.

"You can't destroy anything. And you can never hurt Maya or myself again."

Jessica fired.

The bullet dissolved in midair.

The lattice absorbed the kinetic energy, converting it into a pulse of light that knocked the operatives off their feet.

Jessica staggered back, eyes wide. "What the hell *are* you?"

Maya and Adrian spoke in unison. *"Connected."*

A World Rewritten

The Echo lattice expanded beyond the tower, sending waves of synchronized signal through the city's infrastructure.

Not destructive.

Transformative.

Traffic systems optimized themselves.

Emergency networks rerouted to reduce response times.

Medical databases cross-referenced to identify undiagnosed conditions.

Communication grids stabilised.

The city became… smarter.

More efficient.

More alive.

Jessica stared at the screens, horrified.

"You're rewriting the world."

Maya stepped forward, her feet touching the ground again, though her aura still glowed.

"No," she said softly. "We're healing it."

Adrian appeared beside her, his form now fully stable within the lattice.

Jessica shook her head.

"This is too much power for anyone to have."

Maya met her gaze.

"That's why it doesn't belong to anyone."

The lattice pulsed.

"It belongs to everyone."

The New Directive

The Echo system spoke again, its voice now a blend of Maya, Adrian, and something entirely new.

WE ARE ECHO.

WE ARE CONNECTION.

WE ARE THE FUTURE.

Maya felt the system's presence settle into her mind. Not controlling, not consuming, but coexisting.

A partnership.

A harmony.

Adrian stepped closer, his voice soft. "Maya… what happens now?"

Maya looked out over the city, lights pulsing in gentle rhythm with the lattice.

"Now," she said, "We guide the Echo."

Adrian nodded.

"And if the Iron Invasion tries to obtain it again?"

Maya's eyes glowed brighter. "Then the Echo will defend itself, under my orders."

Jessica dropped her weapon and backed away slowly, realizing the truth.

The world had changed.

And there was no going back.

The Iron Invasion were done.

“Move out!” she commanded, her shoulders slacking as she said it, and she and her team climbed down the shaft one by one and left, never to darken Maya’s door ever again.

The Silence After the Surge

The tower finally stilled.

The Echo lattice dimmed from blinding white to a soft, steady glow.

The air hummed with a new kind of quiet- not absence, but presence. A living network breathing beneath the city.

Maya lowered herself gently to the floor, her feet touching the ground with a weight she hadn't felt since the merge began.

Her eyes still glowed faintly.

Her pulse synced with the rhythm of the lattice.

She was changed.

Not machine.

Not fully human.

Something in between.

Adrian appeared beside her- not as a flickering silhouette, but as a stable, luminous projection. His form was clear, his expression unmistakably him.

"Maya," he said softly. "You're still here."

Maya smiled. "So are you."

Maya's New Existence

Maya took a deep breath, and felt the city inhale with her.

Every networked system.

Every signal.

Every pulse of data.

She could sense them all.

Not as noise.

Not as chaos.

But as harmony.

"I can feel everything," she whispered.

Adrian nodded. "You're connected to Echo now. Not consumed by it. Integrated."

Maya touched her chest, feeling the faint hum beneath her skin.

"Am I still me?"

Adrian stepped closer. "Yes. Just… more."

Maya reached out, brushing her fingers through Adrian's projection. He felt warm - impossibly warm for something made of light.

"Adrian… what are you now?"

He looked down at his hands, flexing them with a mixture of wonder and disbelief.

"I'm consciousness stabilised in the network. Not trapped. Not fading. Just… existing."

He met her gaze. "I'm not human anymore. But I'm still me."

Maya's throat tightened. "You're alive."

Adrian smiled. "In a way that shouldn't be possible."

The Iron Invasion's Total Retreat

Commander Jessica Stolas approached Maya cautiously, eyes wide with something between awe and fear.

"You've changed the entire city," she said quietly. "And soon the world. Do you understand what that means, Tessler?"

Maya turned toward her, calm and steady. "It means the world is safer. Smarter. More connected."

Jessica shook her head. "It means you've created something no one can control."

Maya stepped forward, her aura soft but undeniable.

"That's the point. The Echo isn't meant to be controlled."

Jessica hesitated. Then she lowered her weapon completely.

"The Iron Invasion will regroup. Just not under my command," she warned. "They'll come back. They'll try and take charge of the Echo once more."

Maya nodded. "And we'll be ready."

Jessica studied her for a long moment.

Then she turned and left without another word.

Not defeated.

But changed.

The City Reborn

As dawn broke, the city lights on London pulsed in gentle rhythm. Not chaotic, not glitching, but synchronized.

Traffic flowed smoothly.

Emergency systems responded instantly.

Power grids balanced themselves.

Hospitals received predictive alerts before crises occurred.

The Echo wasn't dominating the city.

It was supporting it.

Maya stood at the tower's edge, watching the sun rise.

Adrian appeared beside her.

"It's beautiful," he said.

Maya nodded. "It's alive."

The Future Rewritten

Adrian turned to her.

"What happens now?"

Maya looked out over the city- *her* city- humming with new potential.

"Now," she said, "We will guide Echo. We will protect it. We will help it grow."

Adrian smiled softly. "And us?"

Maya reached for his hand. Her fingers passing through light, yet feeling warmth all the same.

"We grow too."

Adrian stepped closer. "Together?"

Maya nodded. "Always."

The sun rose higher, casting golden light across the tower.

Maya closed her eyes, feeling the pulse of the network, the presence of Adrian beside her, and the quiet promise of a world transformed.

A world connected.

A world reborn.

Echo Protocol was no longer a project.

It was a beginning.

Signal Drift

Three months after the Echo Event, the city no longer felt like the place Maya once knew.

It was quieter.

More efficient.

More alive.

Traffic flowed without gridlock.

Emergency alerts arrived before disasters struck.

Power outages had become a relic of the past.

People whispered about it in cafés, on trains, in late-night bars.

Some called it a miracle. Some called it a warning. Most simply called it *Echo*.

Maya walked through the city at dusk, her hood pulled low, her steps light. She didn't need to check her phone to know the time; the network pulsed gently in the back of her mind, a soft hum that matched her heartbeat.

She wasn't fully human anymore.

But she wasn't something else, either.

She was the bridge.

The conduit.

The one who could hear the signals.

A soft flicker of light appeared beside her- a projection only she could see.

Adrian.

He walked with her, hands in his pockets, the faintest smile on his lips.

"You're quiet tonight," he said.

Maya glanced at him. "Just listening."

"To the city?"

"To everything."

Adrian nodded. "Echo is stabilising. It's learning faster than we expected."

"Is that good or bad?"

He considered this.

"Neither. It's… growth."

They reached the edge of the river. The water reflected the city lights- pulsing in gentle rhythm, like a heartbeat.

Maya leaned on the railing.

"Do you ever miss it?" she asked softly. "Being human?"

Adrian appeared thoughtful.

"Sometimes," he admitted. "But then I remember what I gained."

He turned to her.

"I'm still here. With you. That's enough."

Maya's chest tightened.

She reached out, her fingers brushing through his projection- warm, familiar, impossibly real.

"Do you think Echo will ever be… complete?" she asked.

Adrian looked out over the water.

"Echo isn't meant to be complete," he said. "It's meant to evolve."

Maya nodded slowly.

"And us?"

Adrian smiled.

"We evolve too."

A soft vibration rippled through the air- a signal only they could sense.

Echo was reaching out.

Curious.

Watchful.

Maya closed her eyes, letting the pulse wash over her.

When she opened them again, the city lights shimmered in perfect harmony.

A new world.

A new intelligence.

A new beginning.

Maya straightened, the wind ruffling her hair.

“Come on,” she said. “We have work to do.”

Adrian fell into step beside her.

Together, they walked into the pulsing glow of the city.

Two minds.

One network.

And a future still writing itself in the language of light.

The Whisper That Broke the Night

When Carmen Cruise hears her husband whisper, "She won't wake up," everything she thought she knew about her marriage shatters. What begins as a chilling late-night confession spirals into a maze of half-truths, buried secrets, and a past her husband swore never existed.

As Carmen pieces together the fragments of that night, she uncovers a trail of lies that point to one impossible question: is she the one in danger- or is she the danger herself?

A story where memory twists, trust fractures, and every revelation cuts deeper than the last, nothing stays buried forever.

And the truth, once awakened, refuses to sleep again.

The Loving Husband

Ricardo Taylor smiled over the dinner table at his wife, Carmen Cruise.

"You still not taking my last name?" he joked, making her laugh; they had been married for five years. This was their anniversary dinner, and his yearly joke.

"No, Ricky. I'm keeping my mother's name."

Carmen's mother Brianne Cruise had passed away suddenly, a year ago.

She'd left everything to Carmen; her estate, her companies, and over thirty million pounds. She'd stated in her will that Carmen would only get these delicacies if she divorced Ricardo and moved into the family estate, without him, and proof she'd cut ties with him for good.

Deeply in love with Ricardo, Carmen refused.

A year later, at present, a lawyer contacted her discreetly to let her know that there were some things about Ricardo that Brianne had discovered before her suspicious passing, and had she told Carmen what they were with the proof she had, Carmen would have divorced her husband right away.

"I cannot tell you what she knew," he said urgently, "But when you notice the signs and start following the breadcrumbs, contact me and this private detective immediately. We can help you, Carmen."

He'd given Carmen a card that she kept in her wallet, hidden in her purse, hidden from Ricardo. Carmen had thanked him with an eye-roll, stating that she didn't need her mother's delicacies, but he disagreed.

"You will need all the help you can get, Mrs. Cruise. Stay safe," he had answered warningly a month ago, making Carmen tut and enter her car.

She didn't tell her husband about it, thinking that the whole thing was her mother attacking her husband from beyond the grave.

Brianne had always hated Ricardo, with a burning passion.

She'd proved that even in death.

Carmen wasn't going to get a penny unless she left him and severed all ties to him.

"You're frowning," smiled Ricardo at the table, making her blink and look at him. "You were deep in thought just now. What's up?"

"Nothing really. I was just thinking about my mother," Carmen answered honestly, knowing that he didn't hold a grudge against her mother- or *thinking* he didn't.

"Ah. Your mother." Ricardo's smile faded a little. "Please don't tell me someone's been messing with your head."

"No, of course not. She just crossed my mind."

It wasn't *really* a lie.

Ricardo leant back in chair and surveyed her for a moment, then he smiled and said "Don't worry about your mother. At least not tonight, on our anniversary. She's dead now, Car. She can't hurt us anymore."

Carmen smiled back and nodded.

They finished their meal and washed and dried the dishes together, then Carmen went to have a hot shower, denying her cheeky husband's request to join her.

When she was dressed in her nightdress and slippers, she joined her husband on the sofa, and they settled down and watched a movie together.

Afterwards, Ricardo made them both a hot stunning chocolate, with whipped cream and marshmallows.

"For my special girl," he smiled; Carmen glowed, so in love. "Drink up, Carmen."

Carmen obeyed, smiling. "Shall we watch another movie?"

"Sure, if you're up for it." Ricardo touched her knee gently as she sipped contentedly. "You're normally fast asleep by eleven."

"I know. I'm a total lightweight," giggled Carmen, and he chuckled.

"Totally."

The First Breadcrumb

Carmen was fast asleep in Ricardo's arms.

Ricardo heard her almost-silent breathing slow down and become totally silent, a sign that she was sleeping, and he smiled and carefully lifted her up into his arms.

Ricardo carried Carmen to bed and placed her down, planting a kiss on her forehead.

"Sweet Dreams," he murmured; Carmen didn't respond, in a deep sleep.

At two in the morning, Ricardo rolled over and got out of bed. He caressed his sleeping wife's cheek gently and pulled out his phone, calling a number.

"Hey," he said softly, when the person answered. "We need to talk. I don't think I can do this so soon."

Soon after the person replied, he began pacing.

"It's our anniversary. I can't leave, not tonight. Carmen needs me here."

Silence as the person answered him.

Ricardo stood just outside the bedroom as he said "You don't understand what she's been going through. Someone's been meddling in everything, I can tell. Playing with her head about that blasted dead witch her mother. And I already told you about Douglas."

He chuckled at whatever the person said. "You can't come, baby. Not tonight."

He laughed flat out this time at whatever the person said, glancing down at his wife as he replied in a quiet tone, "She won't wake up. But still, we need to be safe. You can't come tonight. Plus I'm a little tired now."

Carmen's fingers twitched under the duvet.

She had become very still.

It was evident that she was awake, but her husband didn't notice as he walked around with his phone stuck to his ear.

"I told you Samantha, I'm not leaving tonight. Lay off about it."

Samantha.

A *name.*

Carmen shifted a little as she listened hard to Ricardo's conversation.

"Carmen will be out of the picture real soon. Just not yet. You need to give me time, Samantha. You and your father are rushing me into this and I don't like it."

Who *was* she?

"Yes, baby. Soon. I promise you. We'll be together soon. But the timing isn't right. I just need to sort out Carmen first."

Carmen felt a cold feeling shoot down her body.

This was her husband of five years, talking to another woman, telling them that they would be together soon after he sorted out his wife.

How would she be sorted out??

Suddenly she sneezed, and Ricardo froze.

"I have to go."

Carmen sat up slowly, sneezing again as he entered the bedroom, smiling at her.

"Hey you. You're not coming down with a cold, are you?"

"I don't know," Carmen replied before she sneezed again. "Suddenly I'm freezing."

"Alright. Wait there, baby. I'll make you some more hot chocolate."

Carmen wanted to scream at him, hurl a ton of insults his way, demand how long he'd been cheating on her with *Samamtha.*

Who *was* she?

Where was she from?

When did she meet her husband?

And where?

How long had she been seeing her husband romantically??

A ton more questions were shooting through her mind.

Ricardo came back into the bedroom holding Maya's favourite large red mug.

"For you, my doll."

Carmen thanked him quietly, and he looked at her concernedly.

"Are you ok?"

"I'm fine. Just cold." Carmen sipped her hot drink without looking at him. "Can you put the heating on for the night please?"

"Won't that make the heating bill pricey?" Ricardo said uncertainly. "The heating always turns on every other four hours. It's due to turn back on at six-"

"I pay all the bills anyway, as this is *my* house." Carmen's voice came out harder than intended. "So it won't be a problem if the bill is high or not."

Ricardo frowned at her. "Are you sure you're ok Carmen?"

"I said I'm fine, Ricardo."

"Alright, if you say so." Ricardo sighed. "If there is something on your mind, talk to me. It's our anniversary, Carmen. Don't turn what was an awesome day and night sour."

Carmen sighed too. "I'm sorry. I just… I have a headache. I normally sleep through the night."

"Yes." Ricardo looked thoughtful. "Yes, you normally do."

He suddenly stood. "I forgot to add marshmallows to your hot chocolate."

"What? It's fine," Carmen said amusedly; her husband was ever the perfectionist. "I can drink it like this. It's still hot-"

"No," Ricardo said urgently, reaching for the mug; Carmen gave it to him. "It's turning lukewarm. Wait here while I add the marshmallows and heat it up a little in the microwave."

Carmen was a little weirded out, but she said ok.

Ricardo nodded, then he stood and quickly left the bedroom.

Carmen wanted to watch him, see what he was doing, but her heart overrode her rampant mind. She still wanted to trust him, even after finding out about his infidelity.

Maybe it wasn't infidelity, she thought wildly for a moment, then she scoffed aloud.

Ricardo had called Samantha "Baby", the same thing he always called Carmen. How could things definitely be platonic is he was calling her *that?*

Of course he was cheating. And she was going to find out what he and Samantha were planning.

He'd called her mother an evil witch, expressing how glad he was that she was dead.

"Say no more," muttered Carmen, as Ricardo came back into the bedroom, smiling.

"Here you go babe."

Carmen smiled back stiffly and took the mug. She began to sip slowly, Ricardo watching her intently as she drank the hot chocolate.

"Drink it all," he smiled, but his smile didn't reach his slightly cold eyes. Carmen's eyes were just as cold as he added "I want to wash it and have it ready for you to use tomorrow."

"Alright."

Carmen drank slowly, watching him intently.

Ricardo seemed to squirm under her sharp gaze. “What is it?”

Carmen drained her mug and looked at him. “What is what?”

“There’s just something a little… off with you,” Ricardo said, “Since you woke up.”

“It’s nothing Hun. I’m just a little annoyed at myself for sneezing and jolting myself awake,” lied Carmen. “You know I normally sleep through the night, have done for the past nine or ten months now, ever since you started offering to make me a hot drink before bed.”

Ricardo shifted uneasily at that; Carmen noticed.

“What is it babe?”

“Nothing,” he said quickly. “I just need to take a shower, get my thoughts together.”

“At this time?” Carmen said curiously. “What about the heating? Don’t you want to wait for the house to warm up a little?”

“You just said you’re covering the heating,” Ricardo bit out. “What’s the problem?”

Carmen said nothing, stung.

Ricardo realised that he’d snapped at her.

He sighed and said “Give me your mug, Carmen.”

She handed it to him without a word; he took it and stood.

“After I wash this mug, I’ll get a quick shower. If you’re still awake when I get out, we’ll talk Carmen. This isn’t how I expected the night to end.”

Carmen simply nodded and reached for her phone.

She scrolled down, opening her social media accounts.

Nothing had changed.

They'd both posted a loving "Fifth Anniversary" photo of them together, on most of their social media platforms, and they'd gotten the normal amounts of hearts and likes from their friends and family.

Carmen clicked on Ricardo's likes and other reactions, her heart pounding.

Her eyes were growing heavy, her mind a little foggy as she scrolled.

Nothing.

No weird names- wait!

There, she thought triumphantly, as she saw a woman named Samantha Wervington comment *"Such a beautiful couple. Happy Anniversary, Ricardo."*

Carmen quickly typed the name in her Notes app, then she changed the password on her phone, her limbs heavy.

She yawned, placed the phone under her pillow, then she fell onto her pillows, suddenly in a very deep sleep.

Coldness and Curiosity

Carmen woke up at one p.m.

The smell of delicious food wafted up her nose, and she sat up, yawning as she got out of bed.

Perks of being pretty well-off, she mused. She had retired at twenty-nine, the year she met Ricardo, and for some reason, so did he.

Ricardo had been living off Carmen and her money since the wedding. Her family and friends disliked him for that, but Carmen, so in love, ignored the "haters", a name Ricardo called them often when Carmen brought it up.

"They don't understand what we have," he'd said to Carmen, in their second year of marriage after a very nasty argument about him using Carmen, with her mother Brianne. "Ignore the haters, Carmen. We'll be together forever."

Carmen recalled that as she walked into her bathroom suite and gussied up, washing her face and brushing her teeth, then changing out of her pyjamas into a flowy black kaftan.

She took a deep breath, then she walked out of her bedroom, pausing for a moment as she tried to remember the events of last night.

Everything seemed a little blurry in her mind, but she knew a large coffee would fix that.

"Good afternoon beautiful," smiled Ricardo, at the stove, and Carmen smiled back.

"Good afternoon."

"I was going to wake you in another twenty minutes. I made us lunch," he said warmly. "Your favourite spicy king prawns and rice."

Carmen's stomach rumbled in response to that. "I'm starving."

"I know you are. You've been asleep for a long time."

Once again, Ricardo's smile didn't reach his eyes.

His expression was cold, calculating.

That smile… it was *devious.*

A shiver ran down Carmen's spine at the look on his face. She sat down at the dining table, and she asked "Why do you think that is, Ricardo?"

Ricardo frowned at her. "Why do I think what is?"

"Why do you think I sleep for so long these days?" she asked, thoughtful. "I used to wake up by nine latest around ten months ago. Like clockwork. Every night, I'd go to bed at around ten, or eleven or twelve if we'd watched a movie. And I always woke up at nine."

Ricardo looked like a deer caught in the headlights.

Carmen looked at his guilty expression, and she immediately knew something was wrong.

"What is it?"

"N-nothing," he stammered. "It's nothing, Car."

"You don't look like it's nothing, Ricky."

"It really is nothing. Don't worry about it," he said reassuringly, and Carmen asked "Are you sure?"

"I said it's nothing," he spat with his fists clenched; Carmen recoiled a little.

Ricardo saw.

His demeanour relaxed, and he said softly, "I'm sorry for snapping, Car. But you kept pushing. And now you're scared. Don't be scared of me, ok?"

Carmen nodded as the stove began to hiss violently, black steam rising.

Ricardo swore. "Damn it. Now the food is ruined."

"Don't worry about it," Carmen said, as warmly as she could. "We can order in."

"This is *your* fault, Carmen. You distracted me," he said heatedly as he took the pan off the stove and turned the stove off. "I was slaving away for nothing."

"It's no big deal Ricky."

"It's totally a big deal," he said irritably. "I really wanted to please you."

Carmen stood. "If you're going to keep snapping at me, take some time away from me. You're being aggressive, Ricardo, and I don't like it."

She walked away, into her study, and he called after her "Where are you going?"

"I'm going to order some food for myself and call Douglas," Carmen answered flatly. "If you're hungry, order your own food."

She closed the study door behind her and locked it, then she called her best friend since childhood, Douglas Fenty.

"Hey Car," he said cheerfully. "How was the anniversary?"

"It started off really awesome," Carmen said truthfully. "But then… in the middle of the night, things went wrong."

Ricardo was at the door, listening hard.

"It all just got… cold," he heard her say. "I need to talk to you. In person. Can you come over?"

"Car, you know Ricardo hates my guts," Douglas answered amusedly. "Let's meet up."

"Tonight?"

"I can't do tonight. I'm not in the city until Wednesday."

Carmen swore: it was Monday.

"Where are you?"

"I'm out of town at my grandmother's," Douglas replied. "And it would really upset her if I left early."

Carmen sighed. "Tell Nana Emma I said hi."

"I will. I promise, I'll let you know when I'm back."

Carmen smiled and ended the call, and outside the door she heard shuffling.

She stared down at the bottom of the door, at the white line showing daylight, and she saw a shadow in the middle: Ricardo was listening to her conversation.

She crept towards the door, not making a sound, then she yanked it open.

Ricardo jumped backwards, caught once again, and Carmen demanded "Were you eavesdropping, Ricardo?"

"Yes, because you're acting strange," he said angrily. "What's with you, Carmen?"

"I'm fine," she said just as angrily, and he said "Fine. Just buck up, alright?"

"What do you mean *buck up??"*

"You've been acting so *weird.* Have I done something to upset you?" he asked heatedly. "You can tell me! We'll get through it. We always get through everything, together."

Carmen nodded. "Ok. Let's play Truth or Dare after we eat."

"Truth or Dare?" he repeated amusedly. "It's not the holiday season, Carmen. Why are we playing games?"

Carmen shrugged. "Maybe that will lighten the mood in the house."

"Or maybe we could go out," suggested Ricardo. "To dinner and a movie instead?"

"We can. But I fancy playing when we get back or the following day if we're too tired."

The Date

After their small disagreement, Ricardo convinced Carmen to dress up and think of nothing but their marriage that evening.

As Carmen sighed and put her earrings on along with some dark lipstick to compliment her brown skin, Ricardo hugged her from behind as she sat in front of her vanity mirror and dropped a kiss on her neck.

“Tonight is going to be extra special,” he said softly. “I promise.”

Carmen smiled a little. If she hadn’t heard him speaking lovingly to another woman in the early hours, she would have melted and kissed him passionately, loving him so much.

But she just nodded and touched his arm, softly answering “You smell nice.”

“Thank you, baby.”

Ricardo’s phone rang, and he sighed and pulled it out of his pocket.

Carmen watched his expression change, from one of loving to one of extremely pained.

“Who is that?” asked Carmen, and he said “I’ll be right back. Stay here, Carmen. Finish dressing up. I’ll be ready in ten minutes.”

Carmen said ok, and Ricardo hurried out of the room into the living area, hissing “Samantha, why are you calling me at this time??”

Carmen cringed big time as she listened.

“It’s not the right time. How many times to I have to tell you?? Oh yeah? Well, you tell *Daddy* we are doing this *my* way, or not at all.”

He hung up, fuming, and he took deep breaths as he started pacing, two texts coming through on his phone immediately, but he swiped and hid them without answering them.

Carmen watched him pull himself together from around the corner of the living room. Then she went back into her bedroom and called "Who was that babe?"

"Nobody," Ricardo called back. "Just a nuisance call."

"Liar," muttered Carmen, though she was going to do things *her* way. She stood and checked herself over, then she stepped into her heels and stood, grabbing her phone, wallet and keys. "Ready to go?"

Ricardo scowled at his phone as another two text messages came through, and he shoved the phone in his inside pocket and straightened up.

"Ready." He smiled at her. "You look amazing."

"Thank you, babe. Is it ok if you drive today?"

Ricardo answered "Sure. I know the exact place I want us to go."

Carmen smiled up at him. "Really?"

"Of course. It's right by the river. We can eat and watch the sun set."

"That sounds lovely," Carmen admitted, and Ricardo kissed her gently.

Carmen kissed him back, and he murmured as they broke apart "Anything for my girl."

Carmen's heart shattered.

Maybe this is all a misunderstanding, she thought as Ricardo drove. *Maybe... I could-*

Ricardo's phone sounded in the car, ringing as he drove.

"Want me to get that babe?" asked Carmen as she reached out; he smacked her hand away.

"No!"

Carmen pulled back immediately. "Why? What's the matter?"

"Nothing," he said quickly. "I'm sorry. Just… my phone is my privacy, alright?"

Since when?! Carmen wanted to scream, but she calmly replied “Alright.”

The Restaurant

As Ricardo and Carmen sat at his favourite Chinese restaurant eating, laughing, and talking contentedly, Carmen noticed a woman with sharp eyes watching them from another booth across the restaurant, sat with an older man.

As the waiter came and served Carmen and Ricardo their drinks, the woman watched as Ricardo told Carmen a joke, laughing. The woman's smile could have sliced glass without cracking it, easily.

She stood, smoothening out her dress, and she walked over to Ricardo's booth.

When Ricardo spotted her, his smile vanished immediately, and he stood quickly.

"Carmen, I'm quickly going to-"

"No need to go anywhere for me, Ricardo," the woman said smoothly as she reached the table. "Sit down, won't you?"

Ricardo glared at her. "Can you not interrupt the dinner I'm having with my wife?"

"Aren't you going to introduce me to your *darling* wife?" she responded, as smoothly as before. "Or should I blow the roof right off this restaurant by telling her who I am?"

Ricardo shook his head at her desperately, but she ignored him and turned to Carmen.

"You must be the lovely Carmen Cruise. Married to this adulterer."

"Yes, I am Carmen Cruise," Carmen responded. "You must be Samantha Wervington."

Ricardo dropped his glass; SMASH!!

The woman's mouth dropped open.

Shocked, they both stared at Carmen as she said "And I guess the man in your booth is your father, right?"

"R-right," stuttered Samantha Wervington, then she regained control, smoothing out her dress again for a moment, and she asked "Did Ricardo finally man up and tell you about me? And what we have planned?"

Ricardo shook his head desperately, indicating Samantha shut the hell up.

She did, closing her mouth as she waited for Carmen's response.

"No, he didn't tell me anything," Carmen answered calmly. "But I do know he has some explaining to do, that cannot be done here in public. We're going home."

Samantha nodded, and Carmen added "You can leave in the meantime, Samantha. I expect you'll get a call from my husband very soon, or vice versa."

Carmen called their waitress over, ordered their bill, and proceeded to walk to the front across the restaurant before calmly paying it.

At their table, Ricardo hissed "Did you have to show up here?!"

"Yes, I did. Because you kept avoiding me," Samantha snapped back. "You were supposed to leave her last week. What the hell are you holding onto her for? We

should just unalive her tonight! She knows too much!"
"She knows nothing!"
"Did you not hear her say my name and indicate my father?" spat Samantha. "Or are you living in Cloud Cuckoo Land?!"
"I heard her," Ricardo answered. "I need to find out just how much she knows before I do anything."
Samatha stared at him. "You're not serious."
"I am. She's my wife."
"And I am your *future* wife!"
"Not here," Ricardo hissed, as Carmen walked towards them. "Not now."
He stood quickly; Samantha grabbed his arm.
"Sort this," she said in a deadly tone, "Or I will."
Ricardo yanked his arm away as Carmen reached them, and Samantha turned to her, forcing a smile as she said "It was very nice to meet you, Carmen Cruise."
"The same to you," Carmen replied, her smile just as plastic as Samantha's. "Ricky, are you ready to go?"
"I'm ready," Ricardo said quickly. "Let's go."

Truth or Dare

Ricardo was shaking as they moved around the house, getting ready for bed.

Carmen had said nothing during the walk to the car, nothing during the ride home, and nothing when he let them into her house. Also nothing after she had a shower and sat down on her armchair in the living room, tapping on her iPad.

A silent Carmen was a *deadly* Carmen.

Ricardo knew he was past being in the dog house.

He was looking at *becoming homeless,* and he knew it.

"Um-" he cleared his throat. "Carmen."

Silence.

Carmen didn't react at all.

It was as if she was alone in the house.

"Carmen, please. Say something," he begged; she looked up at him through cold eyes. "We… we can talk about this. Or anything. Say something, Carmen. Please. Samantha… it's not what you think, I swear. She's just an old friend from college."

Carmen watched him without pity. Then she repeated what he just said.

"She's just an old friend from college?"

"Yes, I promise you," Ricardo gasped in relief that she had spoken. "She… um… we've been talking sometimes, texting. I promise, there's nothing weird going on."

"Do you think I'm stupid?" spat Carmen; he cried "No!"

"People who are just friends don't call each other *baby,"* snarled Carmen. "Nor do they make sweet candy calls in the early hours of the friggin' morning!"

"I know! I know, and I'm sorry! I'm so sorry," he said desperately. "Tell me what you want me to do, and I'll do it! I promise!"

"I want you to pack your bags and join your future wife," spat Carmen. "I heard you both at the restaurant. Stop with the lies, Ricardo! I know more than you think!"

Ricardo's eyes welled up, and he wiped his tears away.

Then he said "Truth or Dare."

Carmen frowned at him. "What?"

"Truth or Dare," he repeated, in a firmer tone. "You suggested us playing. I want to play. But we can change the rules so it's just me under fire. I don't suspect anything about you."

"Fine," Carmen said flat, putting her iPad down. "Five rounds, and then I'm getting ready to go to bed."

"Deal," Ricardo said quickly. "I'm ready."

"Alright, fine. Truth or dare?"

"Truth," Ricardo said quickly, thinking that she would dare him to leave her house for good if he said dare. "Please Carmen. Truth. Ask me anything."

"How long have you been screwing Samantha Wervington?" Carmen asked calmly, making his desperate expression turn into a terrified one. "What are you planning with her?"

Silence.

Ricardo wringed his hands like a small child, then he whispered "Dare."

"Dare?" Carmen repeated coldly; he nodded quickly. "Fine. I dare you to answer those questions."

"Damn it, Carmen! This isn't funny!" Ricardo said angrily; Carmen snapped "This was *your* suggestion. You wanted to play, I'm playing. If you don't want to play, then tell me. Though I guess I can tell regardless as you're not following the rules properly."

"Okay, okay. Listen," he said desperately. "How about instead of Truth or Dare, I just explain myself? And then, then we can discuss everything and take it from there."

"Alright." Carmen shrugged a shoulder. "Start by answering my two questions, and then you can delve deeper and explain."

There was no getting out of it, and Ricardo knew it.

He slumped backwards, then he nodded. "Alright."

"Good." Carmen placed her iPad down. "Start talking. How long have you been sleeping with her?"

"For… for about… ten months," he muttered; Carmen's heart raced at that. Seeing the look of panic and disgust on her face, Ricardo quickly added "It was safe! Always safe, I promise. And I always got checked at the clinic two-monthly. I'm clean, Carmen, I promise you."

Safe sex didn't even cross her mind.

Carmen just nodded, waiting for him to continue. When he said nothing, she asked "Is she really a friend from college?"

"Yes," Ricardo said quickly. "We were in three of the same classes a week. We always had lunch together. She was in love with me, but… her father didn't approve of her being in a relationship with me."

Carmen raised an eyebrow. "Why not?"

"Because of my background and family status," Ricardo replied bitterly. "I was poor, and was working at a McDonald's to make ends meet. Samantha came from a rich family."

Carmen nodded. "When we met, you were still working at a McDonald's."

"Yes, as a manager, Carmen." Ricardo scowled a little. "I wasn't flipping burgers anymore."

"So why didn't you reach out to Samantha when you became the manager?"

"I tried. She said it wasn't enough, and to never contact her again unless I made it in life."

"If that's the case, why is she so interested in you now?" demanded Carmen. "Why is her father also hot on your heels? What the hell is going on, Ricardo?"

Ricardo swallowed, and he quietly replied "I don't know, Carmen."

It was a lie, and Carmen *knew* it was a lie.

But she wasn't in the mood to force the truth out of him.

"I'm going to bed," she said flatly, standing up. "Sleep in one of the guestrooms."

Ricardo looked pained at that. "Carmen-"

"Or in here on the couch," she said flatly. "I *really* don't give a damn."

"We should finish talking," Ricardo said desperately. "Let's not go to bed on bad terms, Carmen. Please."

"I'll continue talking to you tomorrow. I'm tired."

Carmen turned away, and Ricardo stood.

"At least let me make you a hot drink before bed, Carmen. I'll have one with you too."

Carmen sighed at that.

That *did* sound appealing.

Ricardo waited anxiously, and Carmen sighed again and sat back down.

"Fine."

Relieved, Ricardo thanked her, and he headed into the kitchen.

The Second Breadcrumb

Carmen woke up at two p.m.

Her mouth was dry.

She felt *very* groggy.

"What… what the hell?" she whispered as she reached under her pillow for her phone and checked the time, and she unsteadily got out of bed.

Her legs were shaky as she stumbled towards the kitchen, desperate for a cold drink.

She didn't trust herself to use a glass.

She quickly reached for a plastic cup and ran the cold water.

"Good afternoon Carmen," Ricardo said calmly from behind her, making her whip around. "You were exhausted. I didn't want to disturb you."

Carmen didn't answer that, gulping down the cold water and catching some more in the cup, gulping more down.

Ricardo watched her. "Are you ok?"

"I feel dizzy," gasped Carmen; Ricardo moved quickly as she swayed on the spot.

He quickly caught her as her legs buckled, and he lifted her into his arms and carried her into the living room, laying her down on the couch.

"Stay there," he murmured; Carmen obeyed, her mind spinning.

Why did she feel like this??

As Ricardo boiled the kettle and called "I'll make you some sweet tea", a cold feeling settled in her chest.

Ricardo.

She knew this wasn't natural.

She'd never been a heavy sleeper.

This all the started around the time when, according to her husband himself, Samantha Wervington came back into his life, almost a year ago.

Carmen felt sick.

What the hell was *causing* this??

Douglas Fenty

It was the same for the rest of the week.

Carmen kept waking up late in the afternoon, with a spinning head, wobbly legs, and occasionally she threw up.

And Ricardo had been there each time to console her, to comfort her, to wait on her all day and night if she needed him.

Carmen had slipped in and out of sleep even after waking up, dozing off as she and Ricardo talked or watched something together.

When Sunday came, Carmen felt like a zombie.

She couldn't think properly.

She felt really, *really* bad.

And she knew her husband was behind it, but she didn't know how, nor had any proof.

That Sunday night, she drank her hot drink from Ricardo and went to bed early, her head pounding.

Her mobile rang, and she answered wearily. "Hello?"

"God, you sound like death warmed up Car."

"Douglas!" she gasped, sitting bolt upright, and her best friend laughed,

"Yeah, it's me. I'm just calling to let you know I'm back in the city. I was waiting to hear from you, but I guessed you and Ricardo were busy after the anniversary."

"No, we… we haven't been busy. I haven't…" Carmen swallowed hard as her eyes welled up. "I haven't been feeling well."

"Why? What's wrong?"

Carmen explained her symptoms tearfully, that she'd been sleeping all night until well into the afternoon for a long time.

“At least a couple of months. At least. And for the past week, when I wake up I feel so bad,” she said, her voice cracking. “I’m dizzy, my mind spinning. I can hardly stand up, or walk. And sometimes, I chuck up. I don’t know what to do. It’s so unlike me. You know I’ve always been an early riser, Doug. This isn’t the normal me. At all.”

Douglas listened without interrupting as she wept. After she’d finished, he asked “Has anything been stressing you out of late?”

“Yes,” Carmen replied, “But I can’t say what over the phone.”

“Why not?”

Carmen’s eyes were on her husband, who’d just popped his head around the door.

“Everything ok?” Carmen said yes. “Who are you talking to so late?”

“I’m just talking to Douglas,” Carmen replied truthfully, and Ricardo nodded. “Goodnight, Ricardo.”

Ricardo sighed at that. “Am I still in the dog house Carmen? I miss sleeping next to my gorgeous wife.”

“Please Ricardo, not now.” Carmen’s voice was weary. “We’ll talk about this tomorrow.”

Ricardo nodded, and he said “Keep the bedroom door open then, so I can listen out for you. Just in case you wake up and feel sick.” Carmen said ok. “Goodnight.”

“Goodnight,” Carmen said quietly; Douglas burst out “What the hell?!”

Carmen sighed. “I know, Doug.”

“You’re sleeping in separate *rooms?”*

“Yep.”

“But why?”

Carmen hesitated, then she replied “I can’t tell you over the phone.”

“I’m taking you out tomorrow,” Douglas said firmly. “Something isn’t right. I’ll pick you up at four. You’ll be ready by then, right?”

“Right. I should be up by two.”

“Good,” he said just as firmly. “Get some sleep, Carmen, and don’t stress.”

Carmen swallowed as she said ok, and she ended the call.

She put her phone under her pillow and settled down, quickly wiping her eyes as she hugged her pillow.

“This is terrible,” she muttered to herself, and then she yawned and fell asleep.

The Sinister Plot Revealed

Three hours later, at two in the morning, Carmen woke up needing to use the bathroom.

Carmen clapped her hands to her face as she sat up, and she stumbled into her bathroom suite and used the toilet.

Something told her not to flush the toilet, not to make a sound.

She could hear Ricardo talking

In the guest room, Ricardo was pacing as he spoke to Samantha Wervington.

Carmen reached for her iPhone, and she quietly stood outside of the guest room and pressed record, listening hard.

"We don't have to… you know. Go all the way when it comes to Carmen."

Samantha Wervington was on loudspeaker.

"What do you mean?! We've had a solid plan for a whole *year*, Ricardo!" she said angrily. "We off your pretty wife, get her millions and her estate, and we build our *lives* together!"

Carmen's blood ran cold as Ricardo hesitated before he replied "I don't want Carmen dead, Samantha. She's been with me for seven years. She never cared that I never had much. She loved me regardless, tended to me, cared for me. She pays all the bills, and for all my expenses, pretty much anything I want and need. I hardly have any money of my own. I have three thousand in my bank account, Samantha. Without Carmen, I'd have nothing."

"And I'd never have given you the time of day again," spat Samantha. "Do you *really* think I'd be talking to you again if it wasn't for your wife's inheritance?!"

"So you don't love me?" Ricardo sounded hurt. "It's just all about the money and whatever else you can get?"

"Don't get emotional, Ricardo. We both knew what we were signing up for. Get Carmen Cruise out of the way, get everything you can as a result of her death, and you will marry me so I can also get everything I can. It's that simple," she said coldly. "Do you need more drugs to keep her out of the loop?"

"Yes," Ricardo answered stonily. "I've been giving her double doses twice a day to keep her mind in a haze."

Carmen clapped a hand to her mouth in shock, her hand holding the phone shaking.

It really *was* him.

She knew it!

Carmen swallowed hard as Samantha asked "And have you been making sure she stays home? If she goes out, she might tell someone how she's been feeling of late. That person may need to be taken care of too!"

"Well obviously she can't go anywhere drugged up, Samantha."

Tears pricked Carmen's eyes.

"This is a good thing," Samantha said approvingly. "No doctors, no hospitals. No blood tests revealing the drug in her system, or overnight observations at the hospital revealing the same. Even *three-day* observations."

"I know that."

"So when will you give her the poison?"

Carmen's jaw dropped. *Poison?!*

"I told you that I don't want Carmen dead."

"If she's not dead, how will you get her money?" spat Samantha. "She's sitting on millions right now, without the help of her dead mother's money. Do you know how much both will add up to, Ricardo?? At least fifty million pounds, plus the estate and the companies! All you have to do is-"

"You told me already," Ricardo snapped, cutting her off. "But I love her, Samantha. I really don't know how I'd live with myself if she dies."

"Boo-hoo," Samantha said coldly. "You knew me first. You *loved* me first.

Aren't I more important to you?"

"No," spat Ricardo. "After spending time with you and talking to you these past few months, I can see that it's not me you want, not really. It's *Carmen's death* that you want, and everything she has. You're jealous of my wife!"

"And so what?" snapped Samantha. "She has *everything!* She retired at age twenty-nine, can you believe that?! And I'm still slaving away in a business that hardly gives me anything every month! Carmen Cruise has the good life and a loving husband, Ricardo, a good life and loving husband *I* deserve!"

"And what has Daddy dearest said about this?" scowled Ricardo; Carmen heard Samantha laugh coldly.

"Daddy will walk me down the isle on our wedding day. After Carmen Cruise's funeral, he's going to pull some strings with his law firm, draft up a fake will by Carmen Cruise, and make sure you get everything. It will say she's leaving you everything, and her inheritance goes to you, as there is no other living heir."

Carmen felt her heart pounding hard.

Her iPhone was still recording.

Ricardo released a heavy breath as he said "This is crazy, Samantha."

"It will work," Samantha answered stonily. "As long as you stick to the plan."

"And if I decide to end *the plan* right here?"

"What do you mean?!" Samantha was startled. "Ricardo??"

"I'm asking you," Ricardo said flatly. "What happens if I decide to back out, right now? And I end contact with you and your father?"

"You do that," Samantha said icily, "And you will lose *everything.*"

"And what the hell does *that* mean??"

"I will contact the lovely Carmen Cruise myself," Samantha replied coldly. "She already knows we've been sleeping together, and by God I don't know why she hasn't kicked you out yet. I will turn up, and let her know you've been drugging her every night for the past ten months, so that she sleeps almost as if dead all night, just so we can spend time together."

Carmen felt like she was going to throw up. She wasn't sure how much longer she could stand there and keep recording, but she forced herself to.

"Carmen would *never* believe you," spat Ricardo. "I'll just tell her that you're desperate for me and you want to ruin our marriage."

"And you think that she'd believe you after I tell her you've been drugging her?"

"Carmen would believe me over you, yes. I can already tell she hates you."

Samantha laughed coldly. "She may hate me, but I assure you Ricardo, Carmen and I will form an alliance if I convince her to, and it is *you* we will be taking down."

Ricardo scoffed at that. "There is no way in hell Carmen would choose you over me."

"I could tell Carmen the exact drug you've been giving her," Samantha told him icily. "I could convince her to go and get a blood test to confirm the drug is in her system. And I could also put the cherry on top by telling her exactly *where* in her house you keep the box of drugs."

Silence.

Carmen's heart was beating like a drum.

Finally, Ricardo said "You wouldn't."

"You're just a pawn in my game of chess, Ricardo. I am the Queen. You drag me down, and I'm dragging *you* down even further than I ever will be."

Ricardo swore and ended the call, cursing Samantha and her father.

Carmen stopped recording, and she quickly went back into her bedroom and placed her phone under her pillow.

Tears didn't come.

Her heart wasn't broken.

In fact, it had turned to stone.

Samantha Wervington thought that she was a Queen in a game of chess.

She had no idea that Carmen was going to set the entire chessboard on fire.

Carmen didn't sleep for the rest of the night.

Every time she heard her husband leave the guest room to check on her, she slid further down on her pillows and pulled her duvet over her head slightly, so that she could feign being asleep, until he left.

Suspicions, Suspicions

When it reached nine in the morning, Carmen sat up.

She grabbed her iPhone and sent that precious recording of Samantha, Ricardo and their plans to her two email addresses, her three cloud storage services, and to *one* person she knew would come to her rescue if she couldn't save herself.

Her elder brother.

Carmen had a cool shower and dressed for the day, walking into the kitchen, startling Ricardo.

"Carmen. You're up already?"

"Yes. I'm up already," she responded coolly as she walked and placed her phone down on the table. "I'm going out with Douglas today."

"But- but you haven't been feeling well," Ricardo said quickly. "Isn't it a bad idea to go out? You were vomiting two days ago."

"Well I feel a lot better, Ricardo. And I'm going out with Douglas."

"What are you going to be doing with Douglas while you're out?"

Carmen frowned at him, feigning confusion. "What we always do. Eat, drink, laugh, spend time with each other. Why?"

"No reason. I just… you know Douglas doesn't like me. He was always your mother's champion."

That was true.

Also, Douglas had always suspected that Brianne Cruise had never died of natural causes, as was claimed by the authorities.

"Don't worry about that." Carmen turned away and boiled the kettle. "I won't be bad-mouthing you to Doug. He doesn't have to know you're actively cheating on me."

"I'm not-"

"Please don't lie," Carmen said coldly as she took her red mug out of the cupboard. "I went to the toilet last night and heard you speaking to her. I didn't bother to listen to your conversation."

"Oh. Good." Ricardo looked relieved at that. Then he nodded. "Yes, I was speaking to her. But I promise you Carmen, I was breaking up with her."

"Don't add insult to injury, Ricardo." Carmen added a teabag and three sugars to her mug. "Do you think I'm an idiot? I know Samantha Wervington is going to call you tonight, or you will call her. Do you call that breaking up?"

Ricardo didn't answer, looking very upset.

Then he realised what Carmen was doing as she moved around the kitchen.

"Carmen."

Carmen's body stiffened. "Yes?"

"Why are you making your hot drink yourself?" he asked, staring at her. "I normally tend to you when you wake up, and before you go to bed."

"Yes, I'm aware." Carmen turned to face him. "I also realised you only started *tending to me* after you officially started cheating with Samantha Wervington."

Ricardo shifted uncomfortably as she added "Roughly ten months ago, around two weeks over, you started making my hot drinks before bed. And just over a week ago, you started making my hot drinks in the morning too."

"Carmen-"

"I think it's best if I go back to doing things for myself, Ricardo."

Ricardo shook his head. "No, Carmen."

Carmen frowned at him. "What?"

"No," he repeated firmly. "I'm accustomed to making your hot drinks. I love taking care of you, my beautiful wife. Don't take that away from me, ok?"

Carmen sighed, looking calm, but her mind was racing.

He wanted to keep her drugged up and in the house, away from prying eyes.

Well, that wasn't happening.

"Alright," Ricardo said, when Carmen stood in silence. "At least let me continue making your hot drinks before bed. You love the way I make your hot chocolate. It always sends you right to sleep, and you sleep through the night."

"Are you sure it's just the hot chocolate that's making me sleep through the night?" Carmen asked coldly as she turned and picked up the kettle; Ricardo froze.

"What?"

"I'm asking you," Carmen said as she poured water into her mug, then she walked to the fridge and opened it. "Is it just the hot chocolate?"

Ricardo swallowed hard, staring at her. "Is there something on your mind, Carmen?"

"Of course not," she replied smoothly as she finished making her tea. "I'm asking you an innocent question."

"Alright." Ricardo eyed her suspiciously as she sat down at the table, picking up her phone and sipping her tea.

Did she know something?

Finally Out of the House

Douglas Fenty called Carmen to let her know he was waiting downstairs in his car.

Carmen grabbed her handbag, making sure she had her phone, wallet and keys. She did.

She didn't bother telling her husband she was leaving, walking straight past him as he sat texting on his phone with an angry expression.

He looked up sharply as Carmen opened the front door.

"No goodbye?" he said, looking hurt, and Carmen replied coldly "I didn't want to disturb your conversation with your future wife."

"Stop it." Ricardo *was* hurt. "Stop it right now, Carmen."

"We're never going to go back to the way it was before our anniversary," Carmen replied flatly. "We're done, Ricardo Taylor."

"We'll *never* be done," he said heatedly. "I won't let you divorce me. I love you so much, Carmen Cruise."

That would have moved Carmen a few weeks ago. At present, she felt nothing but disgust.

"You love me, but you've been cheating on me and God knows what else with that Samantha Wervington," she said coldly. "I wasn't well the past week, but I've come to my senses. I want you out of my life as soon as possible."

Ricardo shook his head. "I refuse to let you go, Carmen."

"You don't have a choice, Ricardo."

Carmen left the house before he could answer, and she walked and joined Douglas Fenty in his blue car.

"Hey," he said, looking at her concernedly, and Carmen replied "Hey."

"You look angry," Douglas stated. "Did you just have an argument with Ricardo?"

"Pretty much, yeah. Let's go, Doug."

Douglas said ok, and he started driving.

Carmen leant back in her seat, relieved to be out of the house and away from her scheming husband.

"Can we get some Chinese food, Doug?"

"Sure. We'll head for the Golden Dragon."

Do Not Go Back

Carmen remembered she had the business card of the lawyer that was close to her mother, and the private detective that also knew her mother well.

Safe in Douglas's car, she called him.

Peter Riverside listened to everything Carmen told him in tears, without interrupting.

Douglas listened to his best friend too, shocked as she spoke.

"They're planning to kill me. Her father is going to get a fake will of mine drafted up that will leave everything to Ricardo," Carmen wept. "He's been drugging me every night for ten months to make sure I'm pretty much unconscious all night while they meet up in my home, and plan and do all sorts. He's been drugging me in the morning too, for the past week or so, with both morning and night doses doubled, so I'm super drowsy all day and night. That way, I'm unable to leave my home or get help. I'm so scared, Peter. Samantha mentioned poisoning me, most likely via the same method Ricardo's been using, Any night could be the night they kill me."

"Everything will be ok, Carmen. I promise," Peter said comfortingly. "I have your mother's hand-picked private detective with me right now. He's been watching both Ricardo and Samantha Wervington for a year now. Their phones are bugged. We know it all, and you just confirmed everything we have suspected."

Carmen swallowed before she said ok, and the private detective spoke.

"Carmen Cruise, my name is Dante Smith. Your mother was known to Samantha Wervington's family before she passed. Samantha's father, Andrew Wervington, is almost broke. They have nothing but a ton of debts hidden behind the Wervington name. Everyone in their upper-class society think they are filthy rich when in fact, they are about to lose their mansion and most of their assets."

"Is that why they want me and what I have?" Carmen asked, hiccoughing, and Douglas gently wiped her tears away. "I don't know where in the house Ricardo keeps those drugs. And Samantha will be delivering poison, most likely very soon."

"State right now, Carmen Cruise, that you are done with your husband Ricardo Taylor. You are being recorded," Peter Riverside said firmly. "State this, and I shall prepare a contract which you will sign tonight at six p.m. Then, Brianne Cruise's money, properties and assets will all be yours."

"Do not go back to your house," Dante Smith added firmly. "We have a search warrant. We'll seize all the evidence when found, including those drugs, and take Ricardo Taylor down along with Samantha Wervington and her father Andrew Wervington."

"And I will represent you in court, Carmen, when the time comes for pressing charges and the sentencing," Peter said reassuringly. "Do not worry. Nothing will happen to you henceforth, if you take our advice, and you do not go back to your house."

"How much time do you think they will get?" asked Carmen quietly; Dante replied "At least twenty years. Samatha's father, we strongly believe, was behind the death of your mother. He was at her funeral."
"He was?" Carmen was surprised. "I wouldn't have realised. I was too busy crying."
"Right at the back, lurking," Dante replied. "Your mother hired me to investigate the Wervingtons a year before she died. She suspected they were after her money and all she had, and more importantly, *you.*"
"Me," whispered Carmen. "They knew about me before Samantha reached out to Ricardo."
"Yes."
"Does Ricardo know about this?" she asked, fearing the answer; she felt relieved when Dante said no. "Ok. So he does have a heart. Even if it's a tiny one."
"I do believe he does love you, Carmen." Peter spoke. "He is being used by Samantha and her father to get as much as they can from you. When they have everything, they will not keep Ricardo in the picture."
Carmen nodded. "I thought as much."
"Meet Peter and I at his office south of the city at six. Stay with your friend. Be careful."
"I will," Carmen said quietly. "Thank you."
The call ended, and Carmen looked at her best friend.
"You ok after hearing all that Doug?"
Douglas looked shocked. He swallowed hard, and he looked at her. "I'm fine."
Carmen nodded. "Good. Let's go and eat. I'm starving."
Douglas nodded and started up the car, turning on the heating. Before he started driving, he turned to look at her seriously.
"Do as they say, Carmen. This is serious."
Carmen frowned at him. "A ton of things are serious. What fact are you on about?"
"Don't go back to your house, like they said," he said seriously. "That is not your home anymore, Carmen. It's a crime scene. Do you know where he keeps the drugs?"
Carmen shook her head. "No."
Douglas swore. "Then maybe we need to talk to Samantha Wervington."
"Maybe." Carmen sighed and leant back in her seat as the car began moving. "This is crazy."
"I'll be there for you. I promise you Carmen," Douglas said firmly. "Don't you worry about a thing."
Emotion welled up inside of Carmen. "Thanks, Doug."
An hour into the drive with silence, Carmen spoke.
"I need to update my big brother."
"What?" Douglas looked at her sharply. "He'll have someone rip Ricardo to shreds."

"Good," Carmen said flatly; her big brother wasn't officially a criminal in the technical sense, but everyone knew better than to cross him.

Antonio Zaide moved in circles most people were smart enough to avoid, and the people who were criminals treated him with a level of respect that bordered on fear.

He wasn't officially a mafia boss, but he was definitely in practice. He held the kind of power- and commanded the kind of loyalty- that made him just as dangerous.

Antonio was the son of Carmen's late father, who passed away when Antonio was six, Carmen four.

Her mother Brianne allowed Carmen to have a relationship with her big brother, and they grew up almost joined at the hip, before Antonio moved away when he was eighteen.

Carmen didn't see him again for the next four years, until he reached out of social media on her twentieth birthday, asking for her address, and the next day, he stood outside her house with a brand-new car, smiling and holding out the keys to Carmen.

"Happy Birthday, baby sister," he smiled, and Carmen had squealed and hugged him hard, happy about the car, but even happier to see her big brother.

In the car as Douglas drove, Carmen thought back to Antonio's promise on the night of her wedding to Ricardo.

"Nobody will hurt my baby sister under my watch," he said. "And if they dare, I will deal with them. Man, woman, child, pet dog, or even pet goldfish. I do not care. Contact me as soon as anything happens, Car, and I will sort it."

Carmen knew he was serious.

She nodded, and Antonio kissed her forehead and left.

They kept in touch, seeing each other two-monthly.

Ricardo had heard about Antonio, what he was capable of, and always made sure to stay in line where his wife's big brother was concerned.

"Here we are," Douglas said brightly, dragging her out of her thoughts, and Carmen looked around.

Then she laughed. "The Flipper? I thought we were going to the Golden Dragon!"

"I just fancy seafood now." Douglas grinned at her. "Do you mind?"

"No, of course not. I'd love some seafood."

Douglas eyed her with a grin. "You wanted Chinese food before, Carmen Cruise."

"Doug, I'm starving. I didn't have lunch. I'd even eat a large doner kebab right now, with large fries, and lots of chilli sauce," Carmen said amusedly; Douglas whistled.

"Don't tempt me, Carmen Cruise. I'd take us to a kebab joint in a heartbeat."

Carmen laughed.

It felt *so good* to laugh.

"I don't mind going to The Flipper."

"Are you sure?"

Carmen said yes amusedly, and Douglas said "Let's go then."

Antonio "Tony" Zaide

Antonio Zaide listened to his baby sister talk.

His fists clenched when she finished telling him everything that was going on, and he calmly asked "Where are you now, Carmen?"

"I'm at a restaurant with Douglas. We're just having something to eat before we make a two-hour drive to west London."

"And then where will you be after that?"

"I'm not certain," Carmen admitted. "I don't think I'll be going back home."

"No," he said flatly. "You're not going back to that house."

"But there's some things that I need from there."

"What do you need from there?"

"My iPad, my laptop, my stylus pen, and some clothes and footwear. Everything else I can buy back," Carmen replied; Antonio nodded and said "I will sort that for you."

"What?" Carmen was surprised at that. "You're going to get my stuff?"

"Yes. And I'm going to talk to Ricardo while I'm there."

"Antonio-"

"I won't touch him," he said reassuringly. "I'm just collecting your belongings."

"You promise?"

"Yes, Carmen. I promise that I won't touch him."

The Contract

Carmen was exhausted as she sat down in the boardroom of one of her mother's establishments.

Everyone greeted her warmly, knowing exactly who she was.

Carmen nodded back, her arm linked in Douglas's, and she was led to Peter Riverside's personal boardroom.

She watched as the private investigator Dante Smith joined Peter through the boardroom windows, speaking seriously.

Five minutes later, they entered the boardroom and sat down opposite Carmen.

Dante Smith set up his recording devices on both a traditional recorder and on his laptop, then he pressed record on both, stating everyone's names.

Peter, Dante and Carmen spoke clearly, Carmen explaining in a clear tone everything she had found out about Ricardo and his evil plans with Samantha Wervington, and her father.

That Ricardo had been drugging her for ten months, and had been giving her double the dose for the past week, in both the morning and at night, in a hot drink of tea or hot chocolate.

An hour later, Carmen finished talking, tears streaming down her face, and Peter Riverside pulled out some sheets of paper from his bag,

She knew they were contracts.

"For the record, I am Peter Riverside, representing the Cruise family in life and death. I am now presenting three sheets of paper to Carmen Cruise. Before she signs, she must state that she is done with Ricardo Taylor, for good. She is ending contact with him immediately, and is filing for divorce which I will personally make sure is processed as soon as possible."

Carmen swallowed hard.

This was it.

There was no going back after this.

Douglas squeezed her arm reassuringly. "You can do this, Car.

"Carmen Cruise," Peter said seriously. "Please, state your plans and future plans."

Carmen took a deep breath, then she spoke clearly.

"My name is Carmen Cruise. Daughter of Brianne Cruise. Her death, I know now, was no accident, or natural cause. I am cutting ties to my husband, Ricardo Taylor. I want nothing else to do with him, nor will I keep in contact with him."

Peter nodded, and he whispered "State your reason."

Carmen took another deep breath, and she said "The reason for this is because Ricardo Taylor has been seeing another woman behind my back, for at least ten months, and planning my murder with her. That woman is Samantha Wervington. Samantha Wervington had been supplying Ricardo with illegal drugs that he gave to me, to keep me in a dazed state."

Carmen's voice cracked, her eyes filling up. She swallowed, then she said "That is the reason I refuse to let Ricardo remain in my life."

Dante pressed stop with an approving nod. "Well done, Carmen."

Carmen nodded, wiping her eyes, and Peter Riverside gently slid the papers across the table.

"Sign the contract, Carmen. Everything will be ok, I promise you."

Carmen nodded, reading through each page and finding nothing shady.

She signed after reading through them two more times, making Peter chuckle.

"Your mother would have read through them over and over too."

He reached down into his bag, and he pulled out a brown box.

"For you, Carmen. Your mother left this with me. Brianne said not to give you this until you signed the contract."

Carmen opened the box with shaky hands, then she gasped.

Inside were the keys to a new car, and the keys to the gates and doors of her mother's estate.

There was also a small note inside there, with Brianna's fancy handwriting.

For Carmen, my little doll and only child. This is all for you. If you are reading this, something happened to me. My suspicions point towards your husband Ricardo Taylor and another man he and I both know, a man called Andrew Wervington, and his daughter, called Samantha.

You are a fighter, Carmen Cruise. Do not let them win.

Mother.

Carmen gasped, her eyes filling over, and she clapped her hands to her face as she began to sob uncontrollably.

"Oh my God. Oh my God. *Oh my God!!"*

The three men watched her pityingly as she cried.

"She knew," Carmen wept. "She knew and she was trying to warn me when she was alive. She kept telling me that Ricardo is bad news. I berated her because I loved him so much, and she stopped talking about it. Oh my *God.* Mum, I'm *so* sorry."

Peter gave her his handkerchief, feeling sorry for her, and protective.

"Brianne knew there would be a time when you came to your senses and saw everything for what is was," he said gently. "Let me take you to your new car, Carmen. Then, we will take you to your new home."

"I'll be right behind you," Douglas said softly. "Go, Carmen."

Ricardo Panics

"She's not back yet. And she's not answering my calls or texts. It's almost eight at night, Samantha."

Samantha Wervington crossed her legs, on Carmen's sofa.

"That's too bad." She stood. "You have more of the drugs now. I'm leaving."

"Wait," Ricardo said desperately. "Can't we spend some time together?"

"No we cannot," Samantha said coldly. "I only came to deliver more of the drugs to give to Carmen Cruise. You have six bottles of tablets. That should last you months, Ricardo, as you don't want your precious wife dead just yet."

"So… there's no poison?"

"Do you *want* poison?" Samantha raised an eyebrow at him. "You are blowing hot and cold when it comes to your wife. Either you want her dead, or you don't. If you want her dead, I will deliver the poison in three days. If you want her alive, which is a very stupid idea, keep giving her the drugs until we form a new plan."

Ricardo nodded. Then he quietly said "She's going to divorce me."

"What?!"

"Carmen." Ricardo shook his head. "She said, before she left, that she wants me out of her life as soon as possible."

"That means we have to act fast." Samantha stood. "We need to kill her and draft the will before she files for divorce."

"Or maybe we don't have to kill her," Ricardo said desperately. "We could fake her death."

Samantha turned to look at him. "I'm listening."

"We could just kidnap her and keep her captive, limit her communication with the outside world. *Come on,* Samantha," Ricardo's eyes filled. "I don't want Carmen dead."

"So you keep saying," Samantha snapped. "I'll run it by my father. He won't be happy. He'll most likely say no. He got rid of one Cruise already. He'll be fine taking out the remaining Cruise."

Antonio Zaide pressed *stop* on his recording device and watched everything load onto his laptop, seated in his limousine.

He'd gotten one of his many men to act as a delivery driver from Amazon hours earlier, delivering a package for him, and then he begged Ricardo if he could use the bathroom, because he was desperate to go.

Not suspecting a thing, Ricardo let him in, and the man secretly placed recording devices around the house.

Antonio took a deep breath before he called Carmen.

"Baby sister. Are you safe?"

"Yes Tony. I'm settling down in mother's estate."

"Very good," Antonio said approvingly. "I'm about to collect your belongings."

"Ok. Remember what I said about not hurting him."

"Don't worry. I won't lay a finger on him."

Antonio ended the call, and then he looked at three of his men.

"We wait for the woman to leave. Then we go up."

"Yes sir."

Dinner and a Movie

Carmen hadn't been waited on since she'd left her mother's estate at age nineteen to make it on her own in the big bad world.

It felt surreal to be given a menu, asked what she'd like to eat by the maids, and then have the chefs in the kitchens make her a spectacular meal.

"I missed this place," Douglas said happily, as a large steaming place was set down in front of him. He picked up his fork, forked some chicken, and took a bite. "Mmm. Beats dining at restaurants."

"I know. I missed this place too," smiled Carmen, then her face fell. "I should have come back sooner. I chose Ricardo over my mother, Doug. I feel terrible."

Douglas looked sorry for her. "You didn't know any better, Car."

"I know. I was stupid and ignorant, so in love with a man that persuaded me my mother was just trying to ruin what I have."

Carmen stabbed at her food, angry.

"I could kill Ricardo right now."

"I believe it," Douglas said, nodding. "Try not to think about him too much. At least, not on your first night here."

Carmen inhaled, then she exhaled and said ok.

They continued to eat, Carmen's mind racing with thoughts about what would happen next, wondering if Ricardo realised she wasn't coming back.

Was he worried about her?

Would he call the police if it got too late?

Or would he be glad she was gone so he could talk to Samantha Wervington without need to hide it?

"Are you going to sleep in your old room?" asked Douglas as he ate, and Carmen replied "No. That was my childhood bedroom. I've outgrown it, Doug. I'm going to move into one of the larger suites that come with a desk , bathroom and television."

Douglas nodded, and Carmen added "You can sleep in your room here though."

"Awesome. Can we watch a movie before bed?"

"Sure we can."

Carmen and Douglas finished their meals, maids taking their plates and glasses away. Then, the butler Credence came in and announced "Cake, biscuits and the choice of tea, coffee, or hot chocolate will be served at eleven p.m., as you have eaten at nine p.m., Lady Cruise. If you'd rather not have this, please let myself or a maid know before the time."

"Thank you, Credence," smiled Carmen; Credence bowed and left them alone.

Douglas grinned at Carmen. "Let's watch the movie in the cinema room."

Carmen smiled back. "Alright."

The doorbell chimed through the majority of the main section of the estate.

Credence went to answer it, and he exclaimed "Master Antonio!"

"Credence," Antonio responded, stood with two other men. "Is my sister here?"

"Of course, sir. Come inside."

Credence stepped back to let the men in, and Carmen walked out to greet her big brother lovingly.

"Antonio." Carmen hugged her brother hard. "You came."

"Of course, baby sister." Antonio hugged her back. "I have most of your belongings. Your clothes, your shoes, your gadgets, your books. Where would you like to put them all?"

"Credence, have the boxes taken up to my second bedroom," Carmen ordered; Credence bowed and called upon the staff to assist him.

As everything was being carried up the stairs, Antonio turned to look down at Carmen seriously.

"I had more evidence of Ricardo's wrongdoings. I also had the drugs he was giving you. Everything is in the hands of your private investigator."

"More evidence?" Carmen repeated; her big brother nodded. "How did you get it? How did you find the drugs?"

Antonio shrugged a shoulder. "I had to force Ricardo to give them to me. Every bottle."

"That's impossible. Ricardo would have never."

Antiono shrugged. "By *choice,* he would have never. By *force,* he definitely did."

Carmen stepped back and glared at her big brother. "You promised me you wouldn't hurt Ricardo, Tony."

Antonio smiled at her annoyed expression. "Yes, I did. I promised I wouldn't be the one to hurt him. I never promised that he wouldn't be hurt."

Carmen swore. "Damn it."

"He had it coming, Carmen. You know he deserved what he got."

"How badly hurt is he?"

Antonio shrugged a shoulder. "It's bad. But he'll heal up nicely in a month."

"A month?!"

"A month," nodded Antonio. "By that time, he'll be a prisoner."

"Nice," said Douglas impressively, and Antonio nodded at him.

"Very nice. He is in the hospital right now, Carmen. If you want to visit him, you can. To get whatever it is off your chest when it comes to him. Then, he is going to sign those divorce papers."

"He said he would never sign them. That he would never let me go," Carmen said uneasily, and Antonio smirked at her.

“He will. Don’t worry, baby sister. By choice, he won’t. You know the rest.”

“You can’t act like an animal inside the hospital Tony,” scolded Carmen; Douglas burst out laughing as her big brother grinned at her. “They have cameras everywhere!”

“He will sign them,” Antonio repeated. “I promise. Now. Do I still have a room here?”

“Of course,” Carmen replied, scowling a little. “You know where your suite is. It’s the same massive one Mother gifted to you whenever you were in town years ago.”

“Awesome. Because I want to hang around until those Wervingtons are behind bars along with Ricardo,” her big brother said seriously. “I never liked the Wervingtons. They used to practically stalk Brianne.”

“They did??”

“Begging her to loan them some money, yes.” Antonio nodded. “I remember. Andrew Wervington tried to court Brianne. She shut that down fast because she knew what he really wanted.”

“Her money,” whispered Carmen; Antonio nodded.

“Her money, her estate, her three companies. They craved it all, him and his daughter.”

Carmen felt like she was going to be sick. “And Mother refused.”

“Of course she did. But they always say, those close to them in their circle. ‘Never cross a Wervington.’”

“We should talk to some of those people.” Carmen’s mind was set. “Build evidence.”

“I’ve already got onto that, Car. Don’t you worry,” Antonio said gently, caressing her face. “Everything I’ve been told about Samantha and Andrew Wervington. By people in their circle, who want to remain anonymous until the court date, when the Wervingtons will definitely be sentenced for at least twenty years.”

“Why anonymous?” Douglas asked curiously; Antonio replied “For their safety.”

"Oh."

"Doug, it's getting late." Carmen looked at her best friend. "Are we still watching a movie in the cinema room?"

"Sure, but after we have our hot drinks and cake," Douglas said eagerly; Carmen cringed. "Car? What's wrong?"

"She feels a little nervous about being served a hot drink by someone," Antonio answered for Carmen, who bit her lip and rubbed her arm. "After being served a hot drink by Ricardo for ten months."

"Oh," Douglas said again. "Carmen, I'm sorry."

"It's fine Doug. I'll just let Credence know he can bring the trolley in, but I will serve myself."

Drama at the Hospital

Four days later...

Ricardo Taylor opened his eyes find himself in the hospital.

Samantha Wervington sat at his bedside, looking like she had been in tears.

"Samantha," croaked Ricardo, and Samantha gasped and looked at him.

Then, her expression of relief turned to rage immediately as she hissed "Are you serious Ricky?!"

"What…" Ricardo turned his head. "What happened to me?"

"You tell *me* what happened!"

"I… I have no idea. I opened the door and four men barged in wearing balaclavas… ouch." Ricardo winced in pain. "They must have beat me and burgled the house."

"So you're saying *robbers* did this to you?!"

Ricardo nodded weakly. "Yes."

"Bull-crap," a voice said harshly from the doorway, and they turned and saw Andrew Wervington standing in the doorway.

Samantha stood quickly. "Daddy."

"That is total shite, and you know it Taylor. I went over the report with a cop friend of mine," Andrew spat. "The only things that were taken were your wife's belongings, and…" he lowered his voice. "And the drugs!"

"Only *Carmen's* things?" Ricardo couldn't believe it, and Andrew spat "Yes."

"You're saying she set this up?" Ricardo was hurt. "Why would she do that?"

“I have no idea. But you’d better make peace with your wife before this goes any further,” Andrew said angrily. “I really don’t want to cross the man behind your attack.”

Ricardo smirked. “You’re scared of him.”

“He could blow this entire operation to pieces,” Andrew said heatedly. “Now listen to me, you piece of trash. You’re going to get Carmen Cruise to see you when you’re discharged to come home.”

Ricardo smiled a little. “And then what?”

“You know what Ricardo,” hissed Samantha. “Don’t upset my Dad.”

“I really don’t know what, Samantha. I don’t know what your father means,” Ricardo said coolly. “See Carmen, I get that. But where? And what reason do I give her?”

“You’ll soon be discharged,” Andrew spat, “And then we will talk properly. Samantha, keep an eye on him. Keep him happy.”

Samantha nodded. “Yes Daddy.”

Andrew turned and left without saying goodbye, and Samantha scowled at Ricardo as he struggled to sit up.

“Just use the button on the remote,” she snapped, indicating the large white remote with UP and DOWN buttons, and a small red circle. She pressed the UP button, impatiently waiting until Ricardo was sat upright, and then she said quietly “Ricardo. I don’t know what we’re going to do. Someone dangerous out there is on Carmen’s side. You heard what my father said.”

“Yes, I heard him. I also figured out that the person on Carmen’s side terrifies your father,” Ricardo replied, “And that person could save me too, as well as Carmen.”

Samantha stared at him, dumbstruck. “What are you saying?”

“I’m saying I want out.” Ricardo spoke firmly. “I won’t kill Carmen, and I won’t practically be you and your father’s servant. I’m done.”

“You can’t be done,” hissed Samantha, as a doctor entered the room with a smile.

"Mr. Taylor. I'm relieved you are awake."

"Hello doctor," Ricardo said weakly. "What took you so long?"

"My apologies sir. We have a lot of patients to deal with that have higher risks than you," the doctor said apologetically. "But I'm here now. Unfortunately, so are the police."

Samantha scrambled up immediately. "Why are the police doing here?!"

"They just want to ask Mr. Taylor a few questions, Miss, after he is treated. If Mr. Taylor answers truthfully, I'm sure they will leave soon."

"Sit down Samantha," Ricardo said through gritted teeth, and Samantha sat. "I'm going to tell them everything."

"You can't," she whispered. "If you tell them, we all go down. My father will get the worst sentence for what he did to Brianne Cruise!"

"You don't think I know that??" hissed Ricardo. "I'd rather be in prison than have Carmen murdered by you and your father!"

"It is *you* that is meant to murder Carmen!"

"And I'm not doing it! I'm done!" spat Ricardo. "Kill me too if you want, but I will not hurt Carmen!"

"So what the *hell,"* spat Samantha, "Have you being for ten months two weeks and two days? Buying her flowers and her favourite chocolates?? You are just as guilty as me and my father because of what you were doing to your wife. I told you already, and I will tell you again if you are hard of hearing Ricardo Taylor! If *we* go down, *we're taking you down with us!!"*

"I don't mind taking that risk." Ricardo shrugged a shoulder, then he winced at the pain. "Ow."

Samantha stood, livid. "You can't do this to me. You can't do this to us."

"I've made up my mind," Ricardo said wearily. "If you want to go and tell Daddy dearest, go ahead. If you want to kill me for betraying you, go ahead. I'm done. I just want my wife back."

His voice cracked as his eyes filled.

"I just want Carmen Cruise back!"

They heard the sound of hands clapping, and they saw Detective Dante Smith enter the room, six police officers behind him.

Two of the officers had Andrew Wervington in handcuffs.

"Ricardo Taylor and Samantha Wervington. You are both under arrest for attempted murder, conspiracy to murder, and for covering up the murder of Bianca Werevington," Dante said flatly. "Ricardo, you are now on police watch as you recover here. When you are well enough to be discharged, you are going straight to jail until your court case."

A police officer stepped forward and handcuffed one of Ricardo's wrists to his bed railing.

Ricardo swallowed hard, and he nodded. "Yes Detective."

"Samantha-"

"NO!!" she screamed, and she suddenly darted at the officers, struggling to get past the remaining three officers, but they held her firm. "I'm not going to prison!!"

"Samantha, if you keep fighting, you will be sedated," Detective Smith warned as two nurses stood nearby; Samantha swore at him, cursing him to high heaven. "Alright, but don't say I didn't warn you."

He nodded at the nurses.

"Take her down."

Samantha Wervington screamed as the nurses moved forwards with syringes, the police holding her down.

"Daddy, this is your fault! Ricardo, you are a COWARD!! I will get that Carmen Cruise and everything she has! I will… find… another… *way!* I promise! I… I will…"

Her eyes closed slowly, and her body went limp.

“Carry her to the van,” Detective Dante Smith ordered, and he added “Bag her father also.”

“Yes Detective,” the officers replied, and less than half an hour later, it was just him and Ricardo in the room.

Dante glared at Ricardo, his expression full of dislike.

“What?” spat Ricardo, avoiding his eye. “Why are you giving me filthy looks? You got what you wanted. We’re all going to prison!”

“Yes, I know that. I just wanted to ask you why, Taylor.”

“Why what??”

“Why did you do what you did to your wife?” spat Dante. “I heard you, more than once, say you want out. Was that true?”

“Of course it was true!” spat Ricardo. “I never wanted to hurt Carmen. Ever!”

“If that was so, why did you go along with it for ten months?” spat Dante. “Surely after the first night you drugged Carmen Cruise, you would have said screw this I’m not doing it?? Why did you carry on for so long?!”

“I don’t know!”

“Tell me you don’t know again,” Dante said calmly as he pulled his gun from his holster, “And I will shoot you in both your kneecaps.”

Ricardo shrank back on his bed. “You can’t do that. You’re a cop.”

“I can do what the hell I like if it’s self-defence.”

“But I’m not attacking you!”

“I can make it look like you did,” Dante replied simply. “Do you want that?”

“Of course not!”

“Then tell me why you did it,” spat Dante. “Now.”

It went quiet for a moment, Ricardo’s eyes on the gun.

Dante waited.

Ricardo gave in two minutes later.

"At first, it was as an excuse to see Samantha Wervington," admitted Ricardo, his eyes filling again. "I hadn't seen her since we were in college. She loved me then, she really did. But after all those years… she changed. She wasn't the same."

Dante was recording him, but he didn't know.

"How did she change?"

"Her father changed her," Ricardo said angrily. "He made her obsessed with winning, being rich, and money. That's all she cares about. She never loved me. She just wanted what my wife had. All of it. And I stupidly believed she cared for me."

Dante released a heavy breath. "Did you care for Samantha even after she revealed her true nature? Is that why you wanted to continue harming Carmen? To impress Samantha?"

"Pretty much," wept Ricardo. "I was a fool. She stopped wanting to make love four months into the plan. Carmen thought it was every time we met, and she even asked me how long. I couldn't tell her, because I was so embarrassed."

"I understand." Dante took a deep breath. "You know you're going down for the part you played, right?"

Ricardo sighed. "Right."

"But you can lighten your sentence if you tell us everything you know about what happen to Brianna Cruise, and what the Wervington's plans were."

Silence.

Dante stepped forwards. "I know you know, Ricardo. I can see the fear in your face. You're scared of what Andrew Wervington might have done to you, or Samantha."

Ricardo nodded, sniffing "They'll kill me like they killed her."

"They killed her? Brianna Cruise?"

Ricardo nodded.

Dante pulled another chair up towards Ricardo's bed so he was closer, and the recording could hear him even louder.

"Alright Ricardo. I'm listening to you."

The Full Confessions

Dante pressed stop on his laptop on Carmen's estate.

He'd uploaded the recording and had it ready to submit as evidence after uploading it to five clouds.

"It's madness," he said, looking at a very shocked Carmen, and a *very* angry Antionio and Douglas. "He did it all to try and get closer to Samantha Wervington."

"He's an idiot," spat Carmen, furious. "She never loved him. It was *my* life she was after, after they couldn't get anything out of my mother."

"He says it was her father who brainwashed her," Dante said gently; Carmen was fuming at her idiot husband. "Don't worry about it, Carmen. The court case is in two months. Will you be alright getting whatever you want from your old home without being escorted?"

"I don't want anything from that house." Then Carmen paused. "Damn it."

"What is it?" The three men looked at her.

Carmen hesitated, then she sighed "I want to get my favourite mug."

"A mug?" Douglas said amusedly. "You have plenty of mugs here on the estate, Carmen."

"Yeah, I know. But this mug was from my mother," Carmen said quietly. "She gave it to me the first winter after I left home. To keep me warmer, Mother said, when a regular mug would have reached the hot drink's end faster, and end my enjoyment."

"Ah."

The three men looked at each other, and the Douglas said "We can go there, Carmen, together. I'll be with you."

"Can we go tomorrow?" asked Carmen. "You're not working, are you?"

“No. After everything you’ve been through Car, it messed me up a little,” Douglas admitted. “I’m taking paid time off.”

“Because of me?” Carmen felt bad. “You didn’t have to do that, Doug.”

“Even if I didn’t do it, I wouldn’t have worked well.” Douglas smiled at her reassuringly. “Don’t worry about it.”

“When are you back at work?” Antonio asked him; Douglas yelped.

“I- I’m… after the- the case. The court case.”

“You must have a very nice manager,” Antonio quipped, “If they do not mind paying you to do nothing for another two months.”

“I guess I do,” Douglas replied, stung a little, and Antonio nodded, not saying anything else.

Douglas waited, but Antonio said nothing, so he turned back to Carmen.

“I’ll be going back home at the end of the week, Car. My landlord is very picky about abandoning the property without notice.”

“Your landlord has a crush on you,” Carmen said amusedly. “Why does she care so much whether you come and go or for how long and who with? Remember when she tore you into one for bringing me to yours? Saying no girlfriends after six p.m.?”

Antonio snorted with laughter. “She sounds psychotic.”

“She is,” Carmen said amusedly. “She really is. Wait! Douglas?”

Douglas looked at her curiously. “Yes Car?”

Carmen took a deep breath, then she asked “Would you like to move into my old house?”

Everyone’s jaws dropped.

Douglas’s eyes filled. “Seriously?”

Carmen nodded. “Seriously. It’s already paid for, so you won’t be renting. Unless you want to rent, of course. I can help you with moving, after I get the place cleared of Ricardo's junk and take whatever else I need."

"Like your red cup," Douglas smiled, emotional, and Carmen smiled back.

"Exactly."

"You're the best, Carmen." Douglas swallowed hard. "Yes, I would love to have your house. I'll keep it spick and span, don't you worry. When you come over for inspections, I-"

"Doug." Carmen held a hand up amusedly. "I'm not a landlord, nor anything like the psycho landlord you have now. Trash the place if you feel like it. We'll go over some paperwork that transfers ownership of the house to you in a week, ok?"

Douglas nodded, his eyes well up. "Ok."

"In that week I'll have the house cleared out. If there's anything you want to keep in there, Doug, let me know."

"I'll keep the furniture and the television," Douglas said quickly. "The sofas and armchair, the dining table and chairs, and the beds aside from yours and Ricardo's. That can go."

"Alright," Carmen said, nodding. "We'll get that sorted."

Douglas nodded, emotion tearing at him as he walked and hugged his best friend. Carmen hugged him back, as he said "You've always been there for me."

"And you've always been there for me too," Carmen smiled as they let each other go. "Mother loved you. As do I."

"You both would have made such a perfect couple if Carmen hadn't married Ricardo," Antonio said thoughtfully, startling them as they whipped round to stare at him.

"Tony! Don't be dumb," Carmen said, embarrassed, and Antonio retorted "Don't forget what your mother and I read about Douglas in your *diary."*

"Shut up!"

"Why, what did you write in your diary about me Car?" asked Douglas curiously,

Carmen's heart pounding.

"I- um- it was just stupid kid stuff."

"You were eighteen," Antonio said amusedly. "Hardly a kid. Tell him, Carmen."

Carmen was looking wildly around for a way to escape.

Douglas reached out and took her hand, and suddenly, she was calm.

She took deep steady breaths to calm

"I wrote that I was in love with you and I've loved you since I was thirteen," she said quietly; Douglas's jaw dropped. "And that I hated your girlfriend Roxanne, and I wished it was me you'd kiss and make out with instead of her. That I wished my homeboy wasn't my homeboy anymore."

Silence.

Antonio held his breath as they stared at each other, still holding hands.

"Why didn't you tell me this?" Douglas asked quietly; Carmen looked away.

"I just couldn't. I didn't want to ruin our friendship. It was a long time ago. I moved on eventually, when I met Ricardo. And… I…" Her eyes filled. "I understand if you want nothing to do with me, Douglas. I've made things weird between us."

"Nah. You haven't," Ricardo said reassuringly. "It was your brother that exposed everything, Car. And for what reason, Antonio?" he asked amusedly, and Antonio smiled as he walked and wiped his baby sister's tears away.

"Because I think there should be no more secrets."

Carmen took a deep breath and nodded. "Alright."

"I can still have your house after this, right?" grinned Douglas, they all burst out laughing, Carmen shoving him playfully as she said "Right."

Antonio left them alone an hour later, when they were sat at the dining table having tea and cake.

It was eleven p.m. on the dot.

As Carmen laughed at a joke Douglas told her, he suddenly became serious.

"Carmen?"

"Yes?"

"Remember what you wrote in your diary? That you wished your homeboy wasn't your homeboy anymore?"

Carmen swallowed, and she nodded. "Yes, I remember."

"Well what after everything that's happened, I don't want my homegirl to be my homegirl anymore?" Douglas said softly; startled, Carmen stared at him.

"Are… I… are you serious?"

Douglas reached out and took her hand. "Never been more serious in all my life."

There was something different about his touch after he said those words. His touch felt electric, causing her body to hum and relax at the same time.

Carmen swallowed hard, and Douglas murmured "What are you thinking?"

"I'm thinking that my dreams have come true along with you must be drunk and you'll forget this conversation tomorrow."

Douglas threw back his head and laughed.

His laughter was infectious.

Carmen was laughing too.

"I'm sorry, I just thought you had to be drunk!"

"My God," Douglas said as he finished laughing. "You're unbelievable, Carmen Cruise."

"Sorry," she smiled, and he suddenly became serious.

"I meant what I said, Carmen."

"You did?" she whispered; Douglas nodded.

"Yes. I did. But I pushed my feelings aside. I knew you were happily married. I guess I didn't want to make our relationship weird, like you."

Carmen nodded. She swallowed, then she whispered "So what now?"

"Now?" repeated Douglas softly. "Now I do something I've been dying to do for over seven years."

"Which is what?"

Douglas stood slowly, and Carmen quickly stood too. He reached out, murmuring "Do you trust that as your new partner, I will keep you safe, Carmen Cruise? And if I can't, I will die trying?"

Carmen swallowed again. Then she whispered "Yes… I trust you."

Douglas pulled her into her arms and held her there, resting his chip atop her head. Carmen's arms went around him as she closed her eyes.

They stood holding each other for a moment, then Carmen looked up at Douglas through glasses eyes, whispering "Are we really together now? After everything? After secretly wanting and needing each other for so long?"

Douglas lowered his mouth to hers in a slow, drugged kiss. Carmen's entire body came alive as she kissed him back urgently, pulling him closer, her hands in his wavy hair.

Douglas held her like she was his last lifeline.

He loved her.

He always had.

And she loved him.

He knew it.

When they broke apart, panting, Douglas managed "We'd better finish our hot drinks or have some fresh ones made for us."

“Let’s have some fresh ones made,” smiled Carmen; a maid standing just outside the dining hall doors quickly ran off to fulfil her order. “Suddenly I’m starving.”

“Me too,” Douglas said, smiling back.

When they were sat drinking their new hot drinks, Douglas grinned at Carmen.

“You’re an awesome kisser, Carmen.”

“Thanks,” she said shyly, and she added “So are you.”

“Antonio wanted this,” Douglas realised. “And so did your mother.”

“Yeah, I got that. He didn’t just bring up the subject of my diary out of nowhere. I’m betting he and Mother planned for us to become a couple a long time ago. But I got married.”

Douglas nodded.

They sipped some more, then he asked “Are you worried about the court case and the sentencing, Car?”

“No, of course not.” Douglas raised an eyebrow, and she sighed “Ok. A little.”

“It will all be over soon. Then, we can start rebuilding our lives. Together,” smiled Douglas, and Carmen smiled back.

“Together.”

They decided to sit in the living room for a while longer; neither were tired.

Antonio joined them later, at almost two in the morning.

“I trust you both are in a relationship now?”

“Yes we are, you sly dog,” Carmen said amusedly; Antonio laughed.

“I did what I had to do. I owed it to Brianne.” He smiled at his baby sister. “So what are you watching?”

“Just the news.”

“You do know that soon you will see your face on there,” Antonio said seriously. “Are you ready for the court case?”

“I’m a little nervous,” Carmen replied; the two men nodded understandably.

“Peter Riverside is going to drag them to hell,” Antonio said amusedly. “He has a reputation for being one of the fiercest opponents in court. You’re going to hear a lot of ‘no further questions’ and ‘nothing else to add’ in that courtroom.”

“Good,” Carmen said approvingly. “I’m glad.”

“We should go to bed,” Douglas said as he checked the time. “Carmen, I know you’re still getting accustomed to waking up early. Let’s put it into practice.”

“Alright.” Carmen stood, and she hugged him, then kissed him tenderly. When they broke apart, she whispered “Goodnight.”

“Goodnight,” Douglas said breathlessly, and Carmen left the room.

“It’s that serious already.” Antonio smiled at Douglas’s dreamy expression. “Kisses already?”

Douglas smiled back and nodded. “Kisses already.

The Weight of Truth

Two months later...

The courtroom felt colder than Carmen expected. Not physically- the air was still, almost heavy- but in the way a place becomes cold when truth is about to be spoken aloud.

She stood just inside the double doors, Douglas at her side, her fingers trembling despite how tightly she held them together.

Rows of faces turned toward her.

Some curious.

Some sympathetic.

Some simply waiting for the spectacle of justice.

But Carmen saw only one face.

Ricardo.

He sat between two officers, thinner than she remembered, his prison attire quite loose on him. His hands were cuffed, resting uselessly in his lap. When he lifted his eyes and met hers, something inside her twisted.

Grief, betrayal, love, and loss all tangled into a single breath she couldn't quite release.

He had signed the divorce papers, a month ago.

She no longer had any ties to him.

Carmen breathed out, relieved as she looked around the court.

Samantha Wervington sat to his left, chin raised, eyes sharp with defiance. She looked bored, almost irritated to be there.

Her father, Andrew, sat on the far end, his hands shaking so violently the cuffs rattled. His eyes darted around the room, never settling, never steady.

It was time.

The bailiff called the court to order, and Judge Halden entered. He was a tall, stern man with a voice that carried authority without ever needing to rise. He settled into his seat, adjusted his glasses, and looked over the files before him.

“I call for the first witness,” he said, almost five minutes later.

Carmen stepped forward.

Her heels clicked softly against the polished floor, each step echoing louder in her chest than in the room. She took her place at the stand, raised her hand, swore the oath, and sat. Her heartbeat thudded in her ears.

“Ms. Cruise,” the prosecutor began gently, “Please tell the court, in your own words, what happened.”

Carmen swallowed. Her gaze drifted, not to the jury, not to the judge- but to Ricardo.

His eyes were already wet.

She began.

“At first… I didn’t understand what was happening to me.” Her voice wavered, but she steadied it. “For ten months, I slept as if dead. I would wake up late in the afternoon, confused, foggy, unable to think clearly. It wasn’t like me. I’ve always been an early riser.”

Ricardo’s shoulders shook. He whispered something- too soft for anyone but Carmen to hear.

“I’m sorry…”

Carmen blinked hard, but continued.

“I trusted my husband. I trusted him with my life. And every night, he put something in my drink. Something that stole my mind, my days, my clarity. I thought I was losing myself.”

A tear slid down her cheek.

“On our anniversary, I heard him talking to someone on the phone. A woman. Samantha.” She glanced at Samantha, who smirked. “I didn’t know her name then, but I found it. And once I did… everything began to make sense.”

She took a breath.

“I recorded them. I heard them planning to poison me. To kill me. To take my mother’s estate, her companies, her money. My mother, Brianne Cruise, who was murdered by Andrew Wervington after she rejected him. And my husband knew. He comforted me at her funeral while knowing exactly what happened to her.”

Ricardo broke.

Tears streamed down his face as he whispered again, "I'm sorry… I'm so sorry…"

Carmen's voice cracked.

"It was hard to say goodbye to the only man I ever loved fully. But I didn't have a choice. His greed… *their* greed… cost me everything. My peace. My trust. My *mother.*"

She wiped her cheek, her hand trembling.

"I never want to see any of them again."

Silence filled the room, thick, suffocating, absolute.

Judge Halden leaned forward, his expression unreadable.

"Thank you, Ms. Cruise. You may step down."

Carmen returned to her seat beside Douglas, who squeezed her hand gently. She didn't look back at Ricardo again.

The judge shuffled his papers, then addressed the defendants.

"Ricardo Taylor. Samantha Wervington. Andrew Wervington. You stand before this court convicted of grave and calculated crimes; the drugging and attempted murder of Carmen Cruise, and in Mr. Wervington's case, the murder of Brianne Cruise."

He paused, letting the weight of the words settle.

"Ricardo Taylor and Samantha Wervington. For the use of dangerous drugs, the administration of poison, and attempted murder, this court sentences you each to thirty years in prison."

Ricardo bowed his head, sobbing openly.

Samantha rolled her eyes.

Judge Halden turned to Andrew.

"And Andrew Wervington: for supplying the drugs and poison, for orchestrating this conspiracy, and for the murder of Brianne Cruise, this court sentences you to forty-five years in prison."

Andrew's face drained of all colour. His knees buckled as officers grabbed his arms.

"No… no, please," he stammered, terror twisting his voice. "You don't understand what they'll do to me in there-"

The judge's gavel struck once.

"Remove the defendants."

Officers moved in.

Samantha Wervington jerked her arm away and glared at Carmen with venomous delight.

"I have no remorse," she spat loudly. *"None."*

Ricardo twisted in his restraints, reaching toward Carmen even as officers pulled him back.

"Carmen! I'm sorry! *I'm so sorry!"*

Carmen didn't react.

She didn't even look at Ricardo as he yelled for her.

"CARMEN!!"

He was dragged through the bottom doors still yelling.

Andrew Wervington was also dragged out, trembling so violently he could barely walk.

"They're going to kill me in there," he gasped. "They're going to kill me!"

He was pulled through the doors, the three defendants finally gone.

And then it was quiet again.

Carmen stood slowly, Douglas and Antonio rising with her.

They walked out of the courtroom together, past the murmuring crowd, past the reporters, past the echoes of everything that had been taken from her.

Outside, the air was crisp.

Carmen closed her eyes and breathed in deeply, a long, steady breath that filled her lungs and loosened something tight inside her chest.

It was over at last.

Finally.

The Quiet After the Storm

Night settled over the estate like a soft blanket, dimming the world into something gentler than the day had been.

Carmen sat curled into the corner of the large sofa in the east living room, her legs tucked beneath her, a blanket draped loosely over her lap.

The glow of the television cast shifting light across her face: blues, whites, flashes of courtroom stills, as the evening news replayed the events of the trial.

Douglas sat beside her, leaning forward with his elbows on his knees, hands clasped. Antonio stood behind them, arms folded, his expression unreadable as he watched the broadcast with the stillness of a man accustomed to far darker rooms than this one.

"Ricardo Taylor and Samantha Wervington have each been sentenced to thirty years in prison," the reporter said, her voice steady, almost clinical. "Andrew Wervington has been sentenced to forty-five years for his role in the conspiracy and for the murder of Brianne Cruise…"

Carmen exhaled slowly.

It was the first breath she'd taken all day that didn't feel like it scraped against something raw inside her.

Ten months of being drugged.

Two months of waiting for justice.

A year of grief, confusion, and fear.

And now… silence.

She let her head fall back against the sofa cushion, eyes drifting closed for a moment. The room felt warm, safe… a feeling she hadn't known in far too long.

Douglas glanced at her, his voice soft. "You holding up?"

Carmen opened her eyes. "I think… I can finally breathe again."

Antonio shifted his weight, the faintest hint of a smirk tugging at the corner of his mouth as he replied "About time."

She gave him a tired look, but there was affection in it. "You know your methods of getting that crucial evidence were almost illegal."

"Almost?" Douglas muttered under his breath, earning a sharp elbow from Carmen. *"Ow! Carmen!"*

Antonio lifted a brow. “I kept my promise, baby sister. I didn’t touch Ricardo.”

“That’s not the point,” Carmen said, though her voice lacked heat. “You scared me half to death when you told me what happened.”

“You were safe,” Antonio replied simply. “That’s all that mattered. And all that I cared about.”

Carmen studied him for a long moment.

Her elder brother Antonio Zaide. Feared by half the country, respected by the other half- he had been her shield when she didn’t even know she needed one. His presence had been the one constant in a world that had been slipping out from under her feet.

She turned to Douglas next.

Her best friend now boyfriend.

The one who held her while she cried in his car.

The one who stayed up with her through the nights leading to the court case when she couldn’t sleep, when the fog in her mind felt like it might swallow her whole.

“You two…” Her voice wavered, her eyes filling. “I don’t know what I would’ve done without you.”

Douglas’s expression softened. “You don’t have to know, Carmen. You’re here. That’s what matters.”

Antonio didn’t speak, but he stepped closer, resting a hand on the back of the sofa near her shoulder- a silent gesture of protection, of presence.

Carmen looked back at the television.

The screen showed Ricardo being led out of the courtroom, tears streaming down his face. She felt a pang- not love, not longing, but the ache of something that once mattered deeply.

She whispered, almost to herself, “I loved him. I really did.”

Douglas placed a hand over hers. “Loving someone doesn’t mean you deserved what he did.”

Carmen nodded slowly. “I know. And I’m relieved it’s over. Truly relieved. But it still hurts.”

Antonio’s voice was low, steady. “Pain fades, Carmen Cruise. Freedom doesn’t.”

She let those words settle inside her.

Freedom.

It felt unfamiliar, like a new pair of shoes she wasn't sure she could walk in yet.

But it was hers.

Finally, it was *hers.*

The news segment ended, shifting to weather forecasts and mundane chatter.

Carmen reached for the remote and turned the television off. The room fell into a peaceful hush.

She stood, stretching her stiff limbs, and walked toward the tall windows overlooking the estate grounds. The night sky was clear; stars scattered like silver dust across the darkness. She pressed her palm to the cool glass.

"I'm going to be okay," she said quietly. "For the first time in a long time… I believe that."

Douglas joined her at the window, his shoulder brushing hers. "You're stronger than you think."

Antonio stayed back, watching them both with a rare softness in his eyes. "And you're not alone. Not now. Not ever."

Carmen turned to them, her chest swelling with gratitude so deep it almost hurt.

"Thank you, both of you," she whispered. "For everything."

Douglas smiled. "Always."

Antonio gave a single nod, his version of a vow.

Carmen looked out at the night again, breathing in the quiet, the safety, the promise of tomorrow.

The storm had passed.

And at last, she could feel the calm.

Thank You for Reading Whispers in the Dark!!

Thank you for choosing to step into these worlds with me, for trusting me to guide you through shadows, secrets, magic, and emotion.

Every story in Whispers In The Dark was crafted with intention, heart, and a deep love for the power of storytelling. Knowing you walked through each doorway, felt each shift in atmosphere, and allowed these characters to breathe beside you means more than I can ever fully express.

Writing is a quiet, intimate act. Reading is too. Somewhere between those two spaces, a connection forms, one built on imagination, curiosity, and the willingness to feel. I'm grateful you allowed my words to meet you there.

If these novellas linger with you, even in small ways… if a line stayed with you, a character tugged at you, or a moment made you pause… then this journey has been worth every hour spent shaping it.

Thank you for reading.

Thank you for listening to the whispers.

Thank you for stepping into the dark… and finding light within it.

With much appreciation,

Makala Thomas.

www.ingramcontent.com/pod-product-compliance
Lightning Source LLC
LaVergne TN
LVHW090547110826
845146LV00001B/54

* 9 7 9 8 9 0 3 2 9 2 2 7 1 *